The Sound of Sirens

TITLE PAGE

Published in the UK in 2021 by
Garrison

An imprint of Leamington Books
Edinburgh, Scotland

leamingtonbooks.com

Distributed in the UK by BookSource, and
Leamington Books

ISBN: 9781914090257

Production Editor: Peter Burnett
Typeset by Joshua Andrew
Editorial: Ambrose Kelly
Cover Design: Cavan Convery

Printed and bound by Imprint Academic, Devon.

DEDICATION PAGE

CHAPTER ONE

That morning I got out of my dead cousin's bunk and went to the mirror. I still wasn't used to being at sea and felt sick half the time. The boat rocked, the boat rolled; a rough sea the radio had decreed. I lurched towards the sink, retching up a throat full of phlegm. After gagging and rubbing the back of my hand across my lips, I gargled some water. In the mirror, the same sunken eyes, the same sullen face stared back.

The step ladder groaned under Uncle Tam's weight. I stepped away from the mirror, but he had seen me.

"Aye, you've got it. A Campbell's face, no point denying it."

He clamped my cheeks between powerful hands, stepped back and held them up like a man showing the size of the one that got away. Outside, the boat chopped its way through the empty sea.

"Get that one up," he said nodding at his son. "If he thinks he'll become skipper lying in his scratcher all day, he's got another thing coming." He climbed back up the wooden steps, and I returned to inspecting my face.

"You look like death," Johnny said, slithering into a pair of salt encrusted jeans.

I watched him getting dressed in the sick speckled mirror.

"You should have been in the galley twenty minutes ago. Your dad was down."

He reached into the drawer at the base of his bunk and pulled out a torch. Holding it close to his face, he examined the black metal casing before pointing the light at me. He turned it off and then on again.

"Look at yourself," he said.

They were bringing the net in and the rest of the crew were watching the tow and making bets on the size of the catch. My eyes followed lumps of kelp, tangled in the green net and dragged from the deep. As I stared into the frothy water, Johnny's voice shouted, "Kill the winch", and the mechanised drum that hauled the net in stopped. There was a sound – a screech like some sea god that the people had forgotten - which reverberated through my guts with such violence that I almost shat myself.

Trapped in the net, he hung in front of us: blanched, plump, encased in oilskin smock, rubber bib and brace trousers. Only the feet hung out, white and succulent, like one of they shellfish that are only just worth the bother of getting into. I didn't know what to do with my hands. 'A bloody waste ay space,' I'd been called more than once since I'd started working on their boat. I watched the gows, their chill cries and shocked white wings wheeling away on the wind.

A curse grated out of Uncle Tam's throat. Johnny bundled his father into the wheelhouse, shouting, "Get him down from there. Get him out of sight."

He had come back. Floating just under the surface, his choked air tubes open, his body putrefied and puffed up with gas and saltwater had moved jellyfish-like toward us. I stepped towards the strung-up body. His naked feet hung at the same height as my face, turned in so that one now rested on top of the other. I pulled a strand of seaweed from my Cousin Joe's big toe. He was dripping on me, his whole waterlogged body. I took my gutting knife and cut him from the net.

Cal covered Joe with a blanket from my bunk – the bunk that Joe had always slept in - but I'd already looked, half expecting his face to twitch into a grimace, his mouth to splutter out salt water before muttering that we didn't think we could get rid of him that easy. The greenish bronze tinge of his face however showed that he was dead. Very dead. But for the orange smock that we all wore, and the initials that Aunt Mary had inked onto his hood to stop arguments about whose oilskins they were, it would have been difficult to recognise him. Still, we all knew, had all known, from the moment he was hauled in. The boat keeled and I found myself holding on to the rails, trying not to vomit.

"C'mon," Johnny said, pulling me up by the arm. "You take his legs."

"Me?"

"You."

Shivering, I staggered over to Joe's body and grabbed the slippery rubber material at the back of his knees. He was so heavy and slick that my hands kept slipping. I'd never been so glad to be wearing gloves.

Johnny arranged the blanket so that Joe's face would remain covered. "One, two, three." He didn't look at me, as we lugged Joe's body across the lower deck and down into the hold. We lay him there amongst the crushed ice and the fish that had been gutted and boxed along with others of their kind.

"Jesus."

Not for the first time, I thought of Joe's body sinking through the depths, buffeted by tides and dragged along the ocean's floor while we told everyone at his funeral how we had woken up to find his bunk empty, that his tabs were missing, that he must have fallen overboard having gone up on deck for a smoke.

Johnny scooped a handful of crushed ice from one of the storage boxes and held it to his forehead until it had melted. He looked at me, his dirty cheeks streaked, a droplet of water hanging precariously from the stubble on his chin. If I didn't know better, I'd have thought he was crying.

The dull rumble of fish tumbling onto the deck told us that the bulging net of the cod end had been opened. After a minute, we heard Cal shouting, "Am I the only one working here?"

Johnny wiped his wet hand on his jeans. "Come on. We should go into the fish room and help."

"Would that be normal?"

"Normal? How can any of this be normal?"

The conveyor belt was alive with twitching tails and gasping gills. Cal had started sorting the different types of fish and ordered his son to go down to the hold. Corky started whinging that he didn't see why he always had to work in the ice room but his dad was having none of it. While the others gutted fish he glanced back at us. The bruised bulges beneath his eyes had faded from the Buckfast purple of a fortnight ago. Now, the only thing to distinguish them from the usual puffy bags caused by lack of sleep, was the scab on the bridge of his nose where the broken bone had burst the skin. Joe had given him a real doing the day before that fatal trip and everyone kent it. No wonder he was jumpy. As if reading my thoughts, he clenched his jaw, jutted his chin at me and left.

It wasn't a good catch: too many unprofitable fish. The discard, those that were the wrong species or too small, were tossed into baskets that would be thrown overboard. For once Cal held back from commenting about how the European Union's fishing quotas were good for nothing, except feeding seagulls. I started gutting a box of cod, the others going about their business in silence. The fish were freezing, my fingers soon numb.

"I canna take this," shouted Corky, his ginger head coming out of the hold. "Am sorry but one ay yous can do it. Dead bodies, man."

Cal stared at him, black affronted. Johnny shrugged and headed down to the hold. I handed Corky my box of gutted fish and watched his shaking hands as he washed out any parts that would contaminate the flesh before throwing the lifeless bodies down the chute.

My own hands worked on automatic, gutting fish after fish. My hands didn't shake or tremble. They were brutally efficient compared to the first time I'd tried this. It was easier to pretend you were a machine, that's what Johnny had telt me, but after twenty minutes I needed a breather. I took off my bloody gloves and looked at my raw fingers. I didn't recognise them. The newly formed calluses and cuts from the gutting knife didn't seem part of me. The right hand held a knife. It pressed the point of the blade down onto the back of the left hand and scraped it slowly across. A white line appeared along which a few beads of blood threaded themselves. Nobody noticed. I watched them working at a speed and with a mindless efficiency that I was only starting to achieve. The right hand hacked down and my skin opened up, like lips coming unstuck in the morning. A hot trickle of blood slithered round my wrist and dripped on to the floor with the guts of the fish.

"What have you done?"

"An accident," I said "I'll get it fixed."

Uncle Tam was in the galley with the First Aid box. "Will you stop bleeding everywhere," he snapped. "This'll sting a bit."

I felt like telling him that it wouldn't, cause that wasn't my hand. It belonged to someone else the moment we left harbour. It fixed nets, scrubbed decks, gutted fish. I couldn't understand how it had got so clever so fast. I watched that hand crawl around doing meticulous tasks with the instinct of an insect.

"Malky."

"Aye, Uncle Tam."

"Joe, how was he? How did he seem?"

"Well, he seemed...fine."

"Peaceful?"

"Aye. Peaceful."

"He didnae hae his boots on."

"No."

"His boots werenae in the cabin?"

"No. They must have come off."

"And his socks? Joe was always one for wearing a couple ay pairs of socks."

"He just went up on deck for a smoke. Mind, his cigarettes and lighter were missing."

"Aye, right enough. It's just strange that he didn't come and see me. He'd always stop in at the wheelhouse. Even when he was foonert." He looked at the great bank of storm clouds to the west. "This is the Lord's work. Joe was always a good loon. His mother will be right glad to have him back."

After thanking him for the plaster, I went down the hold to see Johnny. I thought I heard him talking to himself as I climbed the ladder but there was nothing there but boxes of iced fish. Then through the noise of the engine's dreary drone I heard again, softly spoken words. The fish gaped, their unseeing eyes popping out in permanent astonishment. I looked at the shape of Joe's body under the blanket. The voice spoke of water temperatures in the Hebrides and of a low moving steadily northeast across Cromarty before losing its identity. I put one hand on the ladder's rung before seeing Johnny's radio, sitting next to the chute.

Joe's feet poked out from beneath the blanket that I had woken under that morning. The end of his toes had gone green. I put a bunnet on and tried to rub some warmth into myself. His feet had been the same size as mine and had sprouts of the black wiry hair that covered the arms and legs of all the men in our family. All through childhood I'd inherited football boots and school shoes he had outgrown. Now his feet were horribly swollen. Did the swelling go down? Would an undertaker ever be able to squeeze those feet into a pair of his shoes? I lifted the blanket. The skin on his forearm was goose pimpled, as if he could still feel the cold.

Johnny slipped down the ladder, and I stepped away from the body.

Pretending he hadn't caught me looking beneath the blanket, he snapped, "You got ma lighter?"

His lighter was sitting next to the radio, but I just stood there staring at Joe's bulbous feet.

"You've hid it you wee fucker, haven't you?"

Johnny clenched his eyes, knuckle-white tight. He was older than me, harder than me. He took three jerky steps forwards but stopped at his brother's body.

"You're sweating," he said, reaching out and brushing my clammy forehead with the tips of my fingers. He took a raggedy breath before tugging the blanket over Joe's feet.

"C'mon," he said, "Corky needs a hand fixing the net."

We left the body to rest. The radio filling the hold with the horrors of the world: intrepid investigators whispering news from distant lands to a skull full of secrets.

The next evening, we sailed into the harbour, or the marina, as Tam bitterly cried it due to the increasing number of yachts moored there and the decreasing number of trawlers. Cars moved silently along The Front as stickmen and women waited by the warehouses. Johnny leaned over the side, biting hard on his lower lip.

"Can you see any of the family?"

I shook my head, blinking at the harsh white of the police car as seine nets of rain trawled the town. I wondered if my mum had finished at the chippie. She'd been waiting after my first week at sea and had embarrassed me by openly greeting in front of the others when I got off the boat. Still, if she was there, I could go straight back to our bit. I wanted away from the stinking fish and deckies as quickly as possible.

"What are the filth here for?"

I looked at the bruised bulbous clouds, the endless clawings of the sea searching for a handhold on the harbour wall. I didn't answer. Gows were squawking our arrival to the town and the fisher-folks' houses seemed to have slunk down to the harbour, crowding around like old wives with a secret.

CHAPTER TWO

Probationary Constable Sian Gourlay's tea was steaming the windows. Cautiously, she sipped the brew. Having embarrassed DI Stark at the catering van with her request for a flat white with almond milk, she was determined to get it down. Every day was a reminder that she wasn't in Aberdeen anymore. Still, she didn't see why the catering woman had made such a song and dance about it, asking Stark 'Fa's she on aboot?' as if she'd been the one speaking another language. Valiantly, she swallowed another mouthful of the tepid, tasteless tea.

"Was there an FAI after Joseph Campbell was lost at sea, Sir?"

Stark rubbed a hole in the condensation with the cuff of his trench coat.

"Will we need a forensics team?"

Gourlay was keen to impress. Too keen. After two months doing bog standard operational duties, she'd decided that she wanted to become a detective once her probation was over, and this was her first time out with an actual DI. She'd been on the third coffee round in the office, having typed up witness statements about an argument over an uncut hedge, when Stark had muttered something about needing a driver. Suddenly the other PCs, who'd been too busy to help with the coffee had important jobs to do, while Sergeant Grant said, 'We're not a chauffeur service.' Fingers had stopped typing, coffee cups were held mid-way to mouth. 'I need a driver,' Stark had insisted. 'Joe Campbell's body has been hauled in by his own family and I want to be on the harbour when their boat comes in.' Gourlay had heard about the accident – everyone had - but it wasn't so much the idea of her first body, as the urgency in Stark's voice that made her volunteer to drive him.

"Sir, was he lost in a part of the sea that's in our jurisdiction?"

Stark was getting fed up with her attempts to impress. The male PCs at the station, showing a hitherto concealed investigative ability, had discovered she'd gone to university to study law, but had dropped out after a couple of years. So she was bright enough to get on a course like that and to realise that being a sneaky lawyer wasn't for her, but she didn't need to keep proving it. Still this was probably her first body, and he doubted she'd be expecting one so soon when sent to an outpost like this. Waiting for his answer, she adjusted her hat for the umpteenth time.

"You know, you can take that off."

"Thank you, sir." She placed the bowler on her lap. "I'm still getting used to it, to be honest."

Stark hadn't seen her without the bowler that female PCs were obliged to wear. Even the most depraved uniform fetishists would struggle to find this particular item attractive. With her dirty blonde hair slicked back into a regulation bun, carefully sculpted eyebrows and chiselled cheekbones, she looked more like a ballerina than a bobby. He rubbed his eyes. It'd been three days since the laser eye surgery, hence why he wasn't allowed to drive, but he was still finding the world around him dazzlingly bright.

Huge rollers battered against the harbour wall spouting jets of white water up high as the control tower. The ferocity of a North Sea storm tossing around 300 tonne trawlers as they negotiated the peaks and troughs of a mountain range of water never ceased to fill Stark with a queasy admiration. In the twelve years since he'd been transferred here the sea had taken the lives of five trawlermen. It was the killer no one could stop. In Stark's first weeks working around these fishing towns, in which hardly anyone fished anymore, another Campbell - father, brother, uncle of the men in this crew — had been lost at sea. The same thing had probably happened to the generation before and the generations before that. Names and stories woven into the mesh of fishing folks' lore: the tithe they paid to the life sustaining, life taking sea.

"There's that little creep from The Squeak," Stark said, looking in his wing mirror at a car that had pulled up alongside the undertaker's van. "Didn't take him long. Little parasite."

Stark took in the reporter's battered old Polo, noting with satisfaction the paint work peeling and patchy from the corrosive sea air. Word had already got around - it always did in places like this.

"Is that her, Sir?"

The boat bucked and jerked liked a spooked horse trying to throw its riders. Stark had watched this dozens of times, in seas much bigger than this, but his stomach still lurched at the thought of being out there; his heart went out to the men who had made this their lives, while his head felt glad that he was on solid land.

"Rather them than me," Gourlay said. "Do they even make a living from it these days? Especially with those huge factory boats around."

Stark pulled on his trench coat and got out. He wanted to be able to look them in the eye as they came ashore.

A squall of rain pelted his face. He'd stood on this exact spot twelve days ago, twenty-four hours after the search for Joe Campbell had been called off. The Campbells' trawler had been towed into the harbour having run out of fuel due to Tam Campbell refusing to give up on his boy. It hadn't been Stark's decision to call off the search, but the RCC at Kinloss had pulled back their Sea Kings, and the Coastguard their boats. A couple of trawlers had kept ploughing through the same body of water, but after three days everyone knew it was hopeless. Everyone but Tam Campbell. Stark had never seen a man so possessed. The moment his feet hit the harbour, he'd demanded fuel. In contrast, the rest of the crew were shuffling shells of men. Haunted eyes from days and nights without sleep, days and nights of peering into the endless ocean. Stark had recognised Tam Campbell from church: a man shepherded there by his wife, who during prayers sat bolt upright staring at the translucent glow of Christ's body in the stained glass window, as if daring him to pass judgement. He hadn't recognised the other middle-aged man, but that wasn't surprising given that the fishing folk kept to themselves. For locals like that, with six or seven generations of trawlermen behind him, Stark would always be a newcomer.

Rory Tan, a reporter at *The Squeak*, joined him. After a couple of attempts to light a cigarette in the gobs of rain, he gave up.

"Some coincidence this," he shouted into the storm. "Wouldna be surprised if the auld man was secretly looking for him. But even so. After 12 days and wi the tides the way they are. Virtually a miracle, wouldn't you say?"

Stark knew better than to breathe a word. Rory Tan was a sneaky wee bugger, but he was a good journalist, Stark gave him that. It was his articles that had first got Port Cawdor national news coverage and all the unwanted pressure from the Chief Superintendent which went with that. Since then, journalists from all over the country, confused by how a place like this topped every table for registered addicts and deaths by overdose, had descended on the town before writing sensational articles with headlines like *Hooked* or *Caught in the Net* or *From Herring to Heroin* - as if anyone caught herring anymore. Stark had been expressly forbidden to talk to these people, and the Chief himself had visited Port Cawdor half a dozen times in the last year. Stark had been trusted with organising a community outreach project, which had consisted of a series of talks at assemblies in the High School delivered by a carousel of child psychiatrists, doctors, and mothers of heroin addicts not much older than the pupils. But it had little effect. It was what the town had become famous for. Stark knew how these stories ended. Everyone did. But it was the only show in town, and he could do little more than pick up the pieces as one kid after another became entranced by their own tragedy.

Twelve days ago, the boys had caught Stark's attention: a shifty red haired laddie called Josh McCormack, who'd been issued with so many fixed penalty notices for anti-social behaviour that it was absurd anyone would trust him on a trawler. The other, the brother of the deceased, had been in the cells a few time for fighting. But it was the third laddie, a boy called Malky Campbell, who'd startled Stark. Twelve years ago, Stark had seen his face pressed to the banister's bars as he'd ushered his mother into the sitting room to break the news that her husband's body had been swept up. Over the years, Stark had kept an eye out for Malky Campbell: the whole town did. He'd been in the same year as his Zoe, and had spent the first few years of secondary dropping by their house to pick up homework handouts he'd forgotten. Stark had been wise to his game, but had treated the laddie differently from the other boys who'd shown an interest in his daughters. It must have been a couple of years since Stark had seen the boy, but he'd aged a decade in that time.

Twelve days ago Tam Campbell had demanded the trawler be refuelled, while the three lads had stared at their boots barely able to stand up. Skippers of Tam Campbell's generation had gathered to pay their respects and for a moment no knew what to say. It was Stark who'd told Tam that the search had been called off, that there was no point looking for a person who'd been in the sea over 72 hours.

As one of the crew, unidentifiable in his oils, jumped off the trawler and tightened the hawser around a metal bollard, Gourlay sidled up beside him adjusting her hat.

"Will we need forensics suits, Sir?"

"To go on a trawler that's pulled a body from the sea? It's not a crime scene."

But he wasn't sure about that - what had stuck in his mind about the lads when they'd come ashore after the loss of their brother, cousin, crewmate wasn't that they'd looked exhausted by the search, or distraught about Joe Campbell's death. They'd looked furtive. Frightened, even. It wasn't just Tam Campbell's eyes they were afraid to catch. They hadn't once looked at each other. Stark had watched them stagger on sea legs past the pubs on The Front before skulking off on their separate ways.

Tam Campbell gave him a whole-hearted scowl. "You again."

"I'm afraid so, Mr Campbell. We need to come on board before the undertaker can take your son's body."

"What do you want with him?"

"We need to take him to the police mortuary in Elgin. It's standard procedure. You'll have him back in no time."

The skipper winced like he'd a bad taste in his mouth, hawked and spat into the sea. "I'm awa tae tell ma wife that ah've brought our laddie back. That one can show you where Joe is," he nodded at his other son.

The crew offered no assistance as Stark and Gourlay clambered aboard. They watched Gourlay steady herself, resentful but curious; the first woman they'd seen for a week and an unfamiliar one at that. The ginger-headed laddie pulled a face like he'd caught a bad smell and muttered something coarse under his breath.

"You got something to say for yourself, son?"

The boy growled unintelligibly.

"Sorry, didn't catch that."

"He was just saying, it's bad luck for a woman to come on board," said the older man, whose ginger hair identified him as the boy's father.

"Bad luck? You make your own luck in this world, son."

"Try telling that to Joe Campbell," the older man said.

"He's down here," Johnny Campbell intervened, directing them to follow with a nod of his head before disappearing down a ladder. Stark gave the others a steely stare before following. The sharp tang of the gutting room brought bile into Stark's mouth, and he noticed the last embers of colour extinguish in Gourlay's ashen face. The trawlerman disappeared further into the depths of the boat where the ladder's metal rungs grew icy. They were in the fish storage room, surrounded by huge plastic bins filled with crushed slushy water. The body was on the floor wrapped in a bed sheet.

"We didn't know where to put him," Johnny Campbell sounded apologetic, "So, you know, we thought the ice room made sense."

"You did the right thing," Stark heard Gourlay saying, while he peeled back the bed sheet, noting the swollen copper green face peering out of a tightly tied hood. "When exactly did you pull him from the water?"

He half listened as she went over a series of quick-fire questions that were an obvious distraction from looking at the body. Still it gave him the chance to make a quick inspection. A water-proof jacket, bib and brace trousers packaged the rest of the deceased, except from the swollen feet.

"PC Gourlay, note the thickened and wrinkled skin. That's called maceration. Happens much more quickly to exposed skin." Stark peered over his shoulder to check she was paying attention. You never forgot your first body and the lessons you learned from it. His eyes stuck on Johnny Campbell's yellow wellies.

"Where'd his boots go?"

"Were they in the cabin?"

"No."

"No?"

"They'd have come off in the sea," Johnny Campbell explained. "Or he kicked them off to help stay afloat."

Stark looked at the maceration on the hands, which matched the prune-like effect on the feet. He stood up to take a few photos of the body, but it wasn't telling him anything. Maybe the pathologists would find something.

"Anything for us?" Rory Tan asked, as they returned to the car.

"Buy those poor buggers a pint and they'll tell you the whole story — look like they need a drink."

Stark rapped on the undertaker's window. "All yours."

"Where to now, Sir?"

"We have to accompany that undertaker's van back to the mortuary."

They climbed back into the car and Stark made a small porthole in the condensation to watch the undertakers, with help from the Campbell boys, haul the body bag from the trawler to the waiting trolley.

"Notice anything, Constable?"

Gourlay bit hard on her lip. "It might seem daft Sir, but the hood. Why'd he tied the drawstrings so tight? I typed up the crews' statements. They all said it was a dry, still night. The way he had that hood tied, he could barely have seen where he was going."

Stark was impressed. "There won't be much for forensics to work on, but maybe the P.M. will turn up something."

He peered through the windscreen one last time. Before the deceased had been loaded into the undertaker's van, the crew were already heaving the rest of their catch ashore. The young laddie, Malky Campbell, hadn't looked at the police car once.

CHAPTER THREE

After unloading the catch, I went back with Johnny to their bit. We got through the door to find Tam flopped in his easy chair, sneakily filling his pipe. After a couple of attempts to light it, he lent back coughing a huge claw of smoke into the air. I held my breath, expecting Aunt Mary to burst into the room and give him a lecture about his health, but she continued to shuffle wordlessly through dinner preparations. "There is a god," Tam addressed the smoke with grim satisfaction.

He started chewing and puffing away till the silence and smoke made my eyes water. Listening to the dull percussion of pot lids, ladles and pans from the kitchen, I considered that when in their house, I'd never once seen Aunt Mary sit down - that even when she came into the sitting room she'd always lean against the wall, one ear cocked as if expecting the phone to go, a pot to boil over or someone to arrive at the door. I sat back, watching the smoke swell and rise up, as if at any moment it might break and crash down over us.

"Fancy some fresh air?" Johnny asked.

I found myself on my feet. Before we stepped out, he flicked a comb from his inside pocket, grabbed a handful of gel from a pot that was always at the door and slicked it through his black hair, giving the mirror his Ian Brady stare.

"Your tea'll be out in 10 minutes." Aunt Mary shouted

Johnny paused at the door, and from the kitchen I caught the smell of roast chicken and boiling vegetables. Aunt Mary's cooking was legendary. For a moment I wanted to stay with them, as they picked through the best bits of chicken and shared their memories of Joe.

"We'll be back in time," Johnny replied, but we both kent we wouldn't.

At the scabby end of The Front we met up with Johnny's twin sister, Dawn, whose hair and temper was as short as his. She was with her pal Nicky, who was Johnny's one-time, part-time girlfriend. They leant against the window ledge of the permanently shuttered ice-cream shop. We did a lot of leaning in those days. Leaning and slouching and walking like our legs dragged a ball and chain. Although they had both seen us, neither of the girls glanced in our direction until we were right in front on them.

"Jesus Johnny, I'm sorry," Nicky said, squinting up at him as if she'd just noticed he was there. Dutifully she got up and gave him a squeeze. Johnny kept his hands in his jacket pockets until she let him go.

"Are you carrying?"

"Aye."

"Well then."

"It'll cost you."

"That's no very generous of you."

He slouched towards the park, Dawn slinking along beside him. Nicky glanced at me with eyes so green you'd think they'd been photoshopped, a purple slash of lipstick smiling softly. For a moment, I glimpsed a glint of conspiracy in those eyes and as we followed my cousins she reached out to hold my hand. Nicky was taller than any of us but moved with a permanent stoop as if afraid of bumping her head on a ceiling only she could see. Like the rest of us, she stared at the ground not daring to meet the all-seeing gaze of the mounted CCTV cameras that monitored The Front. Her hand was limp in mine and I in turn held hers as if it were a fledgling fallen from a nest.

No one spoke: what could possibly be said that hadn't been said before? Instead we smoked as if our lives depended on it. As we passed the charred stumps of the Victorian band stand that Johnny and Corky had torched when they were thirteen, I felt, for the first time, that I truly belonged with these people with their distressed denim, torn faces and inarticulate rage. We took a short cut through the graveyard, ignoring the generations of stones bearing our surnames, the same forenames unimaginatively repeating themselves.

Dawn turned around and Nicky dropped my hand.

"There'll have tae be a proper funeral now. Another stupid ceremony to upset Mam," she snarled. "It's not fair on her. Not with dad being sick and going on as if there's nothing wrong with him." I remembered the last service, my Auntie Mary belting out the hymns, her off key voice singing bravely above the rest.

"Eternal father strong to save
Whose arm has bound the restless wave."

Johnny had stood next to me, his body quivering. He'd made gurgling, giggling sounds, as he held onto the pew as if it were a piece of flotsam in a stormy sea.

We cut across the golf course and onto the East Beach, the wind whipping the drizzle into a frenzy. "C'mon," said Johnny, pointing at one of the concrete pillboxes that had been dotted along the coast during the War. We staggered over the shingle towards the nearest block sunk deep into the sand dunes. I crawled head first through the box's gun slit and the wind stopped. Inside, behind the shellproof walls the air was dark and dank, but at least didn't smell of pish. Over the seventy years since it'd been in use so much sand had blown through the gun slits there was only room for us to sit. Scratched into the wall, one of the pillbox's original inhabitants had written *Pte John Hopkins, June 1940*. My fingertips touched the letters, and I wondered what became of him.

"What's it like in there?"

"A time capsule. But it's better than being out in the wind."

The others heaved themselves in. Nicky unzipped her rucksack, her waxy face illuminated as she lit three fat candles and planted them in the sand. She took out an old fashioned radio, some tinfoil, a biro tube and small paper wrap, her heavy lidded eyes never once looking up. The radio DJs, an overexcited boy and compliantly amused girl, discussed the merits of contestants on that summer's Love Island. I imagined them cut off from the world in a sealed tight studio in London, confident that somewhere, out there, nameless people were hanging on their every word.

Nicky sparked a lighter and swept her long black fringe back from her face. When she was done, her lips drooped into the sort of lopsided smile that people give you when coming from the dentists.

She looked at me, the way she used to look at adults, when she was wee and had broken something valuable. For a moment I thought I might kiss her.

At school they'd glided down corridors with their dyed black hair and their devil may care attitude. The three of them had been in a band that had gone through more name than cord changes, but they had attitude, no one denied that. Once I was in secondary, I'd started learning the drums -Corky's instrument. With his ginger hair and his face like someone suffering an anaphylactic shock, he was clearly the loose link. Through saving money from birthdays, Christmases, paper rounds, I'd built up a full kit, but by then they'd sold their instruments, 'bored of their limitations'. By that point I'd realised that their clothes, their moves, their haircuts were all borrowed. Some tough faced lassie, who was always chewing a golf ball sized globule of gum, once called Nicky a Primark Patti Smith. The fight that followed was legendary. But the girl was right, or at least half right, for the sneers seared onto their faces and their absolute disgust with the hand they'd been dealt, that was all theirs. Sure, they all wanted to be like someone else. I on the other hand had spent the last few years at school sabotaging any prospects I had until I could be just like them.

As I watched them smoke, I thought about how different they were to the actors that appeared in the drug awareness videos we'd got shown in PSE – kids with 80s' shell suit tops trying to regionalise their RADA accents. The sort of doe-eyed clueless weans who died after being peer pressured into buzzing aerosols.

They never offered me anything harder than the occasional half-q of soapbar, or a couple of pills when we were out at Enigma, and I never asked. I was the kid cousin, the one who'd be sent down the corner shop when they'd ran out of mixers or matches. And I'd go. I'd run all the way there and all the way back.

Johnny was laughing as he showed me the wrap. "Look. He's used a page fae a scuddie." I squinted at the creased picture of some naked girl sucking seductively on her finger. "It's that attention to detail you have tae appreciate." He leant back against the wall, nodding.

Nicky stretched out at the back of the pillbox, the snickering candlelight rippling over her. She was scooping up decades of sand that had been blown through the gun slits, letting it drain through her fingers, while humming along to the Balearic beats that were blasting from the radio. She smiled sweetly, "Malky come and lie next to me. It's cosy here." I crawled over, resting my head on the tufty, fusty fur of her lapel. She always smelt slightly of candles, looked even more impressively bored in their light. Far gone eyes, breathing dragon smoke through her nostrils, a private smile itching her lips. I dug my fingers into the cold sand trying to listen to her heart. "Sometimes, I pretend I'm at the bottom of the ocean. That I'm lying flat on my back at the bottom of the ocean looking through all that water, and, you know, it's alright down here." She mumbled on about the gentle weight of water, the absolution of costal currents, but her words slurred into each other and I couldn't make out half of what she was saying.

Johnny and Dawn sat guard at the gun slits. Outside, the evening had become wild. They leant together and I heard Dawn whisper, "You can do what you want now. He'll give up the trawling. Joe was always the apple of his eye. This'll be too much, even for him. There's something about the coincidence of it all. You ken how superstitious he is. He'll sell the boat, thinking it's cursed or something."

I shifted my head so it rested on the curve of Nicky's belly. Her body had gone totally slack and she barely seemed to be breathing but the look on her face was as benign as some stained-glass saint on their way to martyrdom. It was then I felt the kick. I sat up and stared at her. Instinctively she tugged her tatty fake fur coat over the bump and stared me into silence. After holding my gaze for a full minute, she rolled over and pulled her knees up to her chest.

"What do you think?"

"What?"

"About *The Abiding Star.* What'll my da do?"

Dawn was studying my face, and I repeated my lines. "There's no money in it anymore and the risks aren't worth it. Even Tam kens that. We canna compete with the big commercial trawlers. He was only keeping on so Joe could inherit the boat and the license. Even Tam's not going to make it to sea once his chemo sessions start. Either he'll sell the boat, or Johnny'll get it ... and he can do what he wants."

Johnny sucked hard on his long sad face. "How many generations of trawlermen has there been in the family? He'll expect me to take over."

"But he kens you hate it," Dawn complained. "You're always going on about how much you hate it."

"Do you mind the pond in our garden?" he asked. "When Dawn and Joe and me were weans, there used tae be goldfish in that pond. Thing was, the pond wasn't that deep and wi all the gows round here the goldfish were always getting eaten. My father though just kept buying more. Me and Joe were daft about them goldfish. Each time he came home wi a new bag we'd spend ages fighting over their names. Every so often my father would ask which ones had died. None of the fish lasted long apart fae this one called Nessie. He had come in the first bag and Joe had named him. He was our favourite. Every morning we'd rush out. 'Is he gone?' 'I canna see him, wait, there he is behind the rock.' 'Where, are you sure, is that really him?' 'Aye.'

"My father started asking after Nessie, laughing and saying, 'He's a lucky one that.' Well, one day he asked Joe how Nessie was and Joe just shrugged and said that for all he knew Nessie had died months ago. See we couldn't make out the difference. From outside the pond they all looked the same. My father just nodded and said Joe was right. I knew he was right an aw but it didn't stop me hating both of them for it. After that we stopped checking on the fish and my father stopped buying them."

We sat deep in candle-flicker silence. I didn't get it. Johnny hated going to sea, but since his brother's death he'd started acting like becoming skipper was his destiny. He stretched out his feet so they rested on mine. I watched his face, bleached and knotted as if it had been carved from one of they logs that travel the sea for years before being thrown up by a storm. "You got any left, Nicky?" He heated the tinfoil, sucking greedily on the coil of smoke as it twisted and squirmed into the plastic tube. A Tornado from RAF Lossie tore across the sky. We peered out. A second one followed, with its grotesque plumage of bombs and missiles.

"It's the end of the world," Johnny murmured from deep within the box.

"Far do you think they're going?" Dawn asked.

No one answered. It was too mad to think of some loon the same age as us surrounded by glowing buttons and dials and millions of pounds worth of technology.

We hung out of the pill box, watching the plane's lights until they disappeared in murky skies.

"Mon," said Nicky, "the rain's almost off. Let's get out of here."

"Aye c'mon John, we could look for shells to put on Joe's grave." Johnny hawked and spat. "Malky, tell him. It's too cold to sit here all night." I just shrugged, playing wi the sand, piling little pyramids of it on the end of my trainers. When I looked up the girls had gone. I stuck my head out the box and watched them heading towards town, Dawn stepping along the concrete blocks that had been sunk in the sand to stop the invading army that never came.

"We're the last buggers on earth," Johnny whispered, "listen now." He rotated the radio's tuning dial. One wave of static after another rolled over us. He smiled: fat yellow teeth, burnt bin bag breath. His opiated eyes peered into mine. The same sullen face, same sunken eyes. "That boat's ours Malky. We're going to make a killing." He turned the volume on the radio right up high so the static sounded like rain on the wheelhouse's roof, a syringe being sharpened on the side of a matchbox: the noise of pins and needles. I held his hand and watched the stumpy candles shiver and gasp. He kissed me on the cheek, and we curled up together listening to the hush of the radio, the rush of the sea, telling each other to be quiet.

CHAPTER FOUR

Port Cawdor was on a headland that the main A road by-passed. Prior to being posted here PC Gourlay had never visited the place, nor had any of her pals. It's got nice beaches, her dad had suggested … you could learn how to surf. The sign welcoming you to the town stated PORT CAWDOR, more than you can imagine. She wasn't sure if this was a threat. Driving through town, PC Gourlay looked miserably at a gaggle of girls braving the drizzle to make the short run between pubs on Bridge Street. It was Friday evening and her shift would be over in forty minutes, but she felt no sense of elation. Sergeant Grant had driven up that street on their first patrol and explained that while he couldn't ban her from certain premises there were a few drinking holes he'd strongly recommend she didn't frequent. By the time he was done, the only places left in town were the bar at the Golf Club and one old man pub that had more dogs dozing on its sticky carpet than customers. She half considered shooting down to Aberdeen to see the girls for the night, but it was two and a half hours by bus, and she was on again at 7 the next morning. In any case, she'd noticed the social invites tail off. Birthdays had passed and the closest she got to the celebrations was looking at the glee-filled photos on Instagram. They'd been warned about this at college: the social isolation. Even when she was off-duty, people saw her as a policewoman now. And there was always someone who didn't want the police around.

"We'll have you on the night shift next weekend," Sergeant Grant had mentioned, as if this was a treat. "You'll see a bit more action then."

She was accompanying DI Stark to interview the captain of the trawler whose nets had pulled in the body of his son. It was the talk of the town, even making a couple of the national newspapers, and Gourlay had been sure Stark would have another detective with him. But when he'd told her to get her jacket, she remembered the scowls and scurrilous comments that followed Stark out of a room. "That man is not well liked." "There's a reason the other detectives won't work with him." "Nothing more than a small altercation and Stark couldn't do the decent thing and sweep it under the carpet." "You canna trust a man like that."

A call came through from control.

Stark snapped up the radio.

"Murray Square? We'll be there in two minutes."

As she u-turned on the busy street, Gourlay wondered if she'd always feel the surge of adrenaline that accompanied the sound of the siren. This was why she'd joined the force: the startled pedestrians' faces smeared by the flashing lights and car accelerating to sixty. When you'd spent two years trudging through the dead language of law followed by too many temping jobs consisting of data entry and other zombie admin tasks, this moment when gravity pressed you against the headrest and you raced towards trouble would surely never get old.

Two months into her probationary period, and she'd been called to Murray Square more times than she could remember. It was the town's bus terminus, with a public toilet whose blue lighting was meant to deter injecting drug users, but, which judging by the state of a girl who'd OD'd there last week, just led to them making even more of a mess of their arms. Gourlay was confident she knew the fastest route, but Stark directed her down an alleyway between shops and suddenly they were driving past the bookies that looked onto the square. She wasn't sure if it was the strobe of lights, the siren ricocheting off the walls, but she'd noticed when called to incidents in public places that everyone struck a pose as if they'd all been cast as anxious onlookers in some TV drama.

"Over there," Stark shouted, and they ran to a crumpled body in the corner of a bus shelter. The splayed limbs, blood pooling around the base of the skull, piss soaked combat trousers made her think she was seeing her second body that week.

"Open your eyes." Stark was down on his knees checking airways, breathing, circulation. "Open your eyes," he squeezed the victim's earlobe. "Ambulance," he snapped at her. "Unconscious, serious head injuries, breathing and pulse normal." She relayed the information.

"I'm now moving the victim into the recovery position."

"Ambulance will be here in five minutes, Sir."

"First Aid kit."

Gourlay sprinted back to the squad car noticing the punters from the bookies leaning on a crash barrier, momentarily forgetting about their race reports and betting slips. After struggling to put surgical gloves onto shaking hands, Gourlay held a gauze pad to the open head wound. It was only then she had a proper look at the victim. Young black male, late teens, closely cropped hair sticky with congealing blood.

"Don't touch that."

She looked at the nine inch blade, serrated on one side, a green logo like a bio-hazard sign on the hilt.

"Never actually seen one of these before," Stark remarked, putting it into an evidence bag. "A body fished out of the sea, an unconscious black lad and a zombie knife all in two days – and I bet you thought Port Cawdor would be a nice, quiet probation."

After a few minutes, the ambulance bustled into the square. Looking down at the third blood soaked pad, Gourlay took a shuddering breath inhaling the stale wet dog smell from the attack victim's hoody. She glanced once more at the pimpled clay coloured face. Stark quickly filled in the paramedics, while she had a last look over the body, before checking the outstretched hand to see if there was any signs of defence injuries or indications that the victim had put up a fight. The middle and forefinger looked broken, but it was the long, partially painted nails that really shocked Gourlay.

Stark followed the crew to the ambulance. Either because there was something more exciting on the screens in the bookies, or because they were worried about being questioned, the punters shrunk back into the betting shop.

"Don't go after them," Stark muttered. "They won't have seen anything. Especially not in front of their friends." He noted their faces: the type of men too lonely to be caught up in online betting. A waitress looked out of the café window, a couple of old wifies with more shopping bags than they could conceivably carry waited in another bus shelter, boys of twelve or thirteen restarted a game of wallie against the closed down library, while an alky, already too ruined to be of use, shook his can at him like a charity worker with a donation box.

Another patrol car blazed into the square.

"Where have you been?" Stark demanded.

"We came as ..."

He raised his hand. "Save it. You're too late. Tape up the area around that bus shelter. Gourlay, come with me."

Stark had spotted a young couple with a rolled up beach mat and umbrella under their arms. Out of towners, the best bet if you wanted anyone to talk.

"Evening, I'm Detective Inspector Jim Stark, and this is my colleague PC Gourlay. You look pretty shaken up, could we get you anything?"

"It's not every day you see someone get a battering like that," the young man had his free arm wrapped protectively over his partner's shoulder. He had a southern English accent and Stark felt pleased to have picked him.

"In your own words, could you describe what you saw?"

"Well it happened so fast. I hadn't really noticed the boy in the bus stop over there, everyone seemed to be waiting around this one. There wasn't really any shouting or anything, but suddenly everyone was looking, and well, the boy was already on the floor. There were three of them, all wearing rubber Halloween masks: a scary clown, werewolf, and what was the other one?"

"It was like an alien or something?"

"Yeah, and the werewolf had a hammer and was hitting the lad with it. The alien had a weapon too, some sort of bar."

"Like a weights bar, you know for dumbbells."

"It was over in like twenty seconds."

"Less. They were so fast ... so violent."

"You were there like three minutes after they legged it. No one knew what to do."

"Which way did the assailants go?"

"Past the toilets and then I dunno."

"Any distinctive clothes?"

"Just trackie bottoms, black jackets, white trainers."

"All of them?"

"Think so. Sorry. Oh, and gloves. Thick gloves like the type bikers wear."

"Thank you. If you could just give your details to my colleague."

"Will he be alright?"

"She. It was a girl."

"Shit ..." The young women glanced at her boyfriend, hesitating for a second. "Before they ran off, it looked like they took something from her. The one with the crazy clown mask, he knelt down and it looked like he was going through her pockets."

Stark wandered over to the bus stop. There were no timetables or routes around the one where the attack took place, indicating that it wasn't in use. The only mounted CCTV camera stared uselessly down at the operational stops. There was a crack on the Perspex about a foot from the ground and a lot of blood spatter. He'd get forensics to have a look but judging by the ferocity of the attack, he was pretty certain it would only be the victim's blood. Stark followed the path by the public toilets, but there were no weapons or anything else that the assailants might have dropped.

"Right, you two," he addressed PC MacKay and PC Carmichael, "Use your questionable charms to get a statement from that waitress before the café closes. Then give the bookies a go."

"Sir."

"Gourlay, make sure no one enters the crime scene until those two are done."

Gourlay watched Stark climb back into the squad car. Was he making calls or just keeping out of the wind? She looked down at the surgical gloves she was still wearing, and which were smeared with the girl's blood. Peeling them off, she surreptitiously deposited them in a bin, unsure why she was glad that no one was looking. To keep warm, she wandered towards the shelter that said 'Aberdeen and Beyond', but the addicts and alkies that hung around the terminus had taken it upon themselves to melt the timetable's plastic covering making it impossible to read. She stood there pondering whether this was a result of the curse of having nothing to do or whether they just knew that they weren't going anywhere so why should anyone else.

"Aberdeen bus isna due for another forty minutes, hen."

"Cheers," she nodded at the old women with their broods of shopping bags gathered protectively around their ankles.

Stark spun the car and came towards them lowering the passenger window.

"Ladies, could we drive you somewhere?"

"Aye, that'll be right. Ah ken your game. Think we might be ay some use to youse, but where were you last week when that lassie was out for the count in the toilet cubicle? Thirty minutes it took you. Almost pished maself so I did."

"Bloody disgrace and now this."

"So you can stick your lift. We'll take our chances with the bus and you can get on with finding the bad bastards that are filling this town with drugs."

The other policemen came out of the bookies, Carmichael shrugging at them as if to say, what was the point of that. They relieved Gourlay who gratefully got into the warmth of the car.

"Bloody impossible women," Stark exclaimed. "They're like everyone else in this town, thinking we can solve everything without their help." A patchy purple Polo pulled into the layby for drop offs. "If he parks there, I've a good mind to fine him." Rory Tan got out of the car, managing to survey the scene without catching Stark's furious gestures. He decided to take a punt on the bookies.

"Aye and they'll have no problem talking to him and all of this will be described in technicolour splendour for the front page of *The Squeak*. PC Gourlay, put a fixed penalty notice on that illegally parked car."

When Gourlay got back to the car, he was still as angry as she'd seen him. Driving out of the bus stance, she asked, "Was the attack drugs related?"

"Undoubtedly. A black kid doesn't just end up getting randomly assaulted in a location like that."

"Is that not … you know, racial profiling."

"PC Gourlay, there are a couple of Pakistani families in Port Cawdor, some Eastern Europeans during the picking season. We had those Syrian families arrive to great fanfare last autumn, but they'd all legged it by spring to the amusement of all the other fishing towns, but there isn't a single black family in the area."

"Could she not be up here on holiday, or an air force family just moved in?"

"It's possible, but the foosty clothes, bad skin? It'll be some kid sent up from London to run one of these county lines. All the publicity this place has been getting, it's not surprising someone would try it, but the Kerrs won't be having competition like that. There've been kids arrested in towns down the coast."

Gourlay steered the vehicle into his reserved parking spot outside the station and sat for a minute listening to the ticking of the cooling engine.

"How are you settling in, anyway?"

"Fine," Gourlay heard her voice say, before considering the evening ahead in her one bedroom rented flat whose walls remained bare, wardrobe remained empty, her stuff still in suitcases and boxes that she hadn't the heart to unpack.

After changing into her civilian clothes, she checked her watch. There was still enough time for her to catch that bus out of here.

CHAPTER FIVE

The next morning, I waited until my mum had gone to work before rolling out of my pit. After the nauseous nights at sea, this was the first decent kip I'd had all week. But the floor still pitched as I stumbled to the toilet. It'd taken a full day to find my land legs after my first time at sea and sometimes I'd wondered if I'd ever trust the ground beneath my feet again.

Someone chapped on the front-door and I froze, my hand about to flush the toilet. I heard the letterbox open and Dawn shouting, "Malky, are you there?" I listened for Nicky's voice but couldn't hear her amongst the noise of the others carrying on. Nicky, who looked at me like she could read my mind. Nicky, who smiled at me like I wasn't all bad. Nicky, whose life I was going to save.

If she'd been there, I'd be half-way down the stairs.

Traditionally, deckies would have a few days shore leave, during which they'd blow all their pay packet getting howling and chasing quines and wrapping their souped up sports cars round lamp posts, before staggering back to a job with the highest mortality rate in the country. The three day binge was in the blood. Fishing folk had been this way for ever. But nobody did three day sessions like our generation.

While listening to Johnny arguing that they shouldn't post my pay, that if I wanted it I should come and find them, I realised I was holding my breath. Eventually I heard something drop through the letterbox. I counted to fifty before flushing.

There was only £100 in the envelope, the notes as dirty and creased as the hands of the trawlermen and market sellers through which they'd passed. As I sealed the money into the envelope and stuffed it in my sock drawer, I thought of Joe's cold sockless feet and the questions Uncle Tam had asked. Right now Joe would be laid out on the mortician's lab. They'd be examining his body, removing his organs, taking samples of his blood and tissue.

Social media was already full of it: I'd never had so many mentions, messages, links to articles shared with me, as if I didn't know what was happening already. Feeling my heart fluttering in my throat, I turned the phone off and for good measure buried it in my sock drawer next to the money.

My holdall, stuffed with clothes from the previous week was stinking out the room, so I flung the window open and went downstairs to fill the bath with hot water and detergent. I soaked the clothes and started scrubbing. The water scalded my hands and the detergent stung my skin, but it was satisfying to feel that I was getting things done. I scoured the stained waterproofs and sweat drenched under-things. The water turned a rusty red and smelt of rotting sea-weed. After pulling the plug I ran fresh water over the clothes, examining them for any stains.

It was while I was hanging the clothes that the police car drove up Cluny Brae - the vehicle shockingly white against the slate and pebbledash grey. Sure enough, they parked outside our row of houses and I heard two doors slam and heavy knuckles rapping on the door. I stood behind the shed knowing that even if they peered through our windows they'd never see me. My clothes flapped in the wind and I stared at my red raw hands until I was sure they'd gone.

I spent the rest of the afternoon lying in bed, distracting myself by reading the prospectuses of universities I'd never bothered applying to, with their entry requirements that I hadn't bothered working for. Right now I'd have given anything to be escaping to a big city at the end of summer. I wasn't mad about the idea of sitting in libraries and lectures all day; I just wanted to be in a place where no one knew my name. Unable to concentrate on the text, I flicked through pages filled with photos of students who looked like they got their five a day, regularly visited the dentists and felt comfortable in their clothes. Every time I heard a car motoring up the brae, I shut the heavy, glossy books, half hoping it'd stop and I'd know what shade of shite I was in.

My mum came home from the chippie with her clothes reeking of vinegar and cooking oil. "Well the town's full ay it. When Mags first telt me I says I'm naw being taken in by that, but aabody kens." She looked keenly at me to see what I had to say for myself. "Poor Joe," she added. "Poor laddie."

He was already dead, I felt like saying.

"The police were round the chippie. Did they catch up with you?"

"I haven't seen them."

"Well, far hae you been?"

"They must have called when I was hanging the washing. I had my headphones in."

"You did the washing?" She looked out the window at the clothes, which had been dry for hours.

"Should be about dry now. I'll get them in."

"Dinna fash yourself," she said, striding to the garden. "I brought you home a pizza," she shouted over her shoulder. "Thought you'd be sick ay fish by now."

The next morning I headed down to the police station. At the desk was a boy, who'd been in Johnny's year at school. Michael Carmichael. Who the fuck calls their son that? He had blonde hair and black eyebrows and you could visibly see the plaque on his teeth. There was something about the ponderous way that he had spoken when he was at school - savouring the polysyllabic words that he didn't quite know how to pronounce - that had made it obvious he would join the police.

"So, what are you here for?"

"I don't know, you were the ones looking for me."

"Aye, we paid your house a visitation."

"I was in the garden."

"Hanging up the washing. We know. Take a seat. Inspector Stark is conducting an interview. He'll be with you in a minute."

"Do I need a lawyer?"

"A lawyer? It's just a witness interview. You're what we call a voluntary attender – someone who might be able to help us tie up a few loose ends."

I sat on one of the blue plastic seats, wondering what they thought I'd witnessed. Michael Carmichael had returned to looking at his computer screen, and although he clearly wasn't doing any work I was wary of striking up a conversation. The place stank of bleach and vomit. On the noticeboard were the usual warnings about leaving valuables in cars or drinking and driving. Amongst these was a slightly blurred and already sunbleached photo of Danny Kerr who had gone missing at the start of the year. Prior to Joe's drowning, the disappearance of Danny was the most exciting thing that had happened up here. The Kerrs were infamous. Fights were averted the moment one person claimed to be pals with them; entry to the town's only nightclub was secured if you claimed to be with The Family; pool balls were cleared from half-finished games if they so much as looked at a table. So the thought of someone facing up to them was too mad for words. Last Hogmanay he'd gone missing and after four days had reappeared staggering along the West Beach, naked and weeping and incoherent. UFO abductions the newspapers dubbed them, on account of the fact that those who had gone missing came back so traumatised that they were unable or unwilling to say where they had been. The same thing had happened to members of other crime families from down the coast - a younger cousin or son kidnapped on the way back from the pub, or a party, talk of there being a black transit van crawling around the area. Speculation was immense. The story was that Danny had been fed LSD and left in a suitcase filled with rats, or that they'd buried him up to his neck on the tideline and left him there for days, or that they'd forced him to remove the teeth and fingernails of another gangland rival.

What was certain was that a fortnight after Danny reappeared his eldest brother and uncle were arrested with thirty grand of heroin in their car. A week later Danny disappeared again. This time for good.

Zoe Stark's dad came into the room. He had silver hair slicked back into a side parting and wore the permanently concerned look of a Science teacher conducting an experiment in front of pupils who are hoping to see the whole thing blow up in his face.

"Malcolm. Good of you to come in."

As I was led into the guts of the police station, a memory from a Highland League match came to me. January. Freezing. Port Cawdor Thistle getting pumped 4-0 and me and Johnny clutching rapidly cooling polystyrene cups of Bovril begging to leave. Uncle James, who'd taken us out for the day, had crouched in front of us. After calling the two of us a fucking embarrassment, he'd explained. "There are four rules in life: you don't leave a team you're supporting early; you don't hit women; you don't vote Tory and you never, ever rat on anybody to the police. Stick by those rules and you'll do alright."

The reek of bleach and vomit grew more powerful as Inspector Stark opened the door to the interview room. The policewifey, who'd been on our boat and who'd probably be a looker if it wasn't for the mingin uniform, sat at the table scribbling in a notebook.

"Son, this is PC Gourlay. She's going to sit in on this meeting if that's ok with you."

It wasn't really a question so I didna bother answering. PC Gourlay gave me the sort of smile a primary school teacher might bestow on a shy pupil, so I gave her a sarky smile back until she went back to whatever she was doing in her notebook.

"This is just an informal chat, so no need for the audio recorder."

I sat on the lone plastic chair, that would have a sweaty arse crack line on it by the time this was over. Inspector Stark took a pile of papers out of a folder, making sure I couldn't see what was on them.

"The autopsy has been completed and once we've got a few things cleared up, the pathologist can return the body to your Aunt and Uncle. That's the main thing. Joe can have a proper funeral and the bereaved can complete the grieving process."

He looked up from the papers. "Thanks," I heard my voice saying.

PC Gourlay was staring at my hands, as if she'd never the likes of them. I took them off the table.

"We've not had a full written report and it'll be a while until we get a toxicology report, but I don't think we'll find out anymore from that, not when the deceased had been in the sea for 12 days."

I frowned, felt as if I was meant to apologise for not bringing in a fresh body.

"Witnesses and the toxicology reports have all indicated that the last three trawlermen lost at sea were either under the influence of alcohol, or heroin. But I don't think that was the case with Joe Campbell. He was too professional to be drinking at sea and we know who the smackheads are around here."

Stark gave me a sly look that was meant to suggest he knew far more than he was letting on.

"Joe wasn't into that stuff," I confirmed.

"It's no secret that Thomas Campbell is sick, that he should have packed in the trawling months ago. The talk of the town was that your uncle was going to make Joe skipper."

"So he had things to look forward to."

"Due to be married to a nice girl."

"It seemed strange that someone as experienced as Joe should go overboard on a calm night, so I was glad when the body turned up. Thought it might clear up a few things."

PC Gourlay snapped her notebook shut, indicating that it was her turn.

"It's never easy to say with bodies found in water, but the pathologist is fairly certain that Joe drowned. They found salt water in his stomach. Fairly typical when someone has been struggling in the sea."

My sweaty hands gripped the side of the chair and I felt that I was sinking through depths so great I might never stop. The pigs were eyeing me the way I'd seen deckies look at weird creatures dredged up from the deep that no one knew how to classify.

"No real surprise there. It's either drowning or hypothermia and at this time of year the former is more likely. Are you alright? Is he alright? PC Gourlay, get the lad a glass of water."

I'd dreamt of this a dozen times. Nightmares in which I struggled to keep my head above the lumps of water, as the lights of the boat moved into the distance and I was left in the endless blackness, the sky sagging with stars that must have felt as far away as salvation. How long did it take for the lights to disappear? Did Joe watch them until they'd vanished: his only hope, the trawler coming back? How long would he have survived? A gulp of salt water here, a slap of ocean there.

"He was my cousin."

DI Stark cleared his throat, his eyes flicking between me and something in the report.

"What the pathologist was most interested in was the blunt force trauma that Joe, *your cousin*, suffered on the back of his head. The back of Joe's skull had sustained two, possibly three blows. We've got some close-up photos of the injuries here." PC Gourlay looked like she was about to take the photos from the folder but at the last second Inspector Stark stopped her.

"Look Malky, son, you don't mind me calling you Malky, do you? Everybody knows Johnny and Joe couldn't stand each other. There are four separate incidents on file when we were called to stop them fighting, and that's just the tip of the iceberg. They'd both have been charged with GBH a couple of times if they weren't brothers. God knows how they survived all those years cooped up on the same boat. Their dad is claiming that when they went to their bunks everything was fine. But only you and Johnny know what happened in that cabin."

PC Gourlay slowly reopened her notebook and selected a sharper pencil from her pocket. "In your own words, tell us what really happened that night?"

I looked down at the floor as if trying to remember, but in truth, that trip had been a nightmare I'd never forget. It was my first time working on the trawler. Within an hour of us leaving the harbour I'd been sick so many times that I was dry heaving, gulping air, trying to focus on something that wasn't constantly rolling. Johnny and Corky were zombified on the buprenorphine they got off the chemists, pretending, and somehow succeeding to convince their dads, that they were only hungover. Joe was raging. Joe was always raging, but this time he had us three useless fuckers to focus his fury on. The whole mood was poisonous: Joe had been trying to convince Tam that Corky was a total liability, a waster, whose presence on the trawler put us all at risk. Tam though was having none of it. That was why Joe'd given Corky a doing the night before we'd gone to sea. He'd figured Corky wouldn't make it to the harbour with a burst face and that he could use this as further evidence of his unreliability. But he hadn't figured how much Corky needed the money.

A day into the trip and Johnny's buprenorphine had gone missing. I'd never seen him so feart. Joe had spent the evening goading him – telling him one moment that he'd thrown the pills overboard, and then minutes later that he was going to show them to Tam, who'd finally have to face up to the fact that his son was a junkie. 'When I'm skipper,' he'd told Johnny, 'you won't get near this trawler the state you're in and, if you do, and it's a big if, you won't spend the first two days of every trip pretending to be sick and making every other bugger do your work.'

Inspector Stark's catarrh cough brought me back to the interrogation room.

"What we want to know is this: did they fight that night? Is that what happened?"

For one vertiginous moment, I saw a way out of this. My lips came unstuck and my tongue felt as heavy as a bone. The pigs leaned their snouts forward as if they thought it was feeding time.

"Could the injuries not have happened as he fell overboard?"

PC Gourlay winced as if I'd just blown smoke into her face, while Stark folded his arms in a manner that was clearly meant to signify his disappointment in my stupidity.

"Three blows to the back of the head. What do you think?"

"Thing is son, this is potentially a murder investigation, and we can't release the body until someone is arrested and charged. That's hard on your Uncle and Aunt, don't you think?"

"Let's go over your original statement. You said that you woke up in the cabin and Joe wasn't there?"

"Yeah."

"Who woke first? You or Johnny?"

"Me. It was my first time at sea and I was being sick all the time. I just about made it to the sink and that woke Johnny."

"Right, and did either of you raise the alarm at that point?"

"No. We had a blether for a few minutes and then went back to sleep. We just thought Joe had gone up to the wheelhouse, or was taking a dump."

"What did you talk about?"

"Johnny said something about the sea sickness getting better after the first few days and how we'd have to celebrate my first time away from shore when we got back."

Inspector Stark looked at the statement I'd made after Joe first went overboard.

"Uh-huh," he said.

Truth was, I had woken feeling sick, but the others had been whining so much about the noise and the smell of me puking that I'd gone up on deck and had stayed there until the skelps of sea squalls made me feel better. When I got back to the cabin, Johnny and Joe were wrestling on the floor. I'd seen this before and for a moment it'd looked like Johnny was going to have him. But Joe was stronger, heavier and hadn't been gutted by three days of withdrawal at sea. He'd rolled Johnny and knelt on his chest his hands around his brother's neck …

Inspector Stark shuffled the papers on his side of the table and for a moment I thought we were through.

"We should probably tell you that we've got forensics combing the cabin. If you're trying to protect John Campbell, you should forget it."

"It'll be much better for you if you make a clean break of it."

"Think he'll stick up for you?"

"This is the one chance you get."

"What about Josh McCormack?"

"What about him?"

"Friend of yours?"

"Of Johnny's."

"So he and Joe probably didn't get on? I mean, seen as Johnny and Joe didn't get on?"

I shrugged.

"His face had been bashed up a fair bit when we first interviewed him. We took photos of that too. He told us he'd been jumped coming back from the pub by some laddies with Fraserburgh accents."

"Never reported it or anything. Know anything about that?"

Inspector Stark scratched the silvery stubble on his chin, the sound like someone continually failing to light a match. On the bottom of her notepad PC Gourlay scribbled in capital letters SIGNIFICANT SILENCES. Her eyes locked on mine and I realised she'd meant me to see this.

"I need a lawyer. I'm not saying anything without a lawyer. I'm seventeen. You're interviewing me without a lawyer and I'm seventeen."

Inspector Stark had been rocking on the back legs of his chair and let the four legs clatter against the floor as he leant towards us.

"This was never an interview, son. You came here of your own accord for a wee chat and can go when you want. But you're right. If you don't start telling us what really happened in that cabin, the next time we meet we'll be interviewing you under caution, and I'd say that finding a lawyer will be the least of your concerns."

After the warning, Inspector Stark took us through the secure doors of the station, asking after my mum and questions about how I thought I'd done in my exams, as if what had just gone on in the interview room had all been an act. But the switch from police detective to Zoe Stark's dad didn't fool me. He held the station door open while asking me what I planned to do with myself, as if I could just walk out of there and in to any future I wanted.

I was almost gone, when he said the word.

"Guilt." He let it hang. "Some folks think they can handle it. But they can't. Not if there've done something really bad, or know someone who has. They think it's just a feeling, something that can be controlled and, perhaps, there've had a taste of it before and think it's … manageable." He sniffed. "But that'd be like someone who didn't take a drink thinking they could handle a bottle of whisky."

I wanted away from him more than ever then. Had a certainty that if he saw my eyes the whole world would come tumbling down.

"Thanks for the advice," my voice sounding more childish than churlish.

"I'll be seeing you," he shouted at my back as I retreated down the road.

CHAPTER SIX

Straight out the station and I got on the phone to Johnny, but he wasn't answering, so I headed down to Nicky's: the harbour we all turned to in a storm. The Burnside Estate was to be regenerated, by which the council meant sold to a developer who, impressed by the sea views, saw the potential in building luxury flats for the type of posh cunts who were filling the harbour with yachts. I passed a billboard on which unlived in faces the size of hot air balloons beamed from advertisements for these luxury homes. A blandly beautiful woman with a pristine smile revealed her delight in the blandly beautiful room. A slightly older man with the smug face of someone who has just taken control of the world leant back on his Scandinavian sofa. But all these images only existed on a computer; the development had been put on hold. For now The Burnside Estate was a series of condemned brutalised buildings that had been beaten up for years but were still standing, waiting for the wrecking ball the way a punch-drunk boxer waits for a knockout blow. Nicky had somehow got a copy of the key for the top floor of a maisonette and had been squatting there since last summer. Riff Raff Road we called it: a dumping ground of undesirables for decades. In anticipation of the continually pushed back demolition, the tenets of the nearby flats had been evicted, which suited Nicky and the rest of us just fine.

The ground floor door no longer existed and I headed up the dark stair well. It took ages for Nicky to open the door and I felt certain she'd been watching me through the peephole. Inside the flat was as cosy as she could make it, with adverts from glamour mags – gaunt girls in expensive rags - covering the holes in the walls.

She led me through a barricade of binbags and salvaged furniture to the sitting room. Her hair looked like she'd just got out of bed, while her face looked like she hadn't slept for days.

"I was just about to shower," Nicky said.

By showering, Nicky meant heating a pot over a primus gas stove and splashing herself with the warm water. While she did this in the next room, I tanned a can of beer from her fridge, which was only nominally a fridge seeing as the electricity had been cut a month after the other tenants had been moved. With the haar shrouding the town, the flat seemed gloomy and Nicky shouted on us to light some candles and put the music on. The sitting room was full of candles. Bodies lifted them from pubs at closing time and brought them as presents. Fat expensive ones the colour of priests' fingers, thin red ones sticking out of spirit bottles, scented ones that mingled with the stench from the maze of binbags and made her room smell like one of they shops for tree-huggers. In the near silence, I sat listening to the splash of water as it was scooped up into her face and oxsters and breasts.

During a night in which the doom accelerator had been firmly pressed to the floor, Nicky had smashed one of the sitting room windows in a misguided belief that she could juggle beer bottles. As the chill air slithered over the broken glass, I watched the snickering candles around the filled in fireplace, their light reflecting off Nicky's legendary collection of letters in bottles. Every month or so, one of the fishing boats would pull up one of these bottles with their catch. Some of them were new plastic ones, but others were older, thick brown glass bottles with labels and brand names erased from their surfaces. There was even one clear bottle with what looked like Russian letters embossed on the glass. Loons working on the boats gave these gifts to Nicky and in exchange she would let them hang at her flat or would share some of her smack, lulling them to sleep with elaborate stories behind each bottle. These gifts delighted her, but they became worthless if she discovered they'd been opened. The deckies all kent this and stoppered their curiosity, faithfully bringing bottles containing messages that no one but the writer had read.

I'd once asked if she'd ever secretly opened them and she'd looked at me, shocked by how little I had understood. Stupidly, I'd blundered on protesting that some of the messages could be rescue pleas from people marooned on lonely islands or the last words of sinking ship captains, lost through her lack of curiosity. But she'd stopped listening and had instead stared at her collection, mesmerised by the glint of candlelight on the green, brown and opaque glass.

"We are all at sea, filled with stories that will never be told," she whispered. "These bottles are no different from you and me."

Nicky came out of the room that she slept in. With the towel wrapped around her it was easy to see the curve of her pregnant belly. She walked over to the couch that we'd all carried here from the Sally Army store and I felt the heat of her body, her skin smelling of ice-cream and freshly cut football pitches.

"You've naw seen ma brush?"

The cushion sank as she knelt next to me. "I can't find it anywhere," she said, looking behind pillows. The towel edged up her thighs which were smooth and white like the inside of a conker shell.

"Don't even look at me like that."

"Like what?"

She raised an eyebrow, and there was the old Nicky: cocky, cheeky, a total tease. I thought of the graffiti in the boys' toilets at school. On the wall of one cubicle someone had simply written – Nicola Skelton? There was no need to properly form the question. Around it dozens of boys, probably too feart to even look her in the eye, had described all the things they'd like to do to her. If she'd grown up in a big city she'd probably have ended up being a model or lead singer in a group that didn't play in a town whose aboriginals were only happy listening to covers of bands that existed before they were born. But up here, as soon as she hit high school, she was doomed to be chased by all the head cases. With a yelp, she located her hairbrush and rushed through to the next room.

Whilst she did her hair, I scrolled through LCD illuminated images of people living postable lives on social media, but it was hard to concentrate with Nicky behind a half-shut door, wet and singing sadly as if she'd forgotten I was there. Her battery powered ghetto blaster was surrounded by mix tapes that Johnny had made for her over the years. Despite everyone streaming music, mixtapes still had currency; nothing said, "I love you, but I'm too much of a tongue tied Scottish teenager" to ever say those words like a tape filled with songs of misery and misrecordings. I slipped one that said Happy Birthday in Johnny's handwriting into the machine and Down by the Water mingled with Nicky's lament. The batteries in the tape player were running out warping and elongating the tune, slurring the words until PJ Harvey sounded like some karaoke drunk. I slapped the machine but to no effect. Not that I was bothered: the permanently dying sound system and the warbled, strung out lyrics suited Nicky's place just fine.

Leaning back, I looked at the peeling triangles of wall paper that hung from the ceiling, saturated and stained by the dirty rainwater that had leaked through the roof. Every so often a drop would form on the point of the paper before dripping to the floor.

"My stalactites," Nicky said, as if introducing me to one of the wonders of the world. "I can spend hours watching them." She sat down and fished a squashed pack of tabs from her shirt pocket.

"I've just been in the police station."

"Again?" She pulled a lighter from behind a cushion. "What did they want?"

"They had a pathologist look over Joe ... they found injuries."

"Injuries?"

"Three blows to the back of his head ... blunt force trauma, they called it."

"Shit. That changes everything. Did one ay youse actually do it? I mean he had it coming."

"It was an accident."

"Aye, that'll be right. Three blows to the back of his head? That's some accident. What's Tam saying?"

"I dinna ken. He asked a few weird questions after we pulled the body in."

"Fuck's sake. What are the chances? In the whole sea …"

"Once the police have interviewed him, he'll know about Joe's injuries … he's not daft."

She made a sound like a punctured football when you kick it.

"Christ. He'll blame Johnny. Everyone'll blame Johnny. There's no way he'll get his hands on the boat if Tam thinks he's anything to do with it."

"That's the least of our worries."

"That's easy for you to say," she cradled her bump.

"Have you seen anyone about … that? Should you not have a check-up or something?"

"Why'd you care?" She stared sullenly out of the broken window. "If I went for a check-up, they'd realise what a mess I am. Besides, I'd need to give them an address. They do home visits. Can you imagine a mid-wife coming round Riff Raff Road? There'd be a whole army of social workers just ready to grab him the moment he was born."

"Him?"

"Him," she smiled a secret smile.

"Could someone at the council not sort you out with a flat?"

She wrinkled her nose. "Not after the wreck we left the last place in. They hate me up there."

"But you can't have a baby here."

She shrugged. "Did Johnny never tell you about our plans?"

Plans? We never had plans. We were full of mad schemes of bands, guerrilla art shows and criminal heists. But these were nothing more than dreams and fantasies that made the heart quicken when the granite grey slog of life became too much.

"You ken Souter?" Even though we were in an empty flat in an abandoned block, she whispered his name. "When he was in Peterhead he shared a cell with a man who'd been transferred from some prison down south. He was part of a smuggling ring - serious organised crime. Once he found out Souter was from round here, he wanted to know if he could get his hands on a trawler and a crew who'd be prepared to bring drugs into the country. Soon as Souter was out, he asked me to get him in touch with Johnny. We kent that Tam's poor health meant he widna be going to sea for much longer, but of course there was always Joe in the way. Dull, reliable by-the-book Joe. That is until his *accident*."

I'd heard Nicky say all sorts of messed up stuff before, but this was mental, even for her. And then she whispered the type of money involved. The type of money that would never become available to kids like us.

"So that's why Johnny's acting like he wants to become a skipper?"

She nodded before lighting a fag, enjoying the look on my face.

"You shouldn't be doing that." I protested.

"Small baby, easier birth," she sneered. "It's not like I can keep it. A skint girl squatting in a condemned flat. It'll have to be terminated."

"You don't have to do that."

"Don't you start telling me what I have to do." She drew a circle with her cigarette.

I stared at Nicky's collection of bottles, at the unread ghost like messages forever enclosed.

"Fuck, I don't know what I'm doing. I mind them getting all the girls together at school and showing us this film – The Silent Scream it got called. It was fucking horrible; this footage of a foetus being broken up in the womb and the idea of it screaming. I had nightmares about that for months – like what would it sound like if this thing had a voice. I had this mad idea that the mother would know. That somewhere deep in her soul, she'd always carry that noise." She looked in disgust at the half-smoked cigarette before dropping it in a beer bottle, where it hissed in the dregs.

"Listen, I'll get a job, sell my x-box, give you all my money."

She chuckled at this. Her mirthless gravelly laugh that she'd curated over the years. She told me I was sweet. Told me it would never be enough. She clawed her fingers through the ends of her still damp hair, tugging at the tangles.

"I need enough money for a fresh start, Malky. If I can get away from this shit hole, I could sort myself out. Get clean. Just enough money so I could get a place that a bairn could be brought up in. Too many people ken this address. You have to get your hands on that boat. Use it for smuggling. Souter and Johnny said I'd get a cut of the money for setting them up. It's my only hope."

And she was right. When you live in a squat in a condemned and deserted block, people can bang and kick at your door until you let them in, pelt stones at your windows when you don't. But mostly, all they had to do was shout through the letter box that they had smack and Nicky would open the door. And, as the flat filled, she'd retire into somewhere far behind her eyes, burrow beneath blankets, hibernating with her habit, to a place where nobody could reach her.

I could have said, why don't *you* get a job, but Nicky had worked everywhere: the bakers, petrol station, most of the pubs and the chippie - even my mum eventually agreed with the common consensus that she was the sort of girl you couldn't take anywhere, except to court or casualty. Everyone kent what she was like, and there was no one left daft enough to give her another chance.

I couldn't see what there was I could do, but as she stared at me with that ravenous look, I felt myself prepared to promise anything. It was at this moment that the mobile on Nicky's table – this old school Nokia brick - started buzzing.

She looked at it the way people look at a solitary toddler wailing in public. Eventually she answered.

"Hello … No, she didn't come back … About 4ish on Friday … Yeah, it's still here … course I haven't touched it." Nicky slammed the phone back on the table. "Fuck." She started rummaging through the contents of a cardboard box, piling books, bills, packets of old photos on the table.

"What's up?"

From the bottom of the box, she pulled out a cling film wrapped package about the size of a tennis ball.

"Christ, whose is that?"

"The fellas fae down south - Souter's pals. They've been sending these kids up fae London. Want to see what the markets like. One of them was biding here."

"Jesus, Nicky, you ken what'll happen if the Kerrs catch you?"

"Sounds like they already got Jazmyne. She never came home on Friday and Dawn heard about someone getting jumped in Murray Square."

I looked at the packet of drugs imagining the police, or even worse the Kerrs, kicking down the door.

"Are they making you do it?"

"No, it's not like that. The girl staying here's younger than you. I already told you. I'm desperate. I need the cash."

She picked up a photo of a primary class from the box. Johnny, Dawn and Corky were all ages with Nicky and I excavated their faces amongst baggy school polo-shirts, butterfly clips and jelly bracelets.

"I knew she wouldn't last long. A black girl dealing on The Front. Hardly gonnae go under the radar. Just glad I haven't touched their stash, or I'd be in real trouble." She looked greedily at the package. "They'd never know though, would they? If I just took a wee bump."

I looked at her and back at the primary school photo. It must have been a composite class because sitting beside Nicky was a boy with a helmet haircut, missing his front teeth, a grin like Dracula. He was wearing beige cords and a baggy Dennis the Menace T-shirt that I'd ended up inheriting. I looked for his name. Joseph Campbell. On her other side was Johnny. There was something conspiratorial in the way he and Nicky leant together, as if one of them had just cracked a joke about Joe. Poor stupid Joe, who had only ever wanted to go to sea, who was happy with the life he'd been given and the skin he was in.

"Drowned, suicide, overdose, overdose," Nicky pinged the faces of four of her classmates with her long black nails. "What choice do I have?" She dropped the photo on the floor and held onto us, her face wet against my chest. I looked at the picture, tried to see something damned in the faces of the dead children, something sinister in the way they looked at the camera, something suggesting that each carried within them a little timed bomb that was always destined to go off.

"I'll get my hands on that boat for you." She smiled at me with that bright bruise of a mouth, those blank blacked-out eyes.

The children in the photo stared back at us. I wanted to sit beside them on varnished gym benches, amongst the smell of plasticine and plimsoles and crayon-coloured dreams. They smiled like they had nothing to fear.

CHAPTER SEVEN

Jim Stark, barricaded behind the sports section of the newspaper, chanced a glance across the remnants of the breakfast table at his wife. She was reading The Northern Advertiser, known to all as The Squeak, and sighing dramatically at the paper's content.

"Another assault in Port Cawdor." She read the by-line in a tone that suggested Stark was personally responsible.

He'd read the article. The vivid description of the attack in which the black girl in hospital, was described as brandishing a machete. No one on the policing team had got any witness statements claiming anything like that, but the finger prints on the zombie knife were all hers. She was in an induced coma, her pockets empty, except for a receipt from a McDonald's on Kingsland Road, Hackney that pretty much confirmed his suspicions. The Squeak had commented that dealers from London were infiltrating towns along the coast, and Stark wondered if this was guess work, a leak from the station, or if Rory Tan had his own sources.

"Fighting in broad daylight. Weapons. London gangs. It's getting worse."

Stark had received more or less the same message from Chief Superintendent Jackson along with the news that the National Crime Agency were aware of county lines activities in Port Cawdor and would be interviewing the girl when she regained consciousness.

"Is Zoe going to surface any time soon?" He asked attempting to shift the subject.

"She was back late," his wife responded, "Let her sleep it off. You're only young once."

Zoe was almost eighteen, and Stark was still getting used to it. Head Girl in her last year at school and with offers to study Medicine at a selection of Russell Group universities, she'd always been the perfect daughter. Almost too perfect. Stark was worried about the inevitable rebellion and had hoped it wouldn't come until she was far away from here.

"It'll affect your chance of getting a transfer," Linda Stark steered the conversation in the direction all their conversations motored towards. "It's the end of August that it needs to be submitted by, isn't it? You need to get Jackson to agree to it this time. For all our sakes."

Stark nodded. She was sick of school: the cheeky kids, weak head, lack of aspiration. She wanted to move back to Edinburgh to be near her elderly parents. But it was Sophie their elder daughter's decision to get a summer job in Oxford at the end of her second year at university that had piled on the pressure. She'd spent Easter studying down there too, which meant she hadn't come back to the Port since a few days around Christmas. Stark was proud of her getting a place at a university like that, but he'd always felt her decision to study at the other end of the country when there were perfectly good universities in Scotland was a rejection of them. He understood. It wasn't easy being the daughter of a detective in a town like this. Soon it would be Zoe's turn to leave, and they both feared she'd go the same way. That was why she was allowed to stay in bed past 11 when Stark had made this breakfast for them all.

"It's Joseph Campbell's burial today," Linda Stark said with a rustle of the papers. "I feel sorry for his mother. A son dead and the town full of rumours."

Stark wasn't to be drawn. He knew they sat around the tables in the staff room at school dissecting the crime reports in the paper, commentating on which former pupils had appeared in court, while plugging Linda for any gory details.

"What was he like at school?"

Linda Stark sipped her orange juice. "A bit of a plodder. Set on going to sea so thought studying was pointless. He wasn't badly behaved though. Not like his siblings. They were wild enough. Still are from what I hear."

Stark drained the dregs of his coffee. They'd hit a brick wall with the Campbell case. The pathologist believed that the blunt force trauma on the back of Joseph Campbell's head was most likely the result of an assault, but there was no corroborating evidence, and the crew were sticking to their original stories. It looked like it would be categorised as an accidental death, and knowing how difficult it would be to prove otherwise, one part of Stark hoped it'd just be swept away. The only new lead had been a packet of buprenorphine found in a zipped pocket in the deceased's trousers. Inquiries had uncovered that both John Campbell and Josh McCormack got these on prescription from the chemists to help manage their drug problems and the theory was that Joseph Campbell had taken the drugs from one of them and a fight had ensued. But that's all it was. A theory. As Sergeant Grant had repeatedly observed, it was just about possible that the deceased had slipped, banged his head and been so disorientated he'd fallen overboard. That forensics hadn't found a single spot of Joe Campbell's blood wasn't hugely surprising given he'd been wearing a wooly bunnet beneath the tightly tied hood and the vessel was scoured clean by crashing waves and North Sea storms.

The tightly tied hood had been of interest from the start. Gourlay was right. It didn't make sense for someone to have tied the drawstrings on their hood so tightly in any weather, but Joe Campbell had gone missing on a still, dry night. The sockless feet provided further evidence for a idea he was developing.

"He was a big lad, Joe Campbell, wasn't he?"

"Aye, he was a strapping laddie."

Stark remembered the step ladder into the boys' cabin. If Joe Campbell wasn't wearing anything on his feet, then he had likely been attacked in that cabin. There was no way one person could have carried Joe up that stepladder and thrown him overboard.

"What was Malcolm Campbell like?"

"Malky? He won't be involved in any of this. He was a nice laddie, who knew the difference between right and wrong. Good at art with a really sensitive appreciation for language. He was in my English class in his second year. He'd have turned out better if it weren't for those cousins of his."

If being a police detective for twenty-five years had taught Stark anything, it was that there was no correlation between being intelligent and being good. Malky Campbell might well know the intellectual difference between right and wrong, but in his experience, lots of young people didn't know the difference between wrong and evil.

"Butter," Linda Stark requested in her teacher's voice. "That's margarine."

His wife pulled the arts section from *The Herald*. Sometimes, he thought it was a punch bag or a poodle that she wanted, and neither role appealed. The pot in which the eggs were boiling was starting to bubble over. He watched the water splutter over the sides and sizzle on the hob.

"They've given the *Medea* that's on in Edinburgh a five star review. I've never seen a good production of *Medea*. So much good theatre coming up at The Festival: *Who's Afraid of Virginia Woolf*, *The Odd Couple*, *Death of a Salesman*. Imagine having all that on your doorstep. Ha, on your doorstep ... we've got most of it in our house!"

He had no idea what she was on about. At times like these, he wondered if they shared anything more than a simmering resentment that occasionally boiled over into open animosity.

Stark got up from his seat and grabbed his coat. "What time are they burying him?" Linda tossed him *The Squeak*. Not until twelve thirty. Perfect.

Out the door he wasn't even sure if he had the brass neck to spy on a funeral, but it'd beat sitting around the house. The only chance they had of turning this into a murder inquiry was if one of the crew cracked. They'd stuck to their original stories in the interview room. Malky Campbell had even repeated some of what he'd said in his original statement word for word. Stark had been in this game long enough to know when people were hiding something. If Joe had sustained the head injuries in the cabin, it would have taken two people to get him up on deck and dump him overboard. Stark didn't care if Malky Campbell could write a touching literary analysis. He was one of the two people in that cabin. It was more a hope than a hunch but Stark wanted to be at the funeral in case one of them snapped.

Walking along the Esplanade, the sea sparkling in the slivers of sunlight, dog walkers nodding familiarly as he passed, tourists optimistically carrying all the apparel necessary for an afternoon on the beach, Stark wished that he did a job in which you could switch off on your day off. But Linda was right, for the good of his marriage, for the good of his family, he was going to have to earn a transfer from here, and the only way he was going to do that was by impressing the chief. He headed down to The Front, where, due to the irregular working hours of the harbour, Monty's would have been serving alcohol since six.

The summer sunshine barely seeped through the pub's frosted glass windows and the interior seemed principally to be illuminated by the flashing buttons of a fruit machine. Balearic trance blared from the jukebox while the barmaid stared into an imaginary sunset, her feet shuffling on imaginary sand. Once his eyes had adjusted to the gloom he felt like making an about turn: three old worthies playing dominoes and a young trawlerman asleep in his work clothes, hand still clutching an unfinished pint, were the only occupants.

"What's it to be?"

"Any non-alcoholic beer?"

"Non-alcoholic beer?"

"Aye."

"Naw."

"A pint of soda water and lime then."

He headed to a seat in the snug from which he could see the whole pub and was settling down with his drink when the toilet door burst open and Johnny Campbell waded back to the bar like a man in sinking sand. Stark thought the boy was wearing eye liner. In fact, he really hoped Johnny was wearing make-up because no one should have bags under their eyes as dark as that.

"Another whisky."

"You've had enough."

"I'm about to go to my brother's funeral … his second in a month!" he laughed as if he couldn't believe it was happening. "One on the house."

"You've already had one on the house."

"Do you think it's easy? Going up there with all of youse looking at me." He addressed the old timers who became even more engrossed in their game. "Aye, I ken what you're saying. That I killed my ain brother. That his coming back to us was some sort of sign. Well I didnae. I didnae."

He turned to the barmaid who had busied herself drying glasses. "Drink," he bellowed banging the bar. "Drink."

Rory Tan shambled into the pub, a mackintosh under one arms and crumpled newspaper under the other. He put the coat over a stool and flattened the newspaper on the bar.

"I'll get this."

He held out a tenner. The barmaid hesitated. She didn't want to be responsible for giving Johnny Campbell any more drink, but she was a 19 year old doing a summer job to save money for a holiday, and wasn't used to knocking back the requests of adult men.

Johnny had retreated behind a stool which he gripped as if he might use it as a weapon to fend off the reporter. "How long have you been here?" He hissed, bulging eyes and bared teeth.

"And a Guinness for me," Tan said, ignoring the question.

"They all think I did it," Johnny swept his arm towards an empty table. "What do you think? Did I kill my own brother?"

The music stopped as the girl put a glass of whisky on the bar and Johnny groped for it, still staring at the reporter. In the silence, Stark could hear the rim of the glass rattling off Johnny's teeth as his shaking hand emptied the whisky into his mouth.

"I don't think you've got that kind of evil in you."

There was an awful pause as the jukebox selected a new disc, the domino players stared at their pieces. Johnny peered at the reporter over the rim of his glass before slamming it onto the bar with such force that it shattered. He raised his bloodied hand as if blessing Rory Tan before staring at his fingers in horror.

CHAPTER EIGHT

Joe's casket was the first I'd carried. The gruff seriousness of the other male relatives as we prepared to lift him didn't seem so different from the solemn way they went about their other heavy jobs. Bursting out of their ill-fitting suits they had about them an uncomfortable air of menace like the bouncers at the town's only nightclub.

My mum had dug out an old suit of my dad's. She'd looked at me differently as I slipped into the shoulder clasping embrace of his jacket, but everyone was looking at me differently that day. Before we'd set off I went through the pockets, sniffed the armpits, searching for something of my father amidst the folds of fabric.

Johnny was totally scuttled and looked like he was wearing eye liner. "I've been up for three days straight," he hissed in my ear.

"I figured it was that, or that you'd climbed out of a volcano or been struck by lightning."

As we lifted the coffin from the hearse I smelt the varnished wood and felt afraid that one of the brass handles might snap off in my fist. Johnny was careening about at the front of the coffin and for a moment looked like he might drop the thing. His right hand was sticky with what looked like blood, which left fingerprints on the pale wood of the coffin.

"The state ay that," Uncle James muttered. "Howling at his ain brother's funeral. His father will be black affronted."

As we walked into the church I stared at the back of Uncle Tam's head. His hair had been cut for the occasion, the barber's razor revealing a white, unweathered line above the bacon pink skin on his neck. The eyes of the congregation were on us and despite the cool, floral air of the church, my face burned. I was wearing an old school shirt, fully buttoned up to the collar. My mum had tightened the knot on the black tie up to my throat and as we walked down the aisle I felt as if it was throttling me. I avoided looking at Lucille, Joe's fiancé, who was holding a disintegrating ball of sodden tissues to her mascara-streaked face. I scanned the church for Nicky, who, for once wouldn't stand out in her black clothes, but there was no sign of her. The place was rammed, which was odd given that Joe had hardly filled the world with laughter and light.

From outside the church you couldn't see the colours of the stained glass windows as a pane of tinted plastic had been put in place to protect them from people like us. Back inside, I was reminded that the windows above the altar showed Jonah and the whale, Noah in his ark and men pulling a bulging net full of fish into their boat. Written below a tapestry showing Christ talking to his disciples was the proclamation, *I will make you fishers of men.* Even the priest's robes had the symbol of a fish from a time when Christians were a secret sect condemned to live with the fear of detection.

We were asked to pray. I clasped my eyes shut and closed my fists, waiting for one small breath on the back of my neck that would tell me I wasn't in this alone. One of Tam's favourite sayings was, *He that will learn to pray, let him go to sea.* It was only recently I'd understood what he meant.

Uncle James tugged on my jacket and I realised it was time to carry the coffin. On account of Johnny being too howling to ken where he was meant to be, I ended up at the front of the casket, and felt Uncle Tam's powerful fingers clasp the back of my neck. I pressed my ear to the coffin, and wondered if Tam was also remembering Joe's bare feet.

During the burial, gows wheeled around in the sky as if we were bringing some tasty morsels up from the deep. Their sarcastic mirthless cackling goaded those below with the suggestion they'd seen all this before. Looking along to where my own father's drowned body had been buried, I tried to remember his face, but all I could see was the photo of him on our mantelpiece.

"He's got a bloody cheek," Uncle James growled. At the far end of the cemetery, amongst the weeping angels and twisted yew trees stood Inspector Stark. "After what he's put this family through."

The Inspector turned the collar of his long black coat against the chill and slipped out of sight. For some reason, I thought of my grey hoodie that they'd taken for sampling and hadn't returned, and which would be sealed in an evidence bag in some air tight vault forever. As cold clods of earth were dropped onto the coffin, tentacles of haar reached landward, reeled around the mourners and held them in a chill embrace.

The wake took place in Cawdor Thistle's clubhouse. It was a place I always associated with Joe. Not because he played football, but because it had two pool tables cramped into a side room that didn't have enough space for both of them and which consequently caused a fight, or at least some significant aggro, every weekend. Joe was the best pool player in town. Only a month ago, I'd seen him stagger into the room, so drunk that he needed the walls to guide him. He'd declared himself open for business and the others, those whose money he'd pillaged for years, rolled the balls from half played games into pockets. As usual, Joe played the two tables at the same time. He'd told me to chalk for him and hadn't noticed I'd given him one of the shitey cues. The others, leaning against the broken juke box, sitting on sticky tables or standing with their chins propped up by the butt of their cues, glanced at each other, trying not to get caught smirking at the prospect of revenge. But once Joe leant low to break, that concentrated stillness, the sense of someone coiled up and ready to strike came over him. Sure, he was barely able to stand without the help of the pool table and demanded I buy him a drink using mime rather than with words, but he struck ball after ball into their designated pockets. He started licking his forefinger before each shot and dabbing it on the faded, chalk dappled gauze before pocketing another ball, while we all watched the white, as if drawn by some magnetic force, roll back to rest on the damp spot he'd left on the table. After 20 minutes he'd won three games on both tables. It was the same on the trawler or around the harbour: every movement responding to the rhythm of the task with the graceful economy of a man totally at ease with his environment.

"Joe," Corky said, raising his glass before sloshing the frothy head of his pint into his face. "Cunt that he was."

Aunt Mary shot us a sharp look. She was herding a flock of old wifies towards the sandwiches and was too far away to have heard, but the knitting needle glint in her eyes told me everything. The coroner had eventually released Joe's body, but only after the police had interviewed all of us and forensics had gone over the trawler. But apart from Joe's injuries, the police had nothing. No blood spatter, no motive, no conflicting stories. They'd left the case open, but basically had no leads. Aunt Mary though couldn't let it go. The town couldn't let it go. Not something like that. Johnny's name was dirt. Not that anyone was going to say anything in front of Aunt Mary, but she'd have heard whispers, picked up on looks. Police harassment. Police insensitivity. That was what the rest of us talked about, but I could see she was forming her own theories.

She'd already snapped at Corky that he was to remove his baseball cap, which, to be fair, was decorated with a cannabis leaf motif. I glanced at him, obliviously staring into the universe of his pint glass with a glaikit smile on his face. The sides of his ginger hair had been shaved short and chevron shapes had been sheared along his temples, their resemblance to some post-operative scars further adding to the impression that he was recovering from a lobotomy.

"Only a year older than Corky, than us."

By us Corky meant him, Johnny, Dawn and Nicky. They often commented that Joe was middle-aged from his early teens. All he'd ever wanted was to become a skipper. Long before he was old enough to go out on *The Abiding Star* he could argue about over-fishing, quotas and the Common Fisheries Policy. He understood when and where nets should be shot and kent how the engines and radar worked. He preferred the adults' company, their stories, the fishing lore. He even used old Doric words to describe the weather, or the contents of a catch. A salmon was never simply a salmon when it could be a brannock, a lax or a rawner. No one kent what any of these words meant apart from the old timers and it was dead embarrassing hearing Joe going on in this way in front of normal people.

Joe found big cities, full of people whose genealogy was a mystery, disturbing. Even a place the size of Aberdeen freaked him out. Any man who made a bit of effort buying clothes that fitted, who didn't do a manual job, who actively sought out music that wasn't on the radio, who read anything that wasn't a tabloid or something to do with mechanics, who couldn't play darts or pool or any other pub game designed to make drinking with people you didn't like just about tolerable, was, he'd suggest, very possibly a homosexual. Johnny's entire personality was pretty much designed to wind his brother up.

I supped on my Tennents and watched the other men from our family, sitting a couple of feet from each other, locked in their own wee worlds, stroking the condensation from the side of their pints, like the sweat on the skin of a loved one. I chanced another look at Aunt Mary, busying herself around the cakes and coffees. She paused mid-way through slicing a scone and scowled in my direction.

"Once this is over, Corky's into paying Pete the Hat a visit if you're up for it?"

I kept stum. Pete was one of the Kerrs. He had a straggly black moustache half covering a face, white as a mackerel's belly. Hanging from nails in his sitting room was his collection of trilbys, stetsons and fedoras. With his family's reputation and his collection of shiny suits Pete clearly thought he looked like a Mafiosi, when he actually looked like someone going to a fancy dress party. Not that anyone was going to tell him this.

Round here, you learnt that he and his family were not to be fucked with from an early age. My first run in with the Kerrs had been aged nine, a day after Christmas while going down to the brae in The Bottom End to see if Rosco's new a scooter really was faster than mine. We were at the top of that hill and had been so focused on the race that we hadn't noticed the man being dragged out the flats. He was wearing a bright red Christmas jumper with the words *Yo-Ho-Ho!* across the chest. Two trackie-clad toughs that I'd later ken as Pete and his cousin Stevie had him by the ankles. By the nick of him, they'd either battered him indoors, or had dragged and kicked him down the six flights of stairs. Floundering on the icy pavement, the man had waved one hand towards us, before Jackie Kerr had stamped on it: the bone in his wrist snapping with the sort of crack I'd only heard when swinging on a branch for too long. The Kerrs had all looked at us then. We had our scooters and were at the top of the brae, but the idea of legging it didn't even flit across my mind. Pete swaggered over. The Kerrs always sauntered or strolled or swaggered. Even the women. Especially the women.

"Want your eyes back," he'd growled.

Thinking of it, he could only have been in his late teens. Back then he'd seemed like a big man, a real man. He'd reached out and taken my scooter, walked back to the others with it slung over his shoulder, like the grim reaper in a grey hoodie. The man from the flats was curled in a foetal position holding his broken wrist with his good hand. I couldn't hear him, but I could tell from his shuddering shoulders that he was sobbing. He didn't see Pete as he came from behind and smashed the metal scooter over his skull. Rosco threw up. The others jumped back and even Jackie Kerr made a what-the-actual-fuck motion. Pete hopped on the scooter and sped back to us tunelessly singing the chorus of a song that in a bowel bothering moment years later I'd identify as the Pixies' *Where Is My Mind?*

He'd given the scooter back to me and said, "Cheers lads." Looking down at the back wheel, he'd said, "You might want to clean that up."

A tuft of blond hair held together with a scab of scalp was stuck in the wheel.

In the weeks that followed, I'd been certain the police were going to turn up at our door, that I was going to have to testify against The Family and that my mum and me would spend the rest of our days in hiding. But the police didn't show and the Kerrs didn't try to knock me off, or intimidate me into silence. And that was the more terrifying thing. They could do something like that in broad daylight and no one said a thing.

"Got other plans," I said.

"Got other plans," Corky mimicked, as if it was impossible to believe anyone could be up to anything other than gouching out with a load of smack heads. Since that day, just the sight of Pete had given me the fear. If he, or his family, found out about the girl who'd been dealing from Nicky's squat, or Johnny's plans to bring gear into the country, we'd be for it. Nothing happened in the town without their say so.

The others, who hung out at Pete's, were the usual bunch of deadbeats, the sort that chanted along with the jingles of every advert, saw wondrous worlds in the wallpaper and conspiracies in the carpets. "Mon, it'll be a laugh," he sniffled. I sat there wondering when he'd become this snivelling wee skelf. On the trawler he'd been better at doing everything than me. At school just being vaguely associated with him and Johnny had made me untouchable, but now I reckoned that if I gave him a good shake bits of him would fly off.

We drank in silence.

"Are you going to miss the trawling?"

He shrugged like it was a dippit question and I guessed he had no idea about Aunt Mary's suspicions.

"If Tam's not going tae sea anymore then Corky'll get a job on one of the other boats." Corky had this unsettling habit of talking about himself in the third person, as if he was a character in a book. To be fair, if I was him, I'd adopt a similar strategy. He sounded confident, but even he must have kent that the whole town thought he was damaged goods and that Tam only risked going to sea with him on account of being pals with his auld man. "Corky minds when me and Johnny were your age, how excited we got coming back intae port. We went out after my first shift tae see a film. John had this rucksack wi him and half way through the film, he goes, 'This is boring, watch this.' He turned the bag upside down and tips aw these crabs into the aisle in front ay us. We just sat back trying naw tae piss ourselves as these daft quines started screaming."

He rocked in his seat, laughing silently at the memory.

"That's what Corky would miss. The craic wi the other deckies. You don't get those sort of laughs in other jobs."

Uncle Tam and Johnny came into the clubhouse. Clearly words had been said and the two of them glowered at the rest of us. With a jerk of his head, Johnny indicated that we follow him outside. As I headed for the door, Uncle Tam grabbed my arm.

"You're not going anywhere wi that waste of space."

He sat me down at a table with Uncle James. I watched Johnny and Corky climb into Mackinnon's cherry red Golf. I waved but Johnny was too busy drumming on the dashboard, while Corky's rusty dusty head was down, counting out his money.

"That chiel is going over his length," Uncle James muttered. "Not fit tae tie his brother's bootlaces. Swanning about at a funeral oot his skull, to say nothing ay that poofy hair ay his."

Uncle Tam's powerful fingers set about filling his pipe. Once lit, the tobacco crackled like old vinyl as he sucked and chewed and spluttered. There were signs all around the clubhouse saying No Smoking, but there wasn't a man in the whole of this town that was going to challenge Tam, not on the day he'd put his son in the ground. In fact people nodded approvingly at this act of belligerence, even those who knew that the pipe was close to killing him.

I stared at the flecks of pastry on the plate in front of me and squeezed my hands between my knees to stop them shaking. Something horrible was about to happen. I sensed it in my uncles' slow, deliberate movements. Both men had removed their jackets and rolled their shirts up to their elbows as if they might, at any moment, be challenged to an arm wrestling competition. Their forearms, when not ushering pints to their mouths or stuffing tobacco into pipes, rested heavily on the table. I thought of the way crocodiles basked in the sun, waiting immobile until snapping into action. I could just about get through an interview with the police, but if they two started an interrogation, they'd see right through me in seconds. Only once the pipe was smoking to Tam's satisfaction, did he turn to me.

"That one, will not take a telling," he prodded the pipe in the direction of the door through which Johnny had left. "He's mair dead to me than his brother will ever be. Aye, the police telt us." He coughed viscously and inspected his fist while I waited for his theory about Joe's injuries. "The pills in Joe's pocket that he'd taken off his brother or the laddie McCormack. If there's one thing I canna stand is a druggie." He coughed again and glugged some of his pint, the cold lager bringing some relief to his anguished face. "I'm not a well man Malky, and none of us are getting any younger."

I nodded relieved that Johnny, was still the target of his ire.

"This summer was to be my last at sea, but I'm done with it now. Joe was always going to become skipper and a bloody good job he would have made of it. I wouldn't let his brother near the job. My conscience couldn't allow that. Placing the lives of men in the hands of a loon who canna even look after himself."

"Flouncing about wi that poofy hair of his," Uncle James added. "So that's it. The end of the line."

There was a long pause during which Tam billowed out great storm surges of smoke.

"Your mother said you'd been talking about going to study books at university." Uncle James said.

I shrugged. Mr C, my regie teacher, had been banging on at me to get they UCAS forms filled in all year but I hadn't bothered.

"Bloody university," Tam spluttered. "Bloody waste of time that's what it is. Getting your mother into even more debt. For what? So that you can show off about the poems ay stuck up English cunts that've never done a day's proper graft. Do you think your mother likes slaving in that chippie at her age?"

I kent what was coming and clenched my jaws like someone waiting to be hit.

"Once they get Brexit done and we're allowed to fish our ain waters, the good times will be back. You wait and see. Your father would be proud. Keeping up the family tradition and looking after your mother. Your father would be gey proud. I could go on for a while yet if I kent I had someone in the family to train, to put through their tickets. Someone to become skipper."

It was hard not to laugh at how desperate they sounded. I could barely walk the length of myself on deck without tripping over something. The number of times I'd almost gone overboard, it was a miracle this wasn't my funeral.

But the boat was ours if I could just sit there and look like I was seriously considering their plans. I watched Tam's tumid nose, the constellations of broken capillaries, the weathered leathery skin of his gnarled hands. And I remembered the years after my auld man had died, how little Tam had done for us when the fishing was good, how the TVs in their sitting room had grown in width at the same rate as his belly. Tam had lorded it over us then, but now that he had throat cancer and his eldest son was dead and the other two were messed up on drugs he thought I'd help him.

"What about Johnny?"

"Johnny?"

"I couldn't take his place. It wouldn't be right."

"I've just been and telt you. That one and me are through. He's not part of this family anymore."

I frowned in a way that I hoped would show how wrong I thought this was. "Could you give me a few days to think it over?"

"Aye, that's best."

"Wise."

"The right decision."

The two of them lifted their glasses and beamed at me. I left them blethering away — the daft auld bastards — thinking I couldn't imagine doing anything better with my life than rocking and rolling over the waves. They discussed my future like men plotting routes on a nautical chart. In their minds this was my inheritance, but all I could think of was the nausea, the salt stiffened clothes, the nostril stinging stench of fish, face scoured red by gale force winds, hands hardening until they barely felt anything at all. Outside the clubhouse, I tried to call Johnny, but he wasn't answering. As I headed towards town in search of him, the haar drifted across the graveyard, wrapping around my ankles, deciding who the sea was going to claim next.

CHAPTER NINE

Gourlay steered into the hospital car park and was directed by Stark towards the spaces reserved for emergency vehicles. He was disappointed to see they were full. Not that this was an emergency, but he wanted to speak to the girl before the NCA officers got to her. As a fine drizzle drifted in from the sea, they found a space in the overflow car park.

"Popular destination," Gourlay said, looking at the brutalist monstrosity that loomed over the town like a massive mausoleum. Over the last week she'd spent a lot of time with Stark. Compared to patrolling the same triangle of roads with PC Mackay or sitting in a speed trap with PC Carmichael, this was riveting stuff. There'd been the interviews for the Joseph Campbell case and now the girl in the hospital who was undoubtedly part of one of these county lines that were getting set up along the coast.

The automatic doors shuddered open as the police approached, and Gourlay felt the ripple of averted faces and furtive glances as they strode through the waiting room. The receptionist was less attentive, and it was only after barking at a man cradling his arm that he'd have to wait his turn like everyone else that she turned her attention on them.

Stark showed his badge. "We're here to see a young lady who was brought in last Friday. Dr Stevenson contacted the station to say she'd regained consciousness and that we could speak to her." The receptionist fluttered her perfectly painted talons at the waiting area to indicate they should sit. Stark didn't budge. The receptionist, captivated by her purple polished nails seemed to be considering whether she should go back to filing them before Stark intervened.

"We're not waiting."

With a sigh, she picked up the phone.

Dr Stevenson led them past the buzz of the vending machines and up to the sixth floor. "She was a bit agitated this morning and is confused about where she is, but other than that she's recovering well. She says her name's Jazmyne, but that's all she's telling us." They stopped outside the ward to use the hand sanitizer. "You've got five minutes."

Each of the four beds in the ward were occupied, but the girl was the youngest there by half a century. Around the beds of the older women were the usual bunches of flowers and 'Get Well Soon' cards, but the girl had nothing apart from a folded up magazine that Gourlay noticed featured photos from a celebrity wedding that had taken place six weeks ago.

"I'm Inspector Jim Stark and this is PC Gourlay, we'd like to have a wee word about how you ended up here."

"We were the ones who found you in the bus station."

The girl shoulders tensed and she looked to the magazine as if it might provide an escape route.

"Now we need to get down a few basic details. Can you tell us your name and address?"

The girl stared sullenly at the drip attached to the back of her hand.

"Jazmyne," the girl's head jerked up at the sound of her name, "We know you're from London."

"What? Are you mad? My name's not Jazmyne. I'm not from London," the girl said in an accent that suggested otherwise.

"So you bide in the toon? Fur aboots?"

The girl winced at the strange dialect. "You're not in trouble. We just want to find out who did this to you and help you get home. You were in a McDonalds in Dalston last week, so we know you're from round there. That's 500 miles away. Long way for a wee lassie on her own." The girl neither confirmed nor denied this. "Can you tell us about the attack?"

"I didn't see nothing."

"Come on Jazmyne, we know that's not true."

"There were three of them. They'd masks on." Jazmyne looked towards her magazine in the hope she could lose herself in it again.

"Had anyone approached you before this happened?"

"I dunno. I was waiting for my bus. Then it happened."

"Could you tell us what you're doing in Port Cawdor, Jazmyne?"

"Which bus were you waiting on? I mean what number, or at least what destination?"

Jazmyne opened her magazine and started reading a horoscope that predicted what would be happening to people five weeks ago. Stark dragged one of the plastic visitor's seats to the bedside and sat down, striking an attitude that suggested he could wait all day.

"I like your necklace," Gourlay attempted. "Would you like me to get you an up-to-date magazine?"

Jazmyne's eyelashes flickered momentarily towards the constable, but, as soon as she saw the uniform she shut them in distrust.

"That's your five minutes," the doctor said.

"Well, that was a waste of time," was Stark's assessment as they renegotiated the hospital's corridors. In the waiting room a couple of plain clothes officers - who Gourlay thought might as well have been in uniform given their sensible shoes, neat haircuts, stolid sense of authority - were arguing with the ward nurse.

"DI Martin Hillman and DC Light, NCA. The girl who was brought in here unconscious. Have you seen her and is she talking?"

"Yes and no," Stark replied. "You got here fast."

"We're in the area … there's a lot going on. Any idea what age she is?"

Stark looked to Gourlay. "Mid to late teens?"

"Name?"

"Maybe Jazmyne."

"And you reckon she's Hackney based."

DI Hillman nodded at his colleague who made a call. "Can you check missing persons for me? First name Jazmyne. Don't know how she spells it, but probably not like the spice. East London area. Black. Mid to late teens. I can hold." The four of them stared at their sensible shoes. "Right. Good. That sounds about right." DC

Light slipped the phone into his jacket pocket. "Jazmyne Davis, reported missing eight days ago from a foster home in Haringey. Third time this year. She's sixteen."

As the men discussed similar cases of London teenagers arrested or beaten up in the other fishing towns, Gourlay spotted the rack of colourful magazines in the hospital shop. She found herself buying four of them before striding back to the ward.

"Here," she said to Jazmyne who was still staring at the five-week-old horoscope. Gourlay pulled the curtains around the bed. "But first you have to give me something. We know your name's Jazmyne Davis. We know you're in care in Haringey and that you're sixteen. That makes you the victim here."

Jazmyne tore her eyes away from the glossy smiling faces on the magazines' covers.

"At least tell us where you were staying."

"Fuck you. Think I'm a snitch."

"Do you know what they'll do to you?" Jazmyne closed her eyes. "Whoever you're protecting – they're using you. Sending you up here on your own to sell drugs. It'll be someone else next week. Some poor exploited kid getting their head panned in to make them money."

Jazmyne looked up and this time at Gourlay and not the faces on the covers of the magazines. "I'm gonna get touched. The olders, I already owe them money. They'll mess me up. But if I don't go back, they'll get my sister. And she's only thirteen."

"Look, I can't promise you anything. It's my first month in the job. But if you can give us any intel, there's ways we can protect you."

Jazmyne bit her lower lip.

"We can get you and your sister out of the home you're in. Somewhere far away from London."

"I can give you the address of the trap house. And describe some of the olders. But I'm not saying anything until my sister's safe."

The curtains were yanked back with a shriek, as a furious looking ward sister hissed, "Do you people never give up?"

"Just giving Jazmyne these," Gourlay said placing the magazine on her bedside table. The girl grabbed her bicep and pulled Gourlay close enough that she could feel the heat in her breath.

"There's this man. He's got a tattoo of a crab on his neck. He's Albanian or from someplace like that. Don't let him touch me or my sister. I've seen what he does to people."

Stark, who'd spent enough time in the hospital's waiting room to know that the spluttering foamy mess produced by the vending machine tasted as much like coal as coffee, watched the NCA men wince at their bitter brews. Truth was he'd been waiting for the type of news they'd given him. Since arresting Jackie and Steven Kerr six months ago with a substantial haul of heroin in the boot of their car, Stark had known this day was coming. It'd all been too easy, and as the Chief, his wife, the editorial in *The Squeak* praised the efforts of the police, Stark had felt like an imposter. What had any of them actually done? Nothing more than follow up on an anonymous tip off. And who was in the position to provide them with that type of information? Ten days later, an associate of the MacLarty family with serious form was dumped in front of a billboard on the outskirts of Aberdeen. The billboard was part of a campaign encouraging people to pass on information to the police with the slogan *Shop a Dealer*, underneath which had been spray painted *Shot a Squealer*. The MacLarty enforcer, he'd been told, was barely recognisable due the exit wound from a bullet to the back of his head. The proximity between the two events was too much to be a coincidence and putting two and two together, the police came to three career criminals off the streets and thank you very much. But there were too many loose strings: the kidnapping and subsequent disappearance of Danny Kerr, the series of what the paper's called UFO abductions that had happened to younger members of other crime families from the fishing towns, the use of a firearm which forensics linked to shootings in London. Stark had policed Port Cawdor long enough to despise the Kerrs, but better the drug dealers you know than the drug dealers you don't. Following the arrests the drought that had hit the town had been biblical; addicts had scoured the streets, their desperate need to score leading to break-ins at the chemists. While nature might abhor a vacuum, drug dealers love it. Of course the economy of supply and demand meant that the scarcity didn't last long, but the last five months had seen more ODs with the purity of the heroin seized sometimes being of a far higher quality than anything they'd previously seen. Remove the Kerrs and this place was easy pickings for any OCG with lots of money to be made from the young men off the boats, rig workers on leave and bored young mums left at home while their men worked off shore. In truth, in arresting the Kerrs and disrupting their operations, they'd been nothing more than errand boys running jobs for a group of more violent and more connected criminals than what had gone before.

PC Gourlay seemed particularly pleased with herself as she crossed the reception area. Stark would never understand what took women so long in public toilets, but then he remembered that the toilets were on the other side of the waiting room.

"Where have you been?"

"Got Jazmyne a couple of gossip mags."

Stark thought about the type of life the girl had come from, the type of life to which she'd return. It was a kind gesture, but another piece of evidence that suggested Gourlay wasn't cut out for this type of work.

"You won't be able to claim them on expenses."

Gourlay smiled serenely as they said their goodbyes to NCA officers and headed to the car. "Even if I told you she's given me a description of one of the men who sent her here and is prepared to give us an address for their trap house?"

Stark started the motor. "You'll do PC Gourlay. You know, you might just do."

Gourlay removed her bowler and placed it on her laps. She'd been in Stark's company for enough time to know that this was as big a compliment as she was likely to get.

CHAPTER TEN

A few days after the funeral I got a copy of Great Expectations and a bottle of vodka. It was my eighteenth birthday. I'd always wanted to impress everybody by the amount I'd read and the amount I could drink. Before she went to work, my mum made me promise I wouldn't go and see what she called, "The criminal element in your father's family." So I was marooned on the sofa. I channel-surfed until the moral indignation of daytime TV populated by people with cash in their attics and homes in the sun, made me want to ram raid shops, burgle houses, smash their smug tanned faces. By the end of the day I'd got a quarter of the way through the book and three quarters of the way through the vodka.

During the rest of that week, I'd get up at seven, eat breakfast with my mum, talk about my plans for the day. The moment she was out the door I went straight back to bed, stuffing my head with tunes and books and dreams of an impossible future. PC Carmichael and Sergeant Grant called a couple of times.

"Home alone?" They'd say, peering over my shoulder.

"*Home and Away*," I'd correct them.

"We're looking for that cousin of yours."

"Dawn?"

"Johnny."

"Absconded," PC Carmichael ponderously pronounced.

"Thought you'd done harassing him."

"Something's come up … a fresh line of enquiry."

"I'll call if I hear anything."

The police had nothing. If they had, they'd never have let us put Joe in the ground. Forensics had gone over the trawler and found fuck all. They'd bagged the clothes we were wearing when Joe disappeared, checked and double checked that our stories matched, but except for the injuries on the back of Joe's head, they had nothing.

Other than the police, I didn't get any visitors and I didn't much fancy going out neither. Despite no one being charged, the town was full of suspicions and it was weird to have suddenly become the source of gossip: a person whose arrival in a shop was met with the lowering of voices.

After a few days of my mum coming home to find me camped out on the couch her patience was wearing thin. Other than getting stoned, guiding unfashionable teams to unlikely victories in Premiership Manager and making a couple of bowls of Angel Delight, I'd achieved little that week. After twice observing that the devil makes work for idle hands, my mum announced she'd found us a job for the rest of the summer, working as part of the Council's Land Services team.

"I'm going back to sea. Tam's going to train me to become skipper."

She'd snorted at this. "Tam's due his first chemo at the end of next week. You'll take that job and button your lip. You're eighteen now. If you're wanting to run about town like an adult, you'll have to start acting like one and that means paying your keep. I'm not having a laddie of mine turning into a layabout."

As I listened to her wittering on, I felt like the person watching the person who was watching me through a two way mirror. Whether this was anything new or just the amount of blow I'd been smoking would have been hard to say.

"Land Services," Uncle Tam sneered down the phone. "Fucking Land Services when you should be going to sea. We'll see how long you last picking up dog shite and cutting hedges for lazy cunts on incapacity benefits. That's not a job for a Campbell. *The Abiding Star* is still there. Once I'm recovered from this next round of chemo we'll get a crew together and get you started on your tickets."

"I still want to go to sea," I'd protested, "but I need to be making money now. Could Johnny not go with me? He's got his tickets. He could train me up."

"I've telt you before. That is not up for negotiation. What about Cal? He could get a crew together and you could be at sea by next week."

Fuck, I thought. Screw Cal. If he came into the picture, we'd never get to do what we wanted with the trawler.

"No. I'm not going without Johnny."

Duffy, the boss of the council's Land Services and Burial Grounds Department, was great pals with my mum. In the 'interview' he explained that Land Services took on extra bodies during the summer. As the schools were about to break, they needed someone to work in the park. There'll be tourists as well, he'd added, as if that made the job sound glamorous. After the schools went back they'd put me on one of the lawn mowing teams. They laid off most of the seasonals at the end of September, but for the right candidate there was always the opportunity of further employment.

Needless to say, I could barely conceal my enthusiasm.

It was near the end of my first week in the job and Aida – the toilet woman - was sitting on a deckchair, slathered in suntan oil. She'd these huge sunglasses on, making it impossible to know whether she was sleeping or keeping an eye on me. Her trousers were rolled up, revealing shapeless calves the colour of kebab meat. She spent most of her working day watching folks through the tinted glass doors of her toilet room office and had perfected the art of whinging. No one could know how boring it was to sit there day after day. The things men did in toilets: unimaginable. The age of the weans trying to break into the condom machines: shocking. She had a hundred dirty secrets at her fingertips. People would say, "Naw a bad day today Aida" and she'd look at the sky as if it was one of the crosswords she was always failing to finish and say, "I've seen worse." On my first day, she'd called me over and said, "You're one of the Campbells." I'd shrugged; it wasn't as if I could deny it. "Mind that customers pay me for the boating pond. They give you a ticket. Nothing more." She'd nodded in a way that very much said *I've got my eye on you* - but after years doing her job, that might just have been the way she looked at everybody.

I had two more shit bins to empty. I always had more shit bins to empty. My arms were aching, the barrow's wonky wheel making me look like a stroke victim as I fought to keep it right. That and these sky blue work trousers, not to mention the NHS correction boot lookalikes, and it had to be said that I was not looking my best.

I put the barrow down to give myself a breather. Auld Jimmy, the pissy park jakey, was hovering round a bin. He was rummaging amongst the chip papers and beer cans, disturbing the wasps, half-drunk on the dregs of carry outs, before clutching to his chest a glass Irn Bru bottle: 20p at the corner shop, a quarter of his way to the day's first tin of Special. A beatific smile creased his booze bludgeoned face.

Aida waved me over.

"It's a rare day," I mustered.

"Would be better if we didnae have that dog show on. Had one woman in already cleaning dog hairs off a brush in the sinks. I said for the love ay Christ what do you think you're doing? She just turns round and says, 'Using your facilities.' Ma facilities, I says, are for people. These are award-winning toilets I'll have you know. You don't get award winning toilets wi sinks blocked up wi dog hair."

I was too bored to even nod and instead stared at her bowfin face, six blackheads on the end of her button nose, ripe for squeezing.

"Aye, and another thing, we've had reports ay broken glass around The War Memorial, so that'll be some work for you."

We've had reports, I laughed to myself.

The War Memorial was its usual Sunday morning mess. In Memory of the Glorious Dead, glass sparkled in the sun.

After shovelling the glass into a bag, I walked back to the howff. Some weans were smoking in the cabin part of the climbing frame. I'd spent ten minutes clearing fag ends from the sand during the shit bin round and stared hatefully at the back of their heads. When I was a good bit past I heard laughter and turned to see a shower of pish coming down the slide. Leanne Kerr leaned her head out and while pulling up her trackies shouted, "Oy, parkie, you're a wanker."

I was used to being called a wanker, but a parkie - fuck that; it was only a summer job and I was chucking it the moment Tam relented.

I bolted the howff's door and walked through the cobwebbed light. At the back of the shed sat six pristine paddle boats, which some bellend at the council had bought without realising that the pond was too shallow for them. Someone had moved them and I held my breath, peering into the gloom.

"That you, Johnny?" He snuck out from behind the unusable paddle boats. "Where have you been?"

"Thought it best to keep my head down after the funeral. Went down to stay with some pals in London."

"You haven't got any pals in London."

He was wearing a brand new parka jacket, spotless white retro Reeboks.

"Nice gutties. You go all that way for a shopping trip?"

"Never you mind what I was down there for. That text you sent - did the auld man really say that he wanted to train you up to become skipper?"

"Aye."

"You were a fucking nuisance on that boat. Worse than useless. He's off his head."

"Ken."

"And you're still saying you won't do it without me."

"Of course, but like I says, he won't let you near the trawler."

"Now that Joe's buried and the police are off our case he'll come around to the idea of the two of us going to sea together. You'll see. My dad and Uncle Peter are obsessed with keeping that boat and its license in the family. They'd see it as some sort of failure on their part if we weren't forced to waste our entire lives at sea too. "

"Maybe, but I wouldna be so confident that the police have given up. That Detective Stark knows something's not right."

"Wheest, you're being paranoid. They've got nowt."

"Joe's stomach was full of sea water." I whispered. "That only happens when you've gone into the sea alive. You said he was dead. You checked. It was your idea to throw him overboard."

I watched his face chewing on itself like a losing football manager in the final minutes of a big game.

"So, you're calling *me* a murderer?"

For a searing second I thought he was coming for me. I leant down and picked up an oar.

"No. It was an accident."

"Too right it was an accident and dinna you go forgetting it. You were the one that smashed his head in."

"Shut it," I snapped, holding my breath and straining to make out if any of the gardeners had returned to the howff.

It was true. I'd come down to the cabin that night to see Joe kneeling on Johnny's chest, his sinewy hands throttling his brother. I'd shouted, but Joe had maintained his grip as Johnny writhed on the floor, stamping his feet in a bid to throw his brother off. I was sure I'd shouted. But people had shouted before. Joe had given me a look, a glance to remind me that I was the kid cousin, an irrelevance, good for reading books and nothing much else.

My grip on the oar tightened as I remembered the impact of clubbing Joe's head with the torch that I'd carried down from the deck. Maybe it was the look he'd given me that did it, the fact he'd tuned his head on me knowing full well I would do nowt. I'd held the heavy metal torch in both hands and swung it baseball bat style. He'd been wearing a wooly bunnet that Lorraine, his fiancé, had knitted him, and this seemed to soften the blow. But, the impact had been enough to knock him off his brother. He'd crawled around like a short-sighted man searching for his glasses. As he'd started getting to his feet, I'd brought the torch down on his head again. The impact of the second blow had been subtly different. Not so much the sound, but the feeling through my fingers, as the back of his skull offered less resistance.

"I thought he was going to kill you, and then, after I'd hit him once, I thought he'd kill me."

Johnny rubbed his neck. "After he'd nicked my Subs I lost it. Went proper schizo. There was no chance I was surviving another week on the boat without them. Could you imagine the state I'd be in? Joe just kept on at me, whispering in ma ear that now da will see what you're really like. The auld yin could put up with all the stories about me, as long as I showed up to work and put a shift in. I'd hae quit the moment it became unmanageable, I always said I'd gie it up as soon as it became unmanageable... Fuck it, I'm not sorry he's dead."

I thought Johnny had saved us that night. After cracking the searchlight over his brother's head, he'd leant back against the bunk, heaving oxygen into his lungs. Joe didn't move. I didn't move. But once Johnny had got his breath back, he'd checked Joe's pulse, pulled the hood of his brother's waterproof over his battered head, tightened and tied the draw strings so that no blood would drip out. He'd gone up to check that no one was on deck, leaving me with Joe ... the body. A sharp vinegary tang of piss had mixed with the cabin's damp sock smell. The number of times we'd muttered that we wished him dead. But standing there looking at the sprawled heap, I'd have done anything to see a limb twitch, to hear those lips spit, "You little bastard." Then Johnny was lifting his brother with his arms under his oxsters and I held his legs, and somehow the two of us had hauled Joe up the stepladder. He'd given me courage when we'd paused to watch the silhouette of the back of Tam's head in the wheelhouse. We'd lugged the body across the deck and bundled him overboard. As Joe disappeared there'd been a screech from the ocean: a seagull, a selkie, a siren from the depths.

"Whatever happened, we did it together and don't you ever forget it," Johnny insisted.

What kept coming back was Johnny leaving me on deck as he went down into the cabin and returned to hurl Joe's boots, fags and lighter into the sea. The smile he gave me after doing that. Relief. Mad ecstasy. Horrible guilt. All rolled into one. I'd never seen anyone smile that way before.

Since the police interview and Nicky telling us about the plans to use the boat for smuggling, the idea that Johnny knew his brother was alive when we threw him overboard had tormented me, but there was no chance I was asking him something like that.

We were interrupted by the sound of a Landrover tearing across the freshly cut football pitches.

"Shite," hissed Johnny, skittering behind the paddle boats as a great hulk of a woman got out. She was wearing what people call a wife beater, which must have been her having a laugh as I'd like to see the man that tried. Maddie Kerr, Leanne's gran or aunt or cousin, or possibly all three – they had not so much a family tree as a family knot weed that spread and strangled other families in their path. For half a second, I thought about hiding with Johnny, but she'd seen me.

"Alright," she croaked, "you're Leanne's wee pal, eh no?"

"Aye, Leanne. Sort of."

"Says you gie her your pieces." I nodded, thinking of how the half-starved skelf had nicked stuff out of my bag on my first day at work. "Says, she gies you a hand putting out the boats." The woman started doing what looked like hand strengthening exercise. "I worry about her. See she's that small for her age."

"She seems to get along ok."

"But she stands out fae the crowd, you canna deny that. Gets picked on cause she's that in-div-id-u-al." I thought of Leanne Kerr pissing down the slide this morning.

"Aye she's certainly individual." The woman's hands splayed right out. Maddie the Matriarch we called her, head of the infamous Kerr clan, seen as most of the men were dead or in prison.

"Were you not in Danny's year at school? Youse played football together." She stared at the empty play park for a minute. "That boy," she muttered to herself, "broke my heart."

I minded going to Danny's birthday parties up at their red brick mansion. Neverland it sarcastically got cried in town – on account of the rusted rollercoaster and parked up rides from the shows that were always stored in the garden.

She squinted at me, screwed her eyes up in an unconvincing impersonation of someone trying to retrieve a memory. "It's Malky, isn't it? Johnny Campbell's cousin." The hands had crawled out of her jacket pockets and were hooked round the elasticated top of her leggings. "You worked on the boat with him." She took a step towards me. "Him and poor Joseph Campbell. Fucking sin that was." Her obese thighs flexed beneath hideous multicoloured lycra as she towered over me. "You seen him recently?"

"No."

"You sure?"

"Aye."

"Johnny!"

She shouted like someone calling a lost dog.

"Johnny!"

"Aw," she said breaking off from the scary routine. "That's a shame that, cause I want a wee word wi him. A lot of people want a wee word wi him." She gave me a card. An actual fucking business card with the family's name in gold embossed print.

"Tell him no tae be feart. If he does right by us, we'll do right by him." She pointed at her huge chest. "See me, I'm a fucking philanthropist."

I held the card in both hands never once taking my eyes off her. There'd probably been more philanthropic nail bombs.

"Make sure he calls. And now we're acquainted, mind Leanne gets on the boats for free. Nice tae be nice."

As soon as the Landrover was out of sight, I went into the back of the howff and handed him the card.

"What the fuck was that all about then?"

He stared at the card as if he had no idea, but I kent Johnny better than that. If Maddie Kerr had found out about the men from London who wanted us to smuggle drugs into the country then we'd be for it. This was the Kerrs' town. Stuff like that simply did not happen without their say so.

"Is anyone working here?" a voice shouted. I ignored it, but the impatient cunt kept bawling until I headed out.

It was while I was putting a couple of girls into a boat that Nicky appeared, walking past the part of the boatshed on which some sensitive soul had graffitied the words, *Fight for fun. Kick to Kill*. Despite it being July, she was wearing her fake fur coat, in an obvious attempt to hide her bump.

We sat on a picnic table. During my first morning in the job I'd re-varnished all these tables, but the names of bands and gangs had already been re-etched in sharp white letters. Beneath her coat, Nicky was wearing a denim skirt, showing off her long legs. Her black hair whirled in the wind and I felt a pang of pride that this beautiful girl was sitting next to me. Scanning the pond, I wanted all the tourists with their guffey accents, who looked at me like I was good for nothing, to see me with this girl, a hundred times better looking than the dowdy old things they were huckled with.

"So, what brought you down here?"

"Just wanted out of that dump. Besides, heard you looked a sight in your new work clothes."

I couldn't stop looking at her pregnant belly and every time I did, she tugged her coat over the bump. Although I knew nothing about these things, I guessed she was pretty far gone if she still planned on having an abortion.

"Not seen you in weeks," I said.

"Skint," she replied. "Besides … I'm trying to sort things out. Trying to sort my head out. …"

"That guy still dealing from your place?" By way of an answer, she sniffled, wiped her nose with the back of her hand. "There's a name for that. It's called cuckooing."

"It's not like that. I'm using them as much as they're using me … I'm just trying to save some money seen as no one else is helping me."

And that was the moment when I should have said, Keep the baby. I've already taken a life, ruined my own. Fuck playing at being gangsters. I'll give you every pound I make from this job. When the time comes, I'll do the training to become a trawler's captain. For you, I can endure the restless waves and the scouring winds. We can get a proper place where you can raise a child, where you can get clean. And for one cavernous moment she stared at me with that ravenous face, as if that was exactly what she wanted me to say. But who was I kidding. I was an eighteen year old part-time parkie, who'd killed his own cousin, while she was a heroin addict, who'd fucked every headbanger in town. Besides, she'd heard enough boys promise the world and deliver nothing.

"Your uncle still saying he won't let youse two take out the boat?"

Her phone buzzed and she pulled out the same navy blue Nokia she'd had in the flat.

"Business calls?"

"Something like that." She twisted around to scan the park. "Listen, have you seen Johnny?" I shook my head feeling like a bad bastard. Nicky leant back and her hand tenderly stroked her bump. "He never answers my calls anymore. Dawn says he's left town. Is that what he's done, panicked and done a runner? What am I supposed to do?" My forefinger traced the initials of lovers, gouged into the picnic table. I didn't dare look at her.

"Maddie Kerr was looking for him. If they know about your London links, we're dead. All of us."

She got up and tucked a strand of hair behind her ear. "Still feart of the Kerrs. Aw Malky, and I thought you were bigger than that. One day you're gonnae learn that there are worse things in the world than the Kerrs." The mobile buzzed again and she strode towards the park's grand Victorian gates, arms crossed in front of her, head bowed against the wind, black hair flapping like a bird in an oil slick. She wouldn't look back. I watched until she was through the gates, just in case.

I dragged the rest of the boats into the shed and said, "Closing time."

"How? You're not allowed to close before six," said a woman surrounded by her yapping Chihuahuas and children.

"It's about to rain," I claimed, un-padlocking the chain and letting the metal shutter crash down on her trauchled face.

Peace at last. I loved that moment at the end of each day, but before my eyes had even adjusted to the lack of light Johnny was on at me.

"And what's Nicky Skelton after?"

"You. You're a wanted man."

"Not by her I'm not. Besides, I'm through with her. Fucked up junkie spunk bucket. I'm sick of her dragging me down."

I thought of them in school, of the couple of times I'd watched their band, chin propped up on the window ledge of a pub I was too young to get in. The bravery to get up on stage and sing your hearts out when all the other bands only played covers of hits with choruses to which everyone sang along. She didn't drag him down then, in fact she seemed to hold him up. Back then he clung onto her as if she were filled with helium and one day might float away.

"I think she could do with a friend right now."

"A friend? She's got plenty of *friends*."

"I don't think so."

"Well if you're so concerned, why don't you be her friend? You're always sniffing round her."

"Fuck you." I chucked my phone at him. "Call Maddie Kerr and fuck off. I'm not wanting her coming here again. That Leanne Kerr has been in the park all day, spying on us."

"Spying on you!"

"Well what else is she doing here?"

"She's a child, it's a children play park. It's not that complicated."

There was never any point arguing with him. I headed up to the paddling pond that I had to drain at the end of each day. When I got back into the howff, Johnny was pale and pacing. He handed me back the phone.

"So?"

"So, I don't know. The Kerrs have offered me a job."

"Does it involve mugging old ladies or pimping out your sister?"

Ignoring me, he filled his lungs. "The Kerrs are in on the smuggling plan."

"Fuck ... you're kidding?"

"No, but it's alright. That gang fae London that Souter introduced Nicky to, they've squared it with them. Dinna ken why they've got the Kerrs involved, but maybe that's how it is with the professionals. They've arranged for us to meet a Dutch trawler in The North Sea. There's a shit load of money involved."

I felt sick at the thought of Joe in a coffin and us using words like *professionals* to describe scum like the Kerrs.

"Malky, this is my big chance. This is *our* big chance …I need away fae this town and everyone looking at me like I'm a criminal."

"Well get a bus ticket. It's a town, not a concentration camp. The roads going out of here aren't just for boyracers to do laps; they actually go somewhere. And there's no barbed wire fence or watchtowers stopping you and all the others who spend all their time whinging about being trapped."

"Aye, and where are you going Mr Park Attendant? Don't tell me you couldn't do with the money. You can play at being skipper. The father'll lap it up."

"Away to fuck. I don't want in on this anymore … when Nicky was talking about those guys, that was all it was: talk."

"We've already got rid of Joe. He was the one in our way. We've done the hard bit."

"Joe was an accident."

"We've established that. C'mon, it'll be a piece of pish. Can you imagine doing shitey jobs like this for the rest of your life? One job and then all the money you'll need."

I thought of Nicky cooped up in that squat with no electricity or gas and the way her hand had contentedly, absent-mindedly cradled that bump. She was right. Social services would take that baby off her the minute it was born. This was it. The chance to make some proper money. I could put down a deposit on a flat, set her up in it - it would be criminal not to.

I caught Johnny's eye and it was magnetic, the thought that we'd be together in a scam so big it'd be famous for years. It well known that the fishing towns were so full of drugs on account of trawlers being used to bring gear into the country. Three years ago, a boat from The Broch had been busted mid-way through a deal and the crew had chucked most of the evidence overboard. For weeks all of us from school had combed the coast looking for suspicious packages.

"I'll think about it," I said, but by the quiver in my voice, he must have kent I was in.

Someone rapped on the metal shutter and a man's voice shouted, "You gonnae open up."

I pulled up the metal shutter to reveal a family of tattie headed trolls that looked like they'd escaped from a nineteenth century American freak show.

"Having a siesta?" said the father of this family. He was wearing a faded Superman T-shirt, which – considering he was a fat fuck whose family looked like they could have made a living as extras in a zombie film – did not need commented on.

A bit of me wanted to tell him where to go. I wasn't just some parkie at the beck and call of him and his mutant weans. I was a boy with prospects. Still I got them in their boats, spotting Leanne who'd teamed up with two freckle faced twins, Kerrs of some sort judging by their pinched sneaky faces.

Once the family were finished rowing, they swarmed, nipping at me to give them a free go.

I pulled one of the boats in but Leanne and the twins grabbed another one and launched it into the water.

"Well fucking have it then. And I hope you all drown." They splashed each other with the oars, not caring about getting wet. After a bit they got out of the boats in the middle of the pond and started capsizing them - probably closest the filthy wee tinks would get to a bath all year.

I sat inside not giving them the satisfaction of knowing I was watching. I could hear Johnny chuckling, loud enough so I could hear him, quiet enough so that no one else could.

"You can shut it an aw," I snapped.

"That's the best entertainment I've had all week. Menaced by midgets" he sniggered.

A crazed voice cut into his mockery, "Hoy, ya wee bastards, I'll have you." The kids legged it from the pond Auld Jimmy in hot pursuit. "I ken where you live!"

"Aye, I ken where you live an aw," said Leanne, squaring up tae him. "We'll burn down your house, ya auld paedo." He took a swipe at her but she was away with a gold ringed finger salute.

"Did you see that? You have tae get on top ay them, son."

I nodded wearily. He was already howling, swinging a polly bag wi the remains of a six pack in the air.

"Good deal at the offay?"

"Six Special for four quid," he said. "But they wee bastards. See in ma day." I looked at Jimmy's faded navy top, an old fashioned Council badge printed on it with Parks Services written underneath. Before I'd started here I'd always ignored him as an old jakey but Aida telt me he'd been a parkie for three decades, before the drink got the better of him and he lost his wife, his children, his job. Three decades! A week in the job and he had my sympathies.

"Used tae be some park this. Four tennis courts, beautiful bandstand, a proper pavilion tae get changed in." He shook his head. "People would come fae miles. It's they young uns. Destroy everything. And the toilets. More like a bloody fortress. There was even a house for the Park Attendant – look at it now. Derelict! And it wasn't a position they just filled with loons straight out of school."

"The weather as well. They call this summer. It's a fucking disgrace."

"Aye, someone up top should swing for it."

He shook the can for the third time, to once and for all confirm he'd finished it.

"Got any glass bottles for us?" I looked at where the lawnmower men hid them.

"Sorry Jimmy, no can do. The gardeners banked them this morning."

"Bastards," he muttered getting to his feet and walking off.

I watched his stooped back, wondered at my petty meanness.

Checking my watch, I reckoned Aida would have knocked off in preparation for her night at the bowling club. I was meant to be on another hour but it was a dreich evening and there was no danger any of the Park Inspectors would be round. Besides, if we pulled off this deal, they could stick their job.

I put my waldies on and started clearing the pond of sunken boats. Johnny came out to give me a hand and we had the boats back in the shed in no time.

"We'll do it," Johnny said, crowding me with those dark sunken eyes.

He placed one hand on each of my shoulders and stared at me with such intensity that I wasn't sure whether he was going to nut me or kiss me.

He nodded as if pleased by what he had seen.

I switched off the lights and locked up, leaving behind the dusty spiders' webs that have outlived their creators and the paddle boats that are too big for a pond as shallow as this.

CHAPTER ELEVEN

Parking on Bridge Street, Stark watched a group of young women slink towards Denizens, a glossy mag glow from their fake tan and tinted hair. From a distance, Stark had thought they were in their mid-twenties, but with a lurching feeling like negative g-force he first realised they were Zoe's friends - and then that Zoe too was in the midst of the flowing hair and hilarity. They swanned past the mahogany faced wall punchers on the door, who welcomed them with a familiarity that Stark found unsettling. Stark knew most of the girls by name and was certain most of them hadn't turned eighteen, while Katy Oliphant's sister was two years younger than the rest. PCs Mathie and MacKay were on duty, and he was half way to putting a call through to the desk when he thought of his wife and the rows they'd had at home every time Sophie's underage evenings in pubs had been curtailed due to the police swooping in to check everyone's ID. Reluctantly, he pocketed the phone and made his way to The Nineteenth Hole perched at the edge of town, overlooking its links course. A typical golf club bar, it had the worn tartan carpet, paintings of Victorian gentleman finishing a round and a couple of venerable grandfather clocks whose hands hadn't moved in years. Judging by the empties on their table, the others had been celebrating the verdict from the High Court. Jackie and Stevie Kerr, the father and son who'd run things in Port Cawdor for decades, had got eight and twelve years each. Steve Grant got up to shake his hand.

"That was some result, sir. The two of them getting away with it for years and all it took was one tip off and then, boom."

Although they'd all changed into casual clothes, Grant continued to wear his leather biker trousers, which he had no need to wear even when he was in uniform given that he'd been indefinitely suspended from using the patrol bike for multiple speeding violations.

"Anyone need a drink?"

Despite someone having just got a round in, they gave Stark their orders. The ruddy faced Rotarians – the sort of men who were actually proud that the police patronised their pub - parted as Stark approached the bar. Men whose minor frauds, embezzlements and off shore investments were all looked after by accountants. Men who insisted on harsh penalties and stiff sentences for proper criminals, voted Conservative and complained when the services they wouldn't pay tax for didn't immediately respond to their needs. Grant was in his element among this crowd – the gruff macho patrolman who ensured that no one who drank here was ever caught in a speed trap. He'd be boasting about the Kerrs' arrest after a few more drinks, about his vital role in apprehending the criminal after the anonymous tip off.

Stark ferried the round of drinks back before returning to the bar.

"And my usual," he directed the barman, who, with his back turned to the punters at the bar, emptied a bottle of non-alcoholic beer into a pint glass. Stark took a grateful gulp.

Gourlay appeared in need of being rescued from the attentions of Carmichael and a PC from Elgin who were engaged in retelling and re-enacting some of their greatest golf matches. But who was he to intervene? They were her age and she was in a town where she knew no one. Stark had been impressed by the relationship she'd built up with the girl in the hospital. The intel she'd got had led to a raid on a trap house in London, but it had been abandoned by the time the police got there. However, the NCA officers said the description of a man with a crab tattoo on his neck matched a person of significant interest.

Stark finished his drink. At the end of the bar, among the beetroot faces and pastel polo shirts, Dr Ross was trying to get his attention. "A good result today," he shouted, lifting a pint glass in acknowledgement of the Detective's work. The man was a nuisance. If it hadn't been for him constantly providing the papers with facts and quotations about what he referred to as the town's drugs epidemic, then the OCG might not have been so interested in muscling in here. Stark understood he was only doing his job: drawing attention to a public health issue in the hope of more funding. But it made the town a target. Depositing his empty on the bar, he went outside for a smoke. Passing the police table he heard Grant declare that he had no idea if Johnny Campbell had killed his brother, but that he was definitely guilty of something – he could tell by the look in his eyes.

People who only ever smoke when they're having a drink often describe themselves as social smokers. Stark recognised that he was an anti-social smoker. He didn't even like cigarettes any more, but he much preferred them to attempting conversations with drunken members of the constabulary.

Gourlay came out speaking to someone on her mobile.

"Didn't know you smoked."

"I don't. This is merely a prop."

"Ha. Well I just pretended I was answering a call to get out of there."

They both smiled, a flicker of solidarity in these shared confessions.

"What do you make of the Campbell case?" Stark asked, setting the test.

"Is that not finished?"

"Is it?"

Gourlay hesitated. "I don't see how Joe Campbell's head injuries could have been the result of an accident. And there's something off about the other Campbell boys – the younger one in particular. But I don't see how we can pin it on them."

She reached out and took Stark's un-smoked cigarette, closing her eyes as she inhaled the smoke.

"Can't we? I've had time to think about this. The missing boots. They could have come off on their own. But, his dad showed me the type of socks he wore. They were heavily elasticated. I've seen bodies come ashore with socks on."

"So?"

"I've always thought Joe Campbell was attacked below deck and that's why he was barefoot."

"None of that's going to stand up in ..."

"But wait. The hood. You spotted it. There's no way he tied his own hood that tightly. He couldn't even see! Someone else did it. Why? To make sure he didn't bleed anywhere. Would it make sense to do that if he was attacked on deck?"

"No. But even if he was attacked below deck, we still don't know who did it."

"If he was barefooted, he would have been in his own cabin. At the very least, his boots would have been. We never found his boots, so whoever did it must have got rid of them. Who was in that cabin? Johnny and Malky Campbell."

"So, they did it."

"One of them. Almost certainly the brother. But here's the thing. There's no way one person could have carried Joe from the cabin to dump him in the sea."

"They both did it."

"Pretty much. Maybe he was unconscious and Malky Campbell thought he was dead. But in effect, two people committed this murder. Did you notice his face when we told him that the autopsy showed Joe had drowned. I kent Malky Campbell when he was a young laddie. He's changed. I've seen people change in that way before. It happens when they've got some awful secret gnawing away inside them."

"A defence layer would tear that to pieces."

"I know."

"So we've got nothing."

"We've got his guilt. He can't hide that away forever."

Gourlay stubbed the cigarette against the Golf Club's wall.

"Did the NCA make any arrests at the address Jazmyne gave us?"

"None. It'd been abandoned. There were traces of heroin and crack cocaine, so Jazmyne hadn't made it up." Gourlay tutted and tapped the ash from the end of the tab. "The description she gave them matched a person they're interested in."

"What'll happen to her?"

"She'll be out of hospital in a couple of days. They've already rehoused her sister at a foster home far away from London. She'll join her there. If we catch the bad bastards that sent her up here she'll have to testify."

Gourlay ground the end of the cigarette against the pub's wall.

"Right, we better show face, or people will start talking."

Stark wasn't sure if she was joking. His mobile buzzed in his jacket pocket.

"DI Hillman?"

"DI Stark. We've got a problem. The registration plates of two vehicles used by the London based OCG that have a county line in your area have just been picked up by an ANPR on the A9. There aren't any cameras north of where they were identified, but we have fairly decent intel that they're heading to Port Cawdor. The man described by Jazmyne Davies, who we believe goes by the name of El or Elhan, is believed to be in one of the cars - other figures potentially higher up the OCG's food chain may also be present. We'll send you a screen grab so you can identify him. These are extremely dangerous individuals with connections to serious organised crime in the Balkans and Puglia. They may be carrying firearms. We insist you do not make any unnecessary attempts to apprehend them and urge extreme caution should they be involved in any criminality. We've scrambled a firearms squad to the hospital in case Jazmyne Davies is their intended target, but they won't be there for thirty minutes."

"I can be there in five." Stark raced to his car, and got in behind the wheel as Gourlay opened the passenger's door. "Where are you going?"

"With you."

Not wanting to waste time arguing, he accelerated down the road filling Gourlay in on DI Hillman's information.

The hospital receptionist's never ending inspection of her indigo talons was once again interrupted by Stark.

"Has this man come through reception in the last hour?"

Languidly she raised her eyelashes to look at the image on Stark's phone. "Who's asking?"

"Police."

Stark pulled out his ID.

"Nah, can't say I've seen anyone like that tonight."

"Is Jazmyne Davies still on ward 16?"

"Yeah, think so."

"Armed officers will be here soon. Direct them to Jazmyne Davies' ward immediately."

Stark and Gourlay jogged through the dim deserted corridors, took three stairs at a time. The recovery unit was eerily quiet: a smell of disinfectant, the rhythmic beeps of a hospital machine, a gleaming floor that no one had walked over since it had been mopped. Stark stepped across the slippy surface and peered into Jazmyne's ward. The old women next to her was reading a crime novel, her bedside lamp providing enough light for the police to see Jazmyne sleeping soundly.

"What do we do now?"

"We wait," Stark replied checking his watch and phone.

Looking again at the face of the man who Jazmyne had identified, Stark noted the flat mid-face, short nose and small eyes of someone with fetal alcohol spectrum disorders. The face stared goadingly at whoever had taken the photo, wads of what looked like a serious amount of money, fanned out for show. Hillman said they'd got it from an Instagram account associated with the gang.

"But what if they show up – we're unarmed."

"They won't try anything with us here," Stark stated, as much to convince himself as the young PC. She leaned against the wall, her pale face shadowy in the dim light that illuminated the emergency exit signs. Was she any older than Sophie? Stark realised he knew nothing about her and most of him thought he'd like to keep it that way.

The ambient noise of a ventilator in the ward behind them was interrupted by a cleaner waltzing down the corridor with her mop, headphones on as she mumbled the words to Moon River.

Gourlay gave Stark as wry smile. "Well, it beats drinking in the Nineteenth Hole."

Stark grimaced. From where he was standing, he could see the lift and could hear the whirling of its cables. He held his breath, his heart racing while the ventilator maintained its regular beat and the waltzing cleaning woman kept time. An electronic bell pinged as the lift stopped. The doors opened and two uniformed policemen burst out. John Mathie and Dougie MacKay, their anxious faces as relieved to see Stark as he was to see them.

CHAPTER TWELVE

We careened into the party like we owned the place, stood looking for floor-space, drink to steal, and girls. There wasn't much spare. A crumpled bottle of cider the colour of dehydrated piss was passed in Corky's direction. He nodded at the girl, whose hand it was attached to, as if he recognised her. She smiled, exposing a run-down graveyard of teeth, while he crushed the bottle to his face.

Blythe Lighthouse was on a headland, at the end of a meandering coastal road whose hedges crowded closer, until branches and leaves swept over your windscreen like a carwash. The actual lighthouse tower had been dismantled a decade ago as coastal erosion meant it was in danger of dropping off its perch and down onto the rocks that for centuries it had warned sailors about. The living quarters of those that had manned the lighthouse were all that remained. The walls of this building had once been painted white but years of North Sea storms had scoured and scabbed the surface. The loose windowpanes, that had not been broken, rattled in their frames at the relentless thump of the techno that regulated all of the nights.

Every year the council boarded up Blythe Lighthouse's windows and put up signs saying *Danger of Death – Keep Out*. Every year the boards on the windows were torn down and the signs stolen as trophies to be hung over bedroom doors.

Blythe Lighthouse was legendary. In the first few years at secondary, people claimed they had been to parties there, but no one believed them. The people who actually went measured the scale of their debauchery not in the number of pints or pills consumed but in the number of days they'd stayed awake. Untouchable girls, who drifted down school corridors sneering at the gym-sweat-Lynx stink of the boys gawking at them, did unspeakable things at Blythe Lighthouse. While something very much like the northern lights curdled the never-quite-night sky, generators and decks, soundsystems and strobe lights were set up by competing teams. Loons came from the other fishing towns and other schools bringing with them the promise of violence and quines who were utterly, eye-achingly new. Every year Blythe Lighthouse shuffled closer to the eroding cliffs, while techno thumped on the walls and the people stomped on the floor and sometimes it felt like we were already falling.

Pete the Hat strode into the main room looking disdainfully at the bodies who were scattered around the crowded mattress and had assumed the type of shapes bomb blast victims might make. Grinding his teeth and baring the whites of his eyes, he stared at the mattress until people made space for him. A few loons from school nodded nervously at me, but I stared right through them. This was what it meant to be known, or at least to be with bodies who were known. Oblivious to the heavy vibes, Corky flopped onto the recently vacated space on the mattress. Resting his head on a girl's lap, he mumbled, "An apple a day keeps the doctor away," as she held a bottle of cider above his face. Every so often he would sit up and slurp greedily from it like some disgusting beardy baby. Eventually Corky noticed Pete's sour face and passed him the bottle. Pete sniffed it, grimaced and poured the remaining cider over Corky's head.

"If cocaine is god's way of telling you, you've got too much money, White Lightening is him saying you haven't enough." Smiling, he produced a wrap and kicked a record sleeve in Corky's direction, ordering him to, "Rack 'em up."

Corky stared at him and for a moment I thought he was going do something stupid. Instead he licked the cider suds from his stubble and said, "Waste of good cider, that."

Pete turned and kicked the bottle hard against the wall, the remaining dregs spraying half the room.

As I skulked over to Johnny, I thought for a moment that Nicky must be at the party: there was that smoky, soapy smell. My nostrils quivered and suddenly I couldn't get enough of that smell, but it was only a couple of candles jammed into whisky bottles in the neuk of the room.

Johnny had been getting mad wi it for days. I hadn't exactly said yes to his plans, but I hadn't exactly said no either, at least not in words he could understand. Besides, the sort of money he was talking about was life changing ... was lifesaving.

Across the room The Viking – head bouncer at Enigma and consequently just about the most important person in the whole town – was pointing us out to a group of men, who looked too old, too sober for this place. One of the guys had been in Pete the Hat's crowd, a nutter called Brian Souter who went out with Nicky when she was 14 and he was in his mid-twenties. He grinned at me, revealing popcorn coloured teeth that looked like they hadn't been brushed in years. The other two were out-of-towners. The type of hard silent men that made me stand straighter, clenching my jaw muscles and wishing I was made of steel, while painfully aware that I was made of burstable skin and breakable bones.

"Do you ken those guys?" I muttered to Johnny, who made an unintelligible noise.

The smaller out-of-towner caught us looking, and indicated I should come over. He had one of those pit-bull faces that people get when their ma couldn't keep off the booze when they're pregnant. The type of face you wouldn't want to get too near for fear he might bite. Crawling up the side of his neck was a tattoo of a crab, one pincer opened as if it were about to grab hold of his ear.

"Want any of these?" He barked, holding up a bag for banking coins, which was bulging with more pills than I'd ever seen before. "Pink Mitsubishis." He looked at the carnage around him. "They're well rapid."

With his stoney face he wasn't much of an advert for his wares, but to be fair, everyone around him was spangled.

"Here." He took five pills from the bag and handed them to me.

"How much?"

"On the house, mate."

I claimed a bottle of tonic that had been circulating and gubbed one. I didn't want to lose the rest, so wrapped them in a Rizzla paper.

"Cheers."

"Say nothing."

Pete Kerr had cleared a space next to Corky by belly flopping heavily onto the mattress.

A fat girl wearing so much make up that she looked like one of the Thundercats gave him a shake. "You alright Pete? Where you been tonight?"

"Don't know," he said. "But it's nice to find somewhere I belong." With that, his eyelids slumped shut and his face assumed the blessed oblivion of someone on an advert for deluxe, king-sized beds.

The man with the crab tattoo stared at him like he thought Pete was a total cunt.

"Your mum works in the chippie. Best fish n chips in Scotland, innit. At least that's what this cunt keeps telling us." He nodded at Soutar. "Tried getting me to eat a battered haggis. That's dutty mate, dutty. Seems a lovely woman. Over generous with the vinegar, but we can't be perfect. I like her. See who I don't like? That Peter fucking Kerr. I don't trust him. Swaggering about with that Stetson on like he's in *The Godfather*."

I looked over his shoulder at Soutar and The Viking to see if they'd heard, but if they had they weren't bothered. Slagging off the Kerrs in public was just something you didn't do, even if you weren't from round here.

The man with the crab tattoo stared contemptuously at Pete, who was pretending to be asleep while the fat girl on the mattress removed his Stetson and stroked his thinning hair.

"The Kerrs are in on this job you're doing for us. I don't like it. The Kerrs — I don't rate them. I want eyes on that boat. You and Johnny are to make sure he doesn't fuck up."

I gestured towards Pete in a way that was meant to indicate the impossibility of this task, but the man was having none of it. His chest puffed up in his sharp white shirt, thick black spider leg hairs grappling around his collar as if they were trying to climb out.

"See, you might think the Kerrs are big time, but it's us you're really working for. You get me? Thing is, your cousin Johnny, I've got plenty of boys like him: the habit they can't afford, the years doing a shit job they're desperate to escape. I get that."

He grabbed my arm and pulled up my sleeve.

"But you're no junkie and according to this big twat, you're bright enough to get out of this dump. So, what you playing at? Because I want youts that are keen and unless you need the money, I want nothing to do with you."

"I need the money," I muttered, terrified that this life line was being pulled away.

He sized me up. A life's time of measuring, weighing, judging had gone into that stare. "Why?"

"A friend of mine's pregnant. She's in a bad place and needs help."

"A good friend, yeah?"

"Aye, sort of."

"You said anything to her about this."

"Because if there's one thing I can't stand is a gobby cunt. A boy needs to keep his mouth shut. Don't say nothing to no one. You get me?"

The Viking and Popcorn teeth snickered, but Crabneck just nodded as if having weighed me he had not found me wanting.

"Souter tells me you're working in the local park. You keep that job until we give you the nod. It looks less suspicious that way. Hell, who'd be a park attendant if they had money coming their way?"

He gave one of my shoulders a hearty slap and walked off.

The second floor was deserted apart from a couple giving it laldy in what once must have been a lighthouse keeper's bedroom. Further along the corridor was another door, which I rammed open with my shoulder. The moonlight spilt over a couple of sleeping bags spread out on the floor. Three children's heads poked out of the top them. Babies really, none old enough to be at school. The pounding techno made the birdshit stained floorboards vibrate. The smash of a breaking bottle, the hum of the generator that those squatting the place had rigged up, a woman invoking god's name as she climaxed in the room through the wall. Looking at their sleep slack faces I wondered if they were so used to this noise that they wouldn't wake up. Either that or they'd been drugged. I tugged the warped wooden door shut, not wanting to know, not wanting to find out.

Eventually I found the toilet, but, as it had no windows and the electricity was off, it was in total darkness. I used the torch on my mobile. There was a girl passed out in the bathtub, one bare leg draped over the side. Mascara gunged eyelashes, collapsed bee-hive hair, lip-gloss smeared off on the back of her hand – Zoe Stark, but not the head-girl, off to med school, captain of the hockey team Zoe Stark that I knew.

Zoe murmured something, which at least meant she wasn't dead. She was wearing a tight half-unbuttoned shirt, her hands clasped in prayer. A ring that looked like it came from a Christmas cracker was on her forefinger, pink hair-band on her wrist. She had perfect ankles but her feet were pink and swollen, dirty plasters round a couple of painted toes. I stepped back and let the mobile's light play over her long splayed legs and up towards a red and white polka dot mini-skirt. Swallowing, I turned the torchlight away. Someone had taken her pants and left her spread like a centrefold.

First thought was to get out of there. I turned my mobile's torch back on and searched the toilet's dirty floor for her pants, but some filthy bastard must have stolen them.

I decided that I should at least fold her legs to one side. Kneeling down, I murmured, "Are you okay? You awake?" She looked like a rag-doll tossed in the corner but her thighs were heavy and warm. I watched her eyes flickering, while her arm made a movement as if she was dreaming of catching butterflies. Her hair was plastered across her sweaty forehead and her breath smelt like cough mixture. I felt sorry for the girl who had put on silver eye-shadow at the start of the night, a light dusting of foundation over her freckles. "Listen. I'm going to see if there's anyone with a car so we can get you home."

As if talking in a dream, she asked: "Who are you?"

"It's Malky Campbell."

"I can't see you."

I shone the mobile's torch on my face.

"Spooky! Where am I?"

"A party. Blythe Lighthouse."

"Fuck. Really? How'd I end up here?"

She stepped out of the bath like a newly born giraffe. She looked damaged, deranged, delicate, which is to say perfect. But in truth she was none of these things. She was just learning the art of looking in pieces, but never so many pieces that there wasn't some idiot who thought he could put her back together again. Having hung out with Nicky for years, her performance seemed amateurish.

"Shoes?" I found a pair of damp flat-soled ballerina-type things. "Torture," she declared. "Haven't spoken to you in years," she said, hot breath sickly sweet on my cheek. "And you used to be so pretty."

"Are you alright?"

"I'll survive, but … could you help me home?"

We slithered downstairs, through the death of the party: desperate chat up lines, minesweepers, helium high-pitched happy hardcore. A few stragglers stared at Zoe, who stood out amongst the hopelessly fat or insane girls normally found at this time. Johnny and Corky had either pulled or, more likely, were holed up somewhere that they wouldn't have to share their gear. Even the scaries with their sharp suits and gorilla gait had exited the building. We excavated our jackets from a pile behind the decks and walked through the doorless entrance.

"Is Johnny Campbell with you?" she said. "Were you on the boat when they pulled his brother in?"

For a moment I saw that swollen copper-green face, those bare, mottled feet.

"He'd been in the sea for a fortnight. It didn't really seem like him." Watching her process this information, I could see she was impressed.

"The tide's out. We could walk home together."

It was 5 miles to town along a barren, featureless strip of scruffy dunes and slippy rocks, but with a head full of pills and her by my side I could think of nothing in the world I'd rather be doing.

"You know everyone's saying Johnny killed his brother." She grabbed my hands so she could face me. "Did he?"

"No. It's just the talk of small town gobshites"

She chewed her lip. "I've never met a murderer before."

"How do you know? You might be holding hands with one." She shrieked and laughed displaying Buckfast stained teeth.

"You're not a murderer. You work in the park and are nice to old ladies and all the art teachers loved you."

"They're the ones you have to look out for," I said, but she'd skipped on ahead. Mental, that this was the same stuck-up Zoe Stark who for the last two years at school wouldn't be seen dead talking to the likes of me. We'd had a thing, at the end of Fourth year. Rosco, hopelessly in love with a girl in Sixth form, had realised that the only boys auditioning to be in the T Birds were so young or camp that giving them the parts next to the swaggering beauties who would be cast as the Pink Ladies would turn the school musical into a comedy. He was right. I'd dropped half a pill to get through the audition and had come out with the role of Kenickie next to Zoe's Rizzo. We'd sizzled – mainly because I was half-cut each night of the show. "Tragic," Johnny had said. "You're not hanging out with us and that pig's daughter," Nicky would add. And for a few weeks of that summer, "Us or her" was all I got from them.

The sun was surfacing and the seed cases of the broom bushes had started popping. A couple of fishing-boats were already far out to sea. I trawled my tongue along furry teeth and massaged my aching jaw, wishing that the birds' incessant cheer at the dawning of another day would stop.

"I hate this time of year. Walking home at six in the morning should be done under the decency of darkness."

"But it's beautiful," she said, throwing her hands up in the air. "Don't you feel blessed?"

"Would you like one of these?" I offered her the pink Mitsubishis.

"Doubly blessed," she shouted, taking two.

I regaled her with my theory about how all of society's problems could be attributed to the unmanning of the lighthouses and the outlet that such a job must have given people who wanted away from it all. She was laughing and I realised I'd never made so much sense.

Every so often amidst the seaside sounds was a strange bellow of misery from creatures without words. It took me a while to understand there was an external source for this noise, but suddenly I remembered walking back from Blythe Lighthouse last summer, the haar nuzzling us, overly familiar and unwelcome as a wet-nosed stray. "The Sirens are calling," Johnny had whooped, whipping his clothes off and running into the sea. I had followed his ecstatic screams as we splashed in the frozen water. We had swum through fog and waves, sound and texture, towards a sandbank which appeared when the tide was low. Johnny had disappeared in the haar and once I was out of my depth I'd felt disorientated and had tread water, shouting his name. For a moment, I hadn't known which way to go, and had thought I was going to drown out there. Hearing the seals as they wailed like the souls of lost men, I'd splashed towards them. A gust of wind had momentarily cleared the haar to reveal Nicky. At first I'd thought she was walking on the water, but she had reached the sandbank and was standing there naked amidst the ribs of a capsized boats, her wet hair scraped back and her body glistening. The seals had rolled into the water and she was calling to them. I'd never imagined human lungs could make a sound like that. Her song had surged inside me pulling my body to her as if it had been caught in a rip tide.

I joined Zoe by the waves. The rising sun was turning the sea a gory red. On the sand banks it lapped around the wrecks of ossified ships, which looked like the skeletons of mythic sea beasts.

"Come on," I pulled her away from the blood tinged water. "This is not a safe place."

The steeple of the town's kirk pierced the horizon. Soon we'd have to negotiate streets, traffic and the awful possibility of interactions with people who were nothing like us.

As if on cue a couple with an improbable number of youngsters scrambled over the dunes. I shivered, certain that the worst thing in the world would be for them to see me. Not even me, I didn't mind that so much as them seeing my eyes. If they were to do that, I felt certain that their whole freshly painted world, their acrobatic dogs and Frisbee throwing tots would be sucked into the blackholes that were my pupils.

"How are we going to do this?" I indicated the approaching town. "The good people of the world are going to work."

As we walked along The Front, I failed to persuade Zoe to put her shoes on or to stop pretending that this massive shell she'd found was a telephone. Bored workers in family friendly cars leered at her long legs, sneered at her dirty feet, as I skulked beside her praying her dad wasn't going to appear.

A black transit van sat outside the chippies. With one of those weird flashes of intuition, I pulled Zoe down so that we crouched behind a parked car.

"What?"

Johnny and the man with the crab tattoo on his neck and a face like an attack dog got out the passenger's side. The driver was another out-of-towner, a man with a claw of black hair and a face like a remedial child's clay work. He looked a bit like what James Bond should have looked like if the decades of alcoholism and getting knocked about by heavies had been allowed to take effect. The three of them daundered down to the harbour like a group of old friends taking a morning stroll. This was weird. Johnny had acted at Blyth Lighthouse like he'd never met any of these scaries.

"What?"

I ducked down by the harbour wall as they boarded *The Abiding Star*. As they climbed down into the hold I realised I'd been holding my breath. We waited for five minutes before Zoe yawned elaborately: "Fuck this. I'm off home. Coming?"

There was no danger I was turning up at the Starks at seven in the morning with Zoe off her face.

I watched as she shimmied across the street, mesmerised by the sway of her skirt and the nakedness hid underneath. For a moment I almost went after her, but the three of them were back on deck and I was feart they'd see me.

At the corner of the fish market, the older of the strangers stopped. He had about him the air of a neanderthal who'd been dragged into the modern age and made to go through a makeover by some stylist on a daytime TV show. He held a cell phone in his hand but you could see he'd have been more comfortable holding a club. After checking the phone, he gave Johnny a handshake that morphed into one of those matey embraces that sports players give to beaten opponents. After more handshaking and shoulder squeezing between Johnny and the man with the crab tattoo, they went their separate ways. A navy BMW Coupe pulled in behind the transit van. A man whose gut spilled over his black biker trousers got out and the three of them shared a pack of fags. I recognised the new arrival but he seemed out of place like a teacher you bump into during the holidays. From where I crouched, I could almost hear the laughter of the out-of-towners' as they pointed at our boat. Johnny had swaggered to the far end of The Front like he ruled the town. I wanted to run after him. Even I knew you didn't shake hands with men like these.

CHAPTER THIRTEEN

While the local MSP crowned the Gala Queen and drunken inbreds from the farms competed in the annual sheep shearing contest, cackling fishwives inspected enormously swollen neeps, and a mannequin, who had been eliminated in the early rounds of last year's X Factor, bleated into a microphone.

"Eliminated from X Factor," Mackinnon hissed as we watched girls crowd round to get his signature. "If he comes anywhere near me, he'll be eliminated from fucking existence."

Thirteen and fourteen year olds stalked about chewing on broken bits of coconut, using the bags they'd won goldfish in as water balloons. A rickety waltzer – half the size of those at a proper amusement park, but twice as scary due to the fact that the people running it could barely maintain consciousness never mind a fast-moving machine - slung screaming kids around as the woman operating the ride shouted over Zombie Nation: 'All you kiddie riders out there, we're gonna hit the sky tonight!" The whole park reeked of fried onions, generator fuel, stale beer, rotting hay and the sheep shitting themselves in terror. The town gala was another of the Kerrs' concerns. Each of the rides was manned by distant family or pals, while they ran the beer tent. They even took a cut of the takings from the boat pond and putting green – "it's just easier that way," Aida had explained.

That morning I'd been in the park before any of them. I'd swept the paddling pond for broken glass, chucked in chlorine tablets and filled it up; emptied all the bins; painted lines on the football pitches and put up nets and corner flags.

I would have loved to have hidden. Not just because I hated all the bodies from school seeing me in these sky blue work trousers and council issue boots, but because yesterday had been exam results day. Up at the war memorial Rosco and Lilly, boys I'd been pals with in school, had appeared with the twins from MacDougal House, who looked to have gone through the sort of transformation that happens in hundreds of Hollywood movies when the geeky secretary or librarian finds contacts, gets a makeover and suddenly, and somehow surprisingly to everyone, becomes ridiculously sexy. They were waving over to Fraggle and Midge: the sort of boys who had fancy allergies, violin lessons, fountain pens and fathers who owned yachts. Fascinated, I watched as the group greeted each other like long lost friends. One of the MacDougal girls popped a bottle of what was probably actual champagne while the other handed round those long skinny glasses.

Rosco and Lilly were just back from inter-railing and it wasn't long until Lilly took off his top to display his bronzed body. His hair, which his parents had never let him grow while at school, had been sun-streaked and he took great delight in flicking it out of his eyes. Rosco at least kept on his top, but he was wearing a black bandana and a T-shirt advertising Stormzy's album *Gang Signs & Prayer*, which on him was fucking hilarious. Fraggle took an actual picnic rug and what looked like a carton of strawberries from his rucksack, while Midge appeared to be carrying a hamper, as if he was a fucking character from Wind in the Willows. I scanned the park wishing that the Young Team who normally hung out at the war memorial would come and smash the lot of them.

The whole town were out on Gala Day and I was sure I'd see Nicky. A few days after she'd come to see me in the park, an advert had appeared on the Post Office's message board for a single occupancy flat in the smart end of town. I'd stared at the cursive, purple hand-writing until the old woman behind the counter had asked if I was alright. It'd taken me ages to muster the courage to phone the number and organise a viewing. Before arriving I'd put on my old school shoes, gargled mouth wash and scrubbed my nails. But the landlady couldn't contain her disappointment at the sight of me. I half-recognised her as someone from school's mum, and as she led me round a swift and unenthusiastic tour she clocked who I was too.

"Which of the Campbells are you then?" she'd asked. "They're prolific enough."

"My mum's Beth Campbell. She works in the chippie on The Front," I said in a hope of distancing myself from Johnny and Dawn.

"So, what age are you supposed to be?"

"Eighteen."

"Any proof of ID?" I'd expected this and pulled out my driving licence. She examined the date closely and frowned. "The flat's not available until the end of August."

"That's perfect."

"You'll have to get a reference from your employer – you do have an employer? And show me evidence of your ability to meet the rent. A pay slip will do. Seen as you're so young and I'm guessing a first time renter, your deposit will be three months' rent, plus you'll have to pay two months' in advance."

I peered out of the window at the triangle of overgrown grass in the back garden. Once the leaves had come off the trees, I reckoned there'd be a view of the sea from there. The garden was perfect. Just the right size for a toddler.

"No bother," I'd replied, as if being asked to cough up two grand was something that happened every day.

"You'll have to keep the garden," she'd added following my eyes.

"I love gardening,"

Giving me a final withering look, she'd said "See if you can come through with all that in a fortnight … if I've not found someone else by then, I'll consider you."

I'd headed out the house and straight down to Nicky's with the news, but no one was answering her door. I'd felt exultant; I was going to be the one to get Nicky out of that dump, help her out when she needed it the most. Even with a bairn on the way I doubted she'd top the list for flats, having, in her own

THE SOUND OF SIRENS

words, put the Boho into ASBO during her previous tenancies with the council. There was no danger she'd be able to put up enough for a deposit in a private property. Too many people kent her Bottom End squat and with the London dealers using it as a base, she didn't even need to leave her couch to score. If she ever wanted clean, she had to steer clear of that scene and a new flat in an area like Mill Hill was the only way to do that. I just hoped the end of August wouldn't be too late.

It'd been a fortnight since the viewing and I still hadn't been able to tell her about the empty flat; the door of the squat was always locked and nothing gives off a more dismal sound than the echoes of someone banging on a door in an abandoned tenement. Her phone was as bad – never a surprise with someone who spent days on end blitzed in a flat with no electricity. Every time I called I got the same automated message: I'm sorry this number cannot be reached. The voice didn't sound sorry at all. All I wanted was Nicky's gravelly voice and husky laughter. All I wanted was to tell her everything was going to be ok.

Zoe, who'd spent the last five minutes exchanging exuberant hugs with the picnic set, sauntered over. We'd met a few times since the night at Blythe Lighthouse, ending up in Denizens or High Spirits seen as they were the only places that sold the gaudy coloured alcopops that she glugged like a person staggering out of the desert. Later I'd pay us into Enigma, or a taxi to Blythe Lighthouse, flashing the cash like a big shot. Looking at my bank account, it was pretty clear that any hopes I'd had of being able to legitimately save the two grand for the flat were nil. But in truth, I'd always known that.

For now, Zoe was wearing a crop top and a pair of cut up denim shorts with purple tights that had been artfully laddered. Draining the dregs of a half-litre bottle of coke that judging by its colour had been heavily doused with vodka, she burped loudly. She had applied so much highlighter to her cheeks that she glowed like a lightbulb.

"Celebrating or commiserating?" I asked.

She belched and made a disgusted face. "Straight As apart from a B in Maths. Got my place at Edinburgh to study medicine. You?"

I shook my head. It wasn't until I'd opened that envelope and seen the series of Cs and Ds, a solitary A in art, that I'd realised I actually gave a shit. Without working, I'd done alright in my Nat 4s, but the years of playing so much GTA that I could have drawn maps of the cities I'd raced through, of skiving every time Johnny was back from the sea, of smoking so much blow the nights before exams that I'd start sentences I was unable to finish, had finally hit hard.

"Got an A in art. Going to college in Glasgow to do a folio for art school," I lied.

"Great," she said, like she almost believed me.

There was no doubt the others were celebrating. They'd been in the same sets as me in the first years of school and weren't anything special. But there they were with their champagne and results while I ran around emptying dog bins and picking up fag butts, looking like a scaffie in my steelies and council-issue work clothes.

Generally speaking, I'd always presumed that everything in my life would be alright – that I wouldn't end up working on the boats or in any of the other zero-hour jobs the town had to offer. My mum's response to the results was to report that Duffy had been in the chippie that week saying how impressed he'd been by me and that there were prospects in Land Services beyond the normal seasonal contract. Prospects! For the first time, the smuggling job looked like a lifeline. The thought I had something else lined up was about the only thing keeping me going.

"I'm going to get a drink off Fabienne," Zoe said.

I watched her take the bottle from Fabienne McDougal with the easy grace of someone used to taking things without anyone objecting. For a few years that crowd would come back from university at Christmas, a couple of weeks in summer and when they bumped into the likes of us while paying for petrol or pints, they'd ask in pretend-concerned voices after the others: the sentinels who stood smoking outside the pubs and who hadn't appeared to have left their posts since the last time they visited.

The woman in charge of the waltzers bellowed, "Scream if you want to go faster!"

I turned over a boat that a toddler had pissed in, explained for the hundredth time that the paddle-boats scrapped along the bottom of the pond and shouted at a group that were splashing some unimpressed looking adults. The other parkie had tactically injured his back and instead of working four days on four day off, I'd ended up being on for sixteen shifts in a row. To say I was scunnered with it all would have been an understatement.

Another hour and things started quietening down at the boating pond, and I'd been told not to even attempt a clear up job until the morning. Word spread that the beer tent had ran out of drink and once the trophies for growing the largest radish and being the fastest sheep shearer had been awarded, the town's aboriginals headed for a top up in the dark familiarity of the High Street's pubs, leaving the park for those too skint, young or howling to have any hope of getting served.

Up the path to the War Memorial some of the older crustie types that you got at Blythe Lighthouse were pushing shopping trolleys loaded with decks, speakers and a generator.

I got the rest of the boats into the shed and locked up.

Even amongst the congregation of waifs and strays it was easy to spot them, as they span around the sound system.

"If you can keep your head, when all around are losing theirs, then my son you can fuck off home."

Corky thrust a bottle of tonic vaguely in my direction. "We're the unmarketable by-catch of humanity," he added. "They'd like to throw us back into the sea."

I gulped the sickly sweet liquid — most of them looked like they'd barely crawled out of the sea. It was going to take a truly heroic effort to make ground on these lot.

Johnny staggered down the hill with his shipwrecked walk.

"Well I feel sorry for whoever has to clear up this mess."

Looking at the smouldering barbecues, the sheep shit on the football pitches and the beer cans bobbing in the boat pond, I said, "I'm not sure I can take much more of this."

"Soon you won't have to," he replied with a know-it-all wink. "We go tomorrow. Tam says we can take the boat."

"You telling me this now?"

"Wasn't to tell anyone until the last minute. And you, don't breathe a word."

I'd spoken to Tam yesterday afternoon, giving him the spiel that Johnny and I had agreed on, about changing my mind after getting my exam results and realising that a life putting weans on rowing boats and emptying dog bins would, indeed, be unspeakably miserable. Uncle Tam had just about managed to supress the smile of someone who kent they'd been right all along.

"Well, in a few weeks, once I've recovered from this chemo session, we'll get started." I'd put on my disappointed face and said, "But I'd really like to get started now. Johnny can show us the ropes; he's got his tickets."

At this point, Johnny, who'd been lurking in the kitchen, came through. He'd spruced himself up and had shuffled forward muttering about how big a disappointment he was, but that he was desperate to get back on The Abiding Star and make things up with the family. Uncle Tam had attempted to glower at him, but now that the police were off our case, he thought his boy deserved one last chance, that he was attempting to reform his character in a bid to become the type of son that his brother had been. The wishful thinking of a dying man. "The Campbell boys going to sea," he'd murmured, dreaming of the generational rightness of it all. For a moment, I'd almost felt sorry for him.

I looked at Rosco and that crew, bobbing about as if they were into the tunes but actually looking awkward as fuck.

"What's everyone spending their money on?"

"Pete's getting a new set of tyres and alloys for his Golf. Reckons he'll be able to break the record for The Bends."

We called the road leading out to MacDougal House 'The Bends' both because of the number of twists and turns in the road and because your face looked like someone in a decompression chamber, as your car smashed speed limits, your brain smeared to the back of your skull.

"Well, you can only fight against natural selection for so long. What about you?"

"First thing I'll be doing is getting my guitar back from that cunting pawn shop. Then I'll buy some Marshall amps. Reckon I'll move down to Glasgow, get a flat, get a band together. I've written some new tunes and just need some studio time."

It was months since I'd heard Johnny speaking about the future other than to say it was all fucked. I didn't believe he'd written any new songs, but was reassured by his lies.

"You?"

There was no way I could tell him about Nicky, so I said, "I hadn't thought that far ahead. But get out of here, that's for sure. Maybe go down to Glasgow as well. I'd like to go to one of those colleges where you do folios to see if you can get into art school."

Jonny nodded encouragingly. "See. It's all going to work out."

As Banjaxed dropped Bicep's *Glue*, the whole merry go round of the Mad Squad danced about with ping-pong eyes, skin on their skulls snare drum tight waiting for the brush for the rush of some weird beat. Johnny jumped to his feet. Minutes before their total abandon had seemed repulsive but suddenly I wanted to join them. I slugged greedily at a bottle of Talisker that Mackinnon had taxed from a caravan that afternoon.

"Are you the youth of today?" He roared at no one in particular.

While they danced, I slipped my mobile out and sent Nicky a message:

Plan is back on. Taking the boat out tomorrow morning. Will have enough money to set you up in the flat I keep texting you about. Hold on and answer your phone! I miss you. M x

A tidal surge of euphoria rolled over me. Banjaxed, who played Enigma on the last Friday of the month, appeared from DJing at the sound system, looking totally smacktastic.

"You got any sweets?" I asked.

"A couple but I'm holding them for Frenchie."

"What about you," I said to Dawn, "seen anyone?"

She gave the park one desultory glance and said, "No."

"No?"

The place was full of multimentalists. Dawn — who had been on the scene since she was fourteen, who could take half an hour getting from Enigma's club door to cloak-room with all the people she had to say hello to, who (like the Queen) never carried any money, but, who (unlike the Queen) ended up as fucked as anyone - was saying no. We glared at each other. "Besides, you're too young to be getting into all this. You need to pick your life up," she said, picking up the stolen bottle of whisky. She gave me a sneaky look and asked, "Have you see Nicky recently?"

"Not for weeks."

"Last half dozen times I've been round no cunt's answered. Last time I was sure someone was standing behind the door watching me through that peep hole. There are some freaky rumours going round about her."

She looked at me for a reaction, but I stonewalled her. "Like what?"

"I'm no gossip."

"Maybe she's trying to get clean," I offered.

"Get clean. Nicky? Why'd she want to do that?" The snicker of a sneer momentarily snuck across her face like she'd set a trap.

Zoe had been waiting for a gap in our conversation, which she filled by waving a fair sized bag of pills in my face. "Think we'll be able to shift these?"

I looked at the park. Girls in luminous boob-tubes wearing YOLO baseball caps and boys in hoodies and anarchist neckerchiefs.

I took the bag from her. Pink Mitsubishis.

"Who'd you get these from?"

She scanned the park and bit her lip.

"This black lad in Enigma with a London accent. I've seen him hanging around the bus stop and The Front."

I had the kind of head rush you get after inhaling poppers.

"Watch yourself. You've no idea who he is."

She shrugged. "They're good, they're cheap."

Seeing that Dawn was listening, I offered her the bag.

"Do you want some?"

She screwed up her nose.

"Don't know." She looked at Zoe. "Your dad know you're into this?"

"Doubt it," Zoe smirked

"Go on." I said

"Well I suppose."

Dawn always did this - made me feel like she was doing us a favour.

I started coming up with a quiver of light on the boat pond, a shiver as if someone had blown cold air on the back of my neck. My fingers and feet kept tapping to a beat that was fizzing down the back of my spine. The skin around my face tightened into the sort of unblinking fish-hooked grin normally only seen on aged Hollywood actresses with botched face-lifts.

I got up on marionette legs and moved down the hill like a puppet whose strings have got tangled. At the speakers, Zoe gave me a big slobbery kiss. As she skipped away it felt like she'd left a limpet on my cheek.

My feet suddenly knew what to do. Even though it had clouded over, a team of topless loons span T-shirts round their heads chanting: "Here we, here we, here we fucking go."

And here we fucking went. My T-shirt was soon wet, what with the sweat and the rain that I hadn't noticed. Maybe it wasn't soon wet at all, maybe it had taken hours. I pulled it off. One of the local loons, his torso covered in so many tattoos of topless women, football club badges and proclamations of enduring love that he resembled nothing so much as the walls of a public toilet, embraced me against his wet muscular body.

"Taps aff," Johnny chanted in my face. "This is getting heavy taps aff."

I concentrated on my breathing. Around me the ground was studded with ancient beer bottle tops, dull shards of glass from pre-historic carry outs, but eventually I found a place to sit. My eyes shimmied up the tree trunks at the back of the park. Carved into the bark were initials, generations of long-lost lovers, strained and stretched as the tree grew so that many were now unreadable. Zoe rushed up the bank and flopped next to me.

"I don't ever want this to stop," she said.

And with the warmth of her thigh pressing against my leg, neither did I.

"You know, everything is going to be alright," she whispered, her breath on my neck sending shivers down me. "Forget about exam results and dead end jobs. Everything is going to be alright."

The whole mad squad frenzied around the sound system. There was a religious fury in the flailing of their limbs and I grinned like I was having some sort of epiphany. "Alright?" I shouted. "Everything's going to be fucking perfect."

We cackled, and for a moment our cracked laughter sounded almost authentic.

CHAPTER FOURTEEN

After correctly predicting the winners of the 5-a-side football, tug-of-war and the courgette growing contest, Sergeant Grant was £30 up on bets with other officers and not shy about it. The Gala was his favourite day of the year: patrolling through the stalls, eating the occasional burger, stopping to have a chat with old school friends. He bathed in the community's approval: proud to be in uniform.

"Thing is," he told the young PC, "There are a lot of good folk round here, don't let anyone tell you any different. Just a shame it's the 5% we spend all our time dealing with. Bloody nuisances. But don't let that give you the wrong impression."

He scanned the hillside by the war memorial, where the usual crowd were gathering. The only prediction that hadn't come through was that the rain had stayed off, and the troublemakers that assembled there at the end of every Gala Day had nothing to drive them home. He wasn't 100%, but he was pretty certain he could see Zoe Stark up there, clutching a bottle of beer despite the ban on such substances in all public places. Grant would never have considered himself to be a malicious person, but it'd give him immense satisfaction to be able to tell Stark about having to give one of his golden girls an on the spot fine.

"You've been spending a lot of time with Stark." Gouraly shrugged – Sergeant Grant had been attempting to draw some sort of a compromising opinion from her all afternoon, but she wasn't biting. "Think you'll apply to become a detective once your probation's over?"

"It's early days."

"Too right. You're three months into your probation. Don't go filling your head with big ideas about running about in fast cars and slick suits. And for that matter, don't think spending time with Stark will help. Man's a has been. I'm not saying all Port Cawdor's troubles should be laid at his feet, but he's totally failed to get on top of the drugs problem. He's a bit of a sad case really. Wife's a torn faced cow, always pressuring him to get a transfer from here. Eldest daughter doesn't come home from uni … other daughter's up there with that shower."

Gourlay surreptitiously attempted to check the time.

"Look at them." The sergeant continued. "In broad day light."

Grant stared at the crowd round the sound system, desperate to identify any activity that could justify making the call to disperse them.

Gourlay didn't see what the issue was and in any case, it was Sergeant Grant who was in charge of policing the Gala Day, and if he found the young people by the sound system so disagreeable, then it was surely in his power to do something about them. Stark had called it right when they were leaving the station. They were a visible presence to appease the early morning dog walking set, but they might as well have been cardboard cut outs. If any day had convinced her that she would apply to become a detective as soon as her probationary period was over, it was today. She couldn't stand parading around with Grant. They'd been told to keep an eye out for the men from the OCG and for any young people who were not from the area, but in truth Sergeant Grant only had eyes for the range of revolting fried food on offer. Other than the Kerrs, who all appeared to be gainfully, and possibly even legally, employed on various rides and stalls, the most suspicious looking person in the park was a man with the sort of rotten teeth she normally associated with serious drug users. But Grant had greeted him like an old friend, the two of them having a good blether, which at one point clearly included some comment about her, which had caused the man to cackle in a way that exposed a whole set of stumpy, stained teeth.

"Golf four two, Golf four two, this is Uniform Bravo, over."

Grant rolled his eyes before speaking into his radio.

"Bravo, this is Golf four two in Ardleigh Park, go ahead, over."

"Golf four two, we've had reports from the public of a young female around six foot, black hair, brown fur coat, suspected of selling drugs by the gates at the Burnside Estate end of the park, over."

"Uniform Bravo, we're on our way. Will report back when we arrive, over."

"Golf four two, received, thank you, over."

Grant unwrapped the napkin where he'd been storing the last half of a burger and, after inspecting the greasy grisly meat, wolfed it down in a couple of gulps, before cleaning his fingertips on the sides of his leather biker trousers.

"Got a job for you two," he said turning to the young PCs.

Gourlay was expecting something a little more covert than simply walking towards the suspect, but Carmichael was marching towards the gates with an unquestioning conviction. A tune dropped at the sound system, the 4/4 beat momentarily matching their steps. The suspect was easy to identify. Lank damp hair hanging over her face, as she looked at the scuffed toes of her Docs, heel of her right boot banging against the wall she was sitting on in time with the distant music. A message came through on her mobile, and the girl spent some time reading it, the tug of a tentative smile pulling at her mouth. The foot stopped, lips pinched and Gourlay realised the girl was watching them through her overgrown fringe. She didn't flinch, but hugged the fur coat tighter to herself as if frisked by a cold wind.

"She's going to run," Gourlay murmured, noticing her heart quicken as she prepared for the chase.

Carmichael marched on, to all the world looking like a man imagining himself on a parade ground about to receive a medal. He stopped in front of the girl who became even more engrossed in the scuffed toes of her boots. Gourlay watched her knuckles tighten as she gripped the wall.

"Evening," Carmichael began. "Any idea why we've stopped here?"

The girl puffed her fringe away from her forehead and glimpsed at them, her eyes the colour of late summer leaves. She was beautiful, Gourlay thought, wondering why she hadn't ran.

"Hiya, Michael, not seen you in ages," she smiled up at him.

Carmichael blushed. "As you match the description of someone selling drugs in this area, we're obliged to carry out a search on you."

The faded green eyes flitted between them with quick, watery, blinks.

"I've done nothing wrong."

"Well then, you won't mind my colleague carrying out a quick search." PC Carmichael stepped back, "Constable."

"I'm PC Gourlay," her voice said as she automatically went through the procedures drilled into her at Tulliallan. She swallowed, attempting to control her quivering voice, attempting to capture the flat impersonal tone she'd heard from experienced officers. "Could you stand up, turn around and put your arms out to the side."

Gourlay found herself mimicking the actions she expected from the girl.

"I've told you. I've not done anything."

"Turn around and put your arms out," Carmichael wheedled. "Or we'll call back up and charge you with obstruction."

The girl eyeballed Gourlay while lumbering to her feet. She stretched out her arms, palms facing skywards. "You people make me mad," she muttered. Gourlay held onto the girl's right wrist and began the search. Up close her fake fur coat reeked of nightclubs, while her hair had the humid smell of classrooms after rainy lunch times.

"Fucking lesbian," the suspect hissed in Gourlay's ear.

"Do you have any sharp or harmful objects in your pockets?"

The girl tutted as if insulted. Gourlay took two cheap pay-as-you-go phones from her pocket.

"Could you tell us why you've two phones in your possession?"

"Is it a crime?"

"It's not a crime, but it's unusual."

"That one's not mine. The Nokia. Found it on the ground over there, didn't I."

Gourlay took a wallet from the suspect's other jacket pocket and handed it to Carmichael.

"Could you tell me how much money you have in this?"

"Dinna ken, a hundred and twenty, hundred and thirty, something like that."

Carmichael flicked through the crumpled fives and tens.

"That's a lot of money."

The girl sniffed. "You might think so."

As Carmichael continued going through the wallet, Gourlay noticed a team of local kids watching them. With a hundred crazies up at the sound system, she suddenly felt exposed.

"Not your lucky day, is it?" Carmichael held up a wrap made from a National Lottery ticket.

A flash of those supernaturally green eyes, as she assessed whether she could kick or charm her way out of this. But her capacity to do either of these things was long gone.

"That's for my ain personal usage."

"Of course it is. Remove your coat, please."

"What?"

"Could you remove your coat?"

"I'm not taking my clothes off in public."

"Under the laws concerning stop and search procedures, we are permitted to ask you to remove an outer coat."

"Fuck you."

Carmichael glanced at the kids, one of whom was filming the search.

"Right, let's take this down the station."

The girl twisted round. "What?"

"We're taking you to the station for a thorough search. Don't try anything silly. If you resist or become aggressive we'll cuff you."

"Fuck you."

A smile bigger and brighter than any she'd seen all day creased Carmichael's face. "And you too my dear. Cuff her."

Carmichael booked her in at the station while Gourlay struggled into a pair of latex gloves in preparation for a more extensive search. PC Stewart, the only other female officer on duty, observed from the door.

"What's your name?"

"Her name's Nicola Skelton," PC Stewart said from the door. "Not the first time she's been in here neither."

"Could you remove your coat?"

The girl slung the tatty article on the metal table in the centre of the room. Gourlay again held onto her outstretched arm as she patted the girl's wooly sweater. Since moving to Port Cawdor this was the closest she got to human contact. As she moved her hands around the waist of the suspect's trousers she felt the bulging bump of her belly.

"You're pregnant?" The defiance seeped out of the girl and Gourlay understood why she hadn't run. "You've not swallowed anything?"

"No."

"I'm going to have to ask you to take off your boots." As Nicky unthreaded the double knotted laces, Gourlay knew instinctively that she was carrying drugs in her socks. She glimpsed at PC Stewart who was busy with her phone.

As she knelt, the suspect shivered like an animal being stalked. Gourlay ran her hand down the girl's black jeans, felt the strong curve of her calf muscles. The tight black jeans ended in a pair of glitter socks that had lost all their sparkle.

"Do you like doing this sort of thing?"

Gourlay looked up at the girl noticing that the unbuttoned jeans, unable to contain her pregnant belly, were held together with one of those elasticated snake belts she'd last seen in primary school. As her fingertips touched a package behind the suspect's ankle bone, she stared apologetically into the girl's desolate, despairing face. For a moment neither of them moved, but then Gourlay slipped a small plastic bag out of the girl's socks and into her own pocket. PC Stewart was still prodding her mobile and the girl was between her and the camera. Gourlay finished off the search.

"Nothing."

"You sure?" PC Stewart's eyes didn't leave her phone.

Clearly pissed off she stuffed the mobile in her pocket. "Need to do a strip search then." She put on latex gloves. "You better not be carrying anything, cause if I find drugs plugged up your arse, and you've made me go there, I'll be fucking raging."

DI Hillman from the NCA and PC Carmichael were busy watching the late kick off when Gourlay found them. "Search has come up clear."

"Bollocks," Carmichael said. "The way she was carrying on, I was certain she was hiding something."

"Maybe we'll find something on the phones," DI Hillman suggested.

"She's had her problems," PC Carmichael said, "but she's never been done for dealing."

"Part of the Kerr set up?"

"Not really. She hangs out with those boys who were on the trawler that pulled the body in. Funny crowd. Even at school. Swanned around like they were rock stars."

"Was she in a relationship with any of them?" Gourlay asked.

"She was always tight with that Johnny Campbell, but I dinna think she was his type if you know what I mean."

DI Hillman picked up the evidence bags with the mobiles. "Wouldn't surprise me if this is a burner phone for the county line gang. Makes sense to recruit locals. Bloody daft sending kids up here from London and expecting them not to get lifted. Let's get her interviewed."

"One thing," Gourlay said as the two men rose. "She's pregnant. Pretty heavily pregnant."

"That'll be one confused wean come father's day," quipped Carmichael.

DI Hillman licked his thin dry lips. "That's good work PC Gourlay. Nothing easier than turning a pregnant woman. Just describe to her what it's like giving birth while handcuffed to a hospital bed."

The two men bustled off to the interview room, leaving Gourlay fingering the cling film wrapped pack in her pocket. Toilet or drain? Toilet would be quickest. She walked out of the response room feeling the sharp corners of the wraps. Behind the locked door of the cubicle she sat on the seat scanning the ceiling for cameras. Hunching over, she unwrapped the cling film before unfolding the first lottery ticket making sure none of the greyish brown powder spilt on the floor. For this to get here people crossed borders with packets in their stomachs, fought turf wars, tortured rivals, bribed police, coerced kids to move it about the country, groomed addicts to sell it on the streets, filled the country's jails. She poured the powder down the pan and did the same with the other five wraps. Nicky Skelton's wane, wasted face filled her head, as she heard her asking: "Do you like doing this sort of thing?" She flushed a couple of hundred pounds worth of drugs, a couple of hundred pounds worth of evidence down the toilet. They'd both been shocked by her answer.

CHAPTER FIFTEEN

Perched on a stool at a couple sized table I stirred the ice in my glass, watching the pub's window reflecting the replay of a goal from last night's football. I looked through the scorer's body as he celebrated in slow motion, arms outstretched and hair flying like an angel swooping down on the street.

It was 7am and outside a dismal dawn seeped through sodden clouds. Due to the irregular working hours of the fishing fleet, Monty's had an early license. Other than the crew of *The Bon Accord*, who were tucking into bacon sandwiches, and the limpets at the bar, the place was dead. I nipped out to the old phone box on the corner to give Johnny the all clear.

Back in Monty's I waited for them to show. I'd been told to leave my mobile at home, so had nothing to look at until an old boozehound lurched over from the bar and clung to the puggy's lager bright lights like a long lost love. He dropped some coins into the slot and serenaded it in a rasping voice. The fruit stopped spinning and a barrage of coins fired into the tray. He bent to scoop up his winnings.

"Been waiting on that one all week," he croaked to the mottled eyes at the bar.

It seemed like a lucky omen. Dawn's car appeared on the street. I took a deep breath and sauntered out the pub. At the door, one of the deckies from *The Bon Accord* muttered: "£20 says they don't make it back."

I didn't react.

The Abiding Star was moored next to the enormous *Fisher Queen*, one of the factory boats that had been putting us out of business for years.

Johnny tutted like an exasperated job centre worker and said, "You give them every opportunity and what do they do?"

He was watching Corky, who was even more of a sweaty, shit-faced, shambles than normal, staggering towards our boat like a man in a storm four sea. On account of his near permanent fucked state, Johnny hadn't told him about the plan until late last night. Typically, he'd been enthusiastic, or at least as enthusiastic as anyone medicated with methadone can be. He'd been brought along purely to make us look like a crew and because the Kerrs saw him as being safe, but he was a total liability.

"Jackie Baird's just put £20 on us not coming back. They're in Monty's the now saying the boat's cursed or that a family like ours make our own bad luck, or some shite."

Johnny laughed. "Jackie Baird will be sitting in that same seat in that same pub in twenty years' time spouting his shite. But we willna. Will we now?"

He was twitchy, wired, I thought on some concoction of uppers, but his eyes looked clear and there was a focus and purpose to his movements.

While we put our bags in the cabin Johnny whispered: "Feels like returning to the scene of a crime, doesn't it?"

"Don't," I said, feeling that icicle trickle of terror that went down my back every time Joe's swollen, miscoloured face flashed through my head.

Pete the Hat was late. Until he appeared, it couldn't even be said we'd done anything wrong, but as we stood there my senses felt like they'd been turned up to ten. The slap of the waves, the smell of rotting seaweed, the gows scavenging the esplanade for scraps. That morning, more than any other, I imagined what we looked like through the grainy images recorded on the CCTV cameras that monitored the comings and goings along the harbour. Hoodie up, head jerking from side to side I watched myself watch the street, sure I'd never felt so alive.

An old worthy of Uncle Tam's vintage skittered out of *The Fisher Queen*. "How are the troops?" He gave us a mock salute, before recognising Johnny and grimacing like a man swallowing cod liver oil.

A Jeep with tinted windows rolled along the front, closely followed by Maddie Kerr's white Land Rover. They parked outside Monty's.

"Other than having an AK47 sticking out the window, could they be any more obvious?"

After a couple of minutes, Pete hopped out of the white Land Rover wearing a baseball cap. Pete hated baseball caps, but there was no way he could be seen getting on a trawler in a trilby.

"What's Maddie Kerr doing here?"

"The Kerrs have put up a quarter of the money. She'll be keeping an eye on things. She's even given Pete a gun. Cunt was flashing it about last night. Went all *Taxi Driver* on us – the wanker."

As Pete walked across the street my heartbeat kept time with the clanging of the rigging on the nearby yachts. If we were to be sprung at any time, it was now.

Pete clambered onto The Abiding Star, evidently bricking it. Seeing a violent man from the town's big crime family looking that shaken up, gave me the fear.

After checking below deck, he said, "It's just the four of us, aye?"

"A skeleton crew," Johnny smirked at his own wit and at Corky's grey, gaunt face.

Pete gave a thumbs up to the white Land Rover. "Let's get moving."

I untied the hawsers and threw them to Corky. As I jumped back onto the deck, a rat scuttled from behind the wheelhouse, leapt into the water and swam for shore. Corky watched it, as if he couldn't believe his eyes. I'd seen him look that way often enough, but this time he had an explanation.

"That," he said, "is as sure a sign of bad luck as you're going to get."

It was only as Johnny steered out of the harbour that the Jeep and Maddie Kerr's car moved off.

"And you deckies claim this is the most dangerous job in the world," said Pete the Hat, watching them go. "We fuck up here and we're dead. End of."

As the harbour walls and the shops became toy-sized I kept murmuring Tam's old saying: *He that will learn to pray, let him go to sea.* I wasn't exactly clasping my hands, but as the steeple of the kirk dipped out of view, I made all types of promises: that this was the last bad thing I would do, that I was essentially a good person, who had just been led astray.

"Phones," Johnny said holding out a bag. "Turn them off and put them in here. Means no cunt will turn theirs on by accident."

Grumblingly, Pete and Corky gave up their phones.

It was a calm enough day, but Pete had never been to sea before and soon he was gripping the safety railing and spewing over the side.

"When's this going to stop?" he wailed.

"It's never going to stop," Johnny cackled like a demented fairground ride attendant.

"It's better down in the cabin," I told him, minding the advice I'd been given on my first time at sea. I watched him skitter across the deck. Corky was already down there trying to sleep off his recent excesses.

Johnny was in the wheelhouse wearing an old captain's hat he'd nicked from Pete's flat. I almost expected to see him puffing on a pipe. It made me think about the last time we'd seen Uncle Tam, entombed in his easy chair, shrouded in smoke, agreeing to the two of us taking the boat.

I looked out of the wheelhouse as a lump of water struck the prow and a fine spray hit the window. We'd left the coast and there was nothing to be seen but endless ranges of peaks and troughs. Suddenly I felt excited by being at sea without any of the adults telling us what to do.

"We're going to be legends after this."

Johnny gave the kind of mirthless chuckle his father used to issue when he wasn't really listening.

"Where are we actually going?"

"The Devil's Hole."

He pointed to a square of the map about 150 miles east of The Firth of Tay. "It's called that because of the trenches in the sea bed. You've not been there."

He inspected the GPS and radar screens in front of him and I looked at them trying to remember things that Uncle Tam or Joe had explained to me, trying to think of something sensible to say.

"Here, I better give you a lesson in how this stuff works. My dad'll be quizzing you when we get back."

Methodically he explained how to get the trawler started and how the various screens helped with navigation, as if any of that mattered.

"And what time are we meeting them?"

"Evening. If there are any problems we can contact them on the satellite phone."

"Then straight back to harbour?"

"Straight back. We'll tell them we had a mechanical or electrical breakdown. You can come up with the story."

"And how are we doing the actual deal?"

"When we're a couple of hundred metres away, they'll drop the packages into the sea. They'll be attached to a buoy. We just need to pick it up."

"What if someone's monitoring us. Will it not look weird? Two boats coming so close together."

"It's a busy fishing ground. These things happen. If there's any sign of the Coastguards, we're to leave it."

"And what's the dingy doing in the hold?"

"If we're being followed and near enough shore, you and Pete are to go overboard with the gear. Not too delighted with the plan to be honest, but needs must."

"Me?"

"Aye. They don't trust Pete and Maddie Kerr doesn't trust anybody with the gear apart from one of her own."

Johnny steered through the waves in a way that seemed to maximise the degree to which the trawler pitched and rolled and gradually that nausea, that fear of making a fool of yourself by being sick at sea, crept over me. I searched for a steady point on the horizon, but we were too far out. At times like these, it felt that you weren't moving forward, that you were just bobbing about on the same spot in the midst of a vast ocean.

I went down to make some tea, but Corky and Pete were too busy doing synchronised vomiting to even consider having any.

Johnny laughed when I told him this and said, "I knew it. Here, give them these. Make sure they swallow at least three of them."

He handed me an amber medicine bottle. On my way to the cabin, I looked at it more closely but the label had been torn off.

Corky had lived the last few years of his life taking anything that he thought might make him feel better and gubbed a handful of the capsules unquestioningly, but Pete looked less certain.

"They're to settle your stomach and help you get some rest."

After dry heaving, he took three pills and washed them down with the tea.

"Why's everything still moving," he complained. "This isn't natural." He closed the curtain in front of his bunk still clinging onto the mattress with one hand. "Gonnae empty the sick buckets. The smell of them is giving me the boak."

After chucking the vomit over the side and filling the buckets with disinfectant I went up to the wheelhouse. Johnny had The Artic Monkeys on and was sitting back in the skipper's chair, trying to work out the chords.

"Nothing to it," he said, "Nothing to it! They were younger than me when they made it." He nodded at the CD player. "But they've got it. Ambition and the will to succeed. That's all you need Malky."

I tried to have a blether about his plans for moving down to Glasgow but he wasn't having any of it. When I brought up Nicky's name, he became animated. "Let sleeping dogs lie. Aye and she's a dog that can do plenty of sleeping and plenty of lying."

"You ken she's pregnant?"

A terse, bitter smile tugged at his mouth. "Wonder who's gonnae take the hit for that."

He turned the volume on the CD player up and went back to accompanying the music on invisible instruments, strutting and posing before an invisible crowd.

Once the album was finished, I said, "I'm going to check on the others."

"Should be asleep," Johnny mused. "Should be asleep for a while yet. You should get some yourself. I'll need you to give me a break for a bit late afternoon."

I'd been up since 5 and with the party in the park and the fear about this mission buzzing through my system, I hadn't exactly had the soundest night's sleep. After reading for an hour I must have dozed off. I was wrenched out of a dream in which I was sleeping on a massive hammock by a sudden sensation that there was somewhere I really needed to be. I went up to the wheelhouse, where Johnny with all the adrenaline from this morning gone, looked fonnert.

"Here," he said, getting up from the marine seat. "Forecast's good. Just keep her going at 12 knots, due South East. Keep your eye on that. If another boat appears and it's moving towards us fast it could be the Coastguard. Moment you see something like that, gie me a shout. Keep your eye out for helicopters as well. I'm done in, but wake me in 3 hours."

Being alone in the wheelhouse was weird. Certainly, I'd never had a moment like this with Tam skippering the boat. He'd hate it. A clueless loon like me being given the controls of his beloved trawler. The wheelhouse still smelt of his pipe. The calendar on the wall featured paintings of the coastline from the local art group that Aunt Mary belonged to, the month still stuck on June, when everything had changed. Above the screens, Tam had a matchstick model of *The Eileen*, my grandpa's boat. The one on which Tam, James and my father had first gone to sea. Through fine mist on the windows I scanned the horizon. Nothing, but sea in all directions. I checked my watch. Five minutes since Johnny had gone. It was going to be a long three hours.

By evening everyone was up. Pete and Corky were a state, but the excitement of what was coming was enough. Johnny kept a closer eye on our radar, while Pete had brought the gun onto deck.

We'd got to The Devil's Hole early, so circled around a bit until the Dutch trawler appeared on our radar. Johnny spoke to a heavily accented voice on our radio before steering us in their direction.

It was against all the rules of trawling to be moving towards another boat. Their lights smudged the drizzle. I could just about make out one of their crew throwing a bright orange buoy overboard and shouted to Johnny that I could see it. Corky brought a pole with a grappling hook on it to the starboard and the boat seemed to slow. The Dutch boat moved away from us, but all eyes were on a light flashing from the buoy they'd dropped into the water. Corky held my belt as I leant over the railings catching the buoy with the grappling hook. Together we pulled it up the side of the boat.

"Put your gloves on and unscrew the top."

Masking tape was wrapped around the top of the buoy and I had to take my gutting knife to it before unscrewing the lid. The sight of what was in my hands knocked the breath out of me. Inside were translucent hermetically sealed plastic packages. I took one of them out and held the brick of compressed white powder up to the light.

"Must be two kilos," said Pete. He rummaged in the buoy. "There should be four more of them. Christ. We've only gone and fucking done it."

"Ten kilos. What's that?" Corky's face looked even more perplexed than normal as he attempted the calculations.

"Half a million, street. More once these lot have cut it."

The trawler's lights bounced off our eyes as we looked at each other. If we'd been anyone else we might even have hugged.

"Get the top of that back on and put it in the hold. Seal it up properly," Johnny handed me a roll of tape. "We're still to get this stuff back to shore."

Sleeping and waking at random hours was a part of being a trawlerman, so it didn't feel strange to be climbing down to the bunk for another kip. Besides, Johnny wanted me in the wheelhouse once we got closer to shore. I was totally buzzing, but in my sleep deprived state I eventually drifted off. I had no idea how long I'd been out of it, but when I woke something was wrong – something was very wrong. The boat felt like it was being buffeted by the waves instead of ploughing purposefully through them. I pulled back the curtain at the side of my bunk. The barely perceptible hum of the trawler's engines was gone.

When I got up on deck, I got my second shock. It was night and the lights that were usually turned on were off. The trawler was adrift and being slapped about by the waves, a silent, powerless lump of metal. There was no one in the wheelhouse, so I jumped down the ladder to our cabin but Johnny wasn't in his bunk. In the other cabin, Pete and Corky were still dead to the world. The last obvious place to check was the engine room, but he wasn't there. I kent what was coming when I looked in the hold – the emergency dingy had gone.

What have you done Johnny, what the fuck have you done?

I climbed back on to the deck and stared into the gloaming. If you went due north from here, you would hit nothing until the Artic. The wind, which slapped my face, had reached out across hundreds of miles of icy sea to skelp me cold and hard in the face. Johnny had betrayed us. If he'd woken me, I'd have gone with him. I'd have gone anywhere with him - even overboard on a dingy a hundred miles from shore. Johnny was dead. What he'd done was suicide; there was no way he could have made it.

I half expected him to have wrecked the equipment in the wheelhouse, but other than the satellite phone, which had been smashed to bits, all was intact. I tried to mind how I'd seen Tam start the engines and miraculously after a couple of goes the boat chugged into life and I got the lights on. It felt weird being momentarily in control of this vessel, this disaster.

My first thought was to search for Johnny, but there was no sign of him or the dingy. It was then I looked at the GPS. I'd thought we would be a hundred miles from shore, but if there hadn't been a thick haar between us and the coast, we could easily have seen the town's lights. This didn't make sense. Johnny had explained that The Devil's Hole was half way to Holland, and we'd left at seven and arrived there early evening. Yet here we were almost home in two hours. For a moment it felt like he had some sea spirit on his side. Then I realised the simple solution. The drop had never been planned for The Devil's Hole. We'd just been going around in circles.

"You sly bugger," I whispered, smiling to myself.

I thought Johnny might have left a message to tell me when he'd gone, to tell me where he was going, but there was nothing in the wheelhouse and despite wracking my brains, I could think of no hint he'd given me.

What was not it doubt was that he'd taken the buoy filled with half a million pounds worth of heroin. It was breath taking. If he got caught, he'd get slaughtered, horribly. Fuck knows what would happen to the rest of us. Corky would hopefully be conscious enough to steer the boat back into the harbour, but then I thought about Johnny. It was impossible to ken how Pete would react, but there was every chance he'd call Maddie or the London gang, who'd doubtless be waiting for our return. If they found out what had happened, while Johnny was still rowing to shore, they'd find him and kill him. Nothing surer. I went back to the wheelhouse and turned the boat, so it was now going out to sea.

The gows flapped in and out of the trawler's light cackling at this decision. One gow in particular hovered permanently by the galley's side, its head twitching round to make eye contact with me. I started thinking about the possibility that the London consortium or The Kerrs had someone at the coastguard monitoring our progress on radar, or that they had a tracking device in the buoy that would tell them exactly where Johnny had come ashore - if he ever made it to shore. I held my nerve for half an hour, but the possibility that Pete would come on deck and think I was part of this flooded me with the fear.

It wasn't easy waking Corky and his shallow breath and mumbles at the unreasonableness of his dreams as they mixed with this reality suggested that the pills Johnny had fed them had been some sort of prescription opiates. His glassy, lifeless eyes tried to focus as I told him what had happened. After nodding for a bit he rolled over onto his side, muttering, "It'll be alright. It'll be alright on the night."

Pete was considerably more bothered. The curtain on his bunk was ripped open. He pulled the gun from the rucksack and unsteadily climbed the steps to the deck. "Campbell you back-stabbing bastard," he bellowed at the darkness before firing a shot into the night. The recoil sent him staggering back and for a moment the deafening bang obliterated the endless struggles of the sea. But soon the old noise came back – the sea and its constant turmoil like a million restless sleepers tossing and turning under a blanket, searching for some comfort. To gain his balance Pete leant against the ladder to the galley and pointed the gun at my face. I searched for a spark of humanity in his opaque, opiated eyes.

"Where is he?"

"I've just got up. The dingy's gone. Do you think I'd be here now if I kent he was going to do this?"

He pressed the barrel of the gun against my forehead.

"If you're in on this, I'll blow your brains out. You can go the way of your cousin Joe."

He paused, his arm shaking. I closed my eyes and for a moment the whole world was condensed to that cold metal muzzle pressing against my forehead. Every part of me strained to know the instance the trigger was pulled. I imagined I could experience a million memories between then and the bullet shattering my brain.

"We need to work this out. Corky's fucked. I'm the only one that can get us back in one piece."

I forced myself to look down the barrel of the gun. He steadied himself on a railing before dropping the gun to his side.

"What's the time?"

"Half ten."

"How quickly can we get to town?"

"Maybe thirty minutes."

"We're half an hour from shore? How does Johnny think he's going to row a dingy that far? Right. Those nut jobs know nothing yet and we're not expected back until morning. You get us in to the harbour and we scarper. Dinna ken about you, but I'm not hanging about to explain this fuck up."

We got Corky from his cabin and propped him up on the skipper's seat where he pressed and prodded the various controls with the concentration of a toddler bought a new toy. I tried to direct his interest towards a stick that I was pretty sure controlled the engines horse power.

"Fuck sake," Pete spat, "This is like the blind leading the barely conscious." When we'd gone down to the cabin, he'd put on his jacket and had reappeared searching his pockets. "Where'd that fucker put the phones?" He turned 360 and catching sight of the smashed satellite phone and the sea on all sides looked like he was about to spew.

"You got yours?"

"Johnny told me to leave it at home in case the police were tracking us."

He gave us a sickly smile. "Maddie is gonnae do us for this. And I'm fucking family."

CHAPTER SIXTEEN

Despite looking like she was made of porcelain, Nicky Skelton had been difficult to break. She'd acted like she was incapable of being interviewed through the night and, to be fair, serious withdrawal symptoms had kicked in at dawn. Warnings that if she didn't tell them her substance dependency history and let them give her drugs to reduce the impact of withdrawal, then she could lose the foetus. Warnings that social services would take the baby once it was born if she didn't testify against those she'd been working for. Promises that the moment she came through, they'd give her metoclopramide for her vomiting, mebeverine for her abdominal cramps, zopiclone to help her sleep.

Stark stared into dilated pupils as Nicky clawed at the sweaty strands of hair plastered to her forehead. Out there in a world with windows and regular meals, his wife would be having a cup of tea and slice of toast before bed.

"So one last time. The phone's not yours, you've no fixed address and the heroin we found on you is for personal use?"

"Exactly."

DI Hillman returned the photos of the OCG to an envelope. "The people who operate the line that keeps sending instructions to this phone are not nice men. I've seen their work. I've seen what they do to people who owe them money or who throw away drugs. We know that some of these men are currently in the area."

Nicky scowled wiping her pink runny nose on her sleeve. Only a year or so older than Sophie, Stark thought, but the state of her. Wracking his memory of his daughters' endless assessments of girls at school, he had a feeling that Nicola Skelton had been critiqued more than once. Stark felt curiously keen to protect the girl who shuffled and snuffled in the interview seat.

"A tissue would be nice. Some methadone wouldna hurt either."

"Look, Nicola."

"Nicky."

"Nicky, you have to start thinking about yourself. You've obviously got addiction issues, and if we don't get any more out of you, we'll charge you for possession. We've got a social worker waiting to speak to you. A child protection plan is going to be put into place. There are people and places that can help you. But you need to show willing. You need to get away from the men who operate this line."

"I've told you before. I don't know them. This isn't my phone."

Stark motioned for DI Hillman to let the suspect stew. They gathered in the staff kitchen, coffees and sugar all round. Stark sipped at the brew, the sweep sugary hit the only thing keeping him awake. Nicola Skelton was stubborn and stupid enough to stick to her story. She'd held out this long. In an hour they'd have to charge her or let her go.

"What now?" The English DI asked.

"Has the kiosk turned up anything on the other phone?" He shouted across the office to the PCs, who'd been trawling though the data from the unlocked phones.

"Nothing overly incriminating. PC Gourlay is going through the intel now."

Stark left the others and went to peer over Gourlay's shoulder. "Anything?"

"It looks like this is her personal phone. There are a few messages about recreational drug use but nothing that connects her to serious crime. There's one thing though. She got a message just before we arrested her:

Plan is back on. Taking the boat out tomorrow morning. Will have enough money to set you up in the flat I keep texting you about. Hold on and answer your phone! I miss you. M x

"Who's M?"

"Just waiting to hear back from the phone company."

Malcolm Campbell, Stark thought. PC Carmichael had mentioned she ran with that crowd.

"And the flat?"

"Some place in Mill Hill that he's wanting to rent for her."

"So, Nicky and ... this M, are an item?"

"Don't know. You can only save a dozen messages on these phones, but she's got a few from him and they're all about this flat and asking how she's getting on."

"That bairn she's carrying. Someone's the father."

"Exactly."

How was a lad of eighteen from a family like his going to afford a deposit and rent on a flat in Mill Hill? With the investigation into Joe Campbell's death hitting a brick wall and Tam Campbell too ill to skipper a boat, he was probably happy to let the boys go back to sea. But trawlermen didn't make that much and never knew how much they were going to make each time they went to sea. How could he be so sure about the money?

"Good work, Sian." Stark glanced at his watch. "Don't think we're going to get anymore from Nicola Skelton. I should have called it a day four hours ago. Remind my wife she's got a husband."

Back in the interrogation room, Nicky was curled in the foetal position trying to burrow her forehead into the cold concrete floor. Stark crouched in front of her, catching a waft of stale sweat. "Here," he said, offering her a couple of pills and a paper cup of water. "These'll help with the cramps." Shaky fingers poked pills onto a dry tongue and with an effort she gulped them down. She wiped the raw rind of her nostrils against the back of her hand.

"Could you not get me a tissue or something?"

"I'll get someone else to do it. I'm heading down the harbour to have a word with Malcom Campbell and those other boys once their boat's in."

The bored defiance that had numbed her features for the past 23 hours spasmed, and she curled back into a ball. It was what Stark had wanted to see. He grabbed his jacket and made for the car.

Foggy wraiths wreathed the Control Tower as Stark strode along the slippery paving stones by the harbour. He'd parked on the front and sat long enough to be sure he wasn't being watched, but even so he'd pulled a wooly bunnet over his head and turned up the collar on his jacket. Amidst the haar and granite harbour walls, he could make out the glow of the harbour master's office.

It took Rafferty a couple of minutes to answer the intercom. Stark had never been in the control tower and once up the stairs squinted at the red and green lights of the harbour's entrance made fuzzy in the fog.

"How do you see anything on a night like this?"

"Out there you don't. These tell you everything you need to know." Rafferty indicated an array of screens.

"Is the Abiding Star out?"

"Funnily enough, it is," Rafferty replied. "First time since they hauled Joe Campbell in. Left this morning. Crew ay daft loons on board if you ask me. Dinna ken what they're about."

"How?"

"Well they headed north from here then south west then south east like they couldn't make up their minds. Then they turned and came straight back. Spent an hour going in circles a mile from here. I radioed a couple of times but no reply"

"How do you know this?"

"This radar follows all the boats. I've been keeping an eye on that trawler. Hauling Joe Campbell's body out of the whole wide sea. Cursed, so it is. Everyone says so."

"So where is it now?"

Rafferty glanced at one of the screens then out through the window. "Five minutes and you'll see its lights."

Stark called the station for back up, his eyes flicked between the dot on the monitor and out through the window. He shuddered involuntarily as the trawler's ghostly lights glowed through the fog.

"Can you go down and meet them? Try to stall them as much as you can."

Rafferty huffed and puffed his way into his Harbour Master's coat and seized a searchlight. The two men followed the funnel of light to where the trawler had docked. Stark peeled off behind a long disused warehouse and crouched behind a pile of rotten rusty lobster cages. The message to Nicky, the boat's unusual movements, presence of the OCG, even the death of Joe Campbell all convinced Stark he'd uncovered a major smuggling operation. Crack this and that transfer would be his. The only problem: he was the only police officer present and there was no way he could take down the crew of the trawler and the probably armed OCG members who must be waiting for them. He glanced at his watch. Six minutes since he'd made the call. Sergeant Grant had taken it, and he'd expressly told him there should be no blue lights. So he'd have no idea when they were approaching, but he reckoned the cavalry should be arriving about now.

The trawler bumped against the tyres that protected it from the harbour wall, and a figure jumped off even before it'd been secured. Stark cursed as Peter Kerr ran towards the Front.

"Where are you?" He muttered into his radio. "Peter Kerr is running towards the Front, can someone pick him up?" He half thought about giving chase but Peter Kerr wasn't carrying a bag, and was quickly shrouded in fog. He waited. Ten minutes since he'd made the call. Rafferty appeared to be talking to a figure on the deck, and he hoped the harbour master would be able to hold them. If not, he was going in. Through the damp air, he heard the sirens that he'd expressly ordered should not be used. As he stood up for a better view, quick footsteps rushed from behind and a heavy wet blackness splintered the night.

CHAPTER SEVENTEEN

Eventually we lined up the harbour lights, using them to steer round the sea wall that was invisible in the fog. Most of the fishing fleet were at sea and there was no danger there'd be any posh cunts out on their yachts at this time of night. Still, it was a bloody miracle we managed to navigate the trawler through the haar without gouging any of the wooden buffers around the walls. Rafferty, the harbour master, stirred the fog with the beam of his search light.

"It's yourselves," he muttered, looking at the name on the side of the boat rather than us. As he secured our hawsers, I looked towards The Front for any sign of the Jeep with the blacked out windows, but unless their headlights were on it would be impossible to make out anything.

"Back already?"

"We had some sort of electrical problem," I said, keeping it vague.

"Did you, aye?" He looked at me sceptically, but left it at that. "Catch anything?"

"We didn't get to the fishing grounds."

"What were you doing going round in circles out there?"

"Oh that's just me trying out a few things. Tam wants me to take my tickets so I can become skipper one day. I was just getting acquainted with the equipment in the wheelhouse."

He scanned the length of the trawler, but Rafferty was no jobsworth and knowing he'd a nice warm office with a decent internet connection and a couple of online games of poker on the go, I was surprised to see him out on a night like this.

"Right," Pete said, emerging from the cabin. "I'm making tracks. Your cousin has just ripped off some heavy fucking guys. When Stevie and my dad get out of prison I might face up to them, but I'm not hanging about to explain this. Maybe they'll find him and this'll blow over, but for Johnny, if he gets caught, he'll wish he'd drowned at sea."

With that he jumped the railings almost colliding with Rafferty.

In the wheelhouse, Corky was slumped over the controls. After waking, he asked, "You got any more of those pills?"

"Get your stuff and go."

Corky grinned at me like this was some sort of game that he couldn't believe I was asking him to play. I wasn't going down with the scuttle-headed fuck-wit and scarpered overboard, passed the empty warehouses of the harbour. The fog birled in a gust of wind and a seagull squawked from its perch on top of one of the CCTV cameras that monitored the comings and goings of the fishing fleet. For once I stared back at the camera's eye, letting it record my last moments on earth. As I approached The Front, I heard the slamming of a car door, the screech of tyres as a shapeless vehicle U-turned on the tarmac and accelerated through the fog. I ducked down a second before its headlight slashed the air around me. On the breathless sprint through Seatown I was accompanied by the commentary of a Crime Watch re-enactment saying he was shot down on his way home. Two cop cars sped past and I hid behind a wheelie bin. Coincidence. Maybe.

The familiar smell of cooking oil, pine wood and women's perfume that welcomed me home was as comforting as the closed door locking me from the world outside. I went up to my bedroom, the Irn-Bru glow of the streetlight shining through my window on the maps of Glasgow, London and New York I'd pinned on the wall. Cities whose famous streets shattered out from famous centres intricate as the cracks around the glass in The Front's smashed up phone boxes. I'd traced the streets and parks and pubs mentioned in songs and wondered what it would be like to live in a world that people sang about. Around the maps were posters of those bands: Warpaint, The XX, Franz Ferdinand, The Libertines. To be living in their cities. I pulled open a drawer and took out a pair of football socks that I kept my money in. I stuffed a few fives and tens in my pocket and grabbed my phone. I took a ragged breath. For a minute I just wanted to climb into my bed and let my mum deal with tomorrow. But this wasn't the type of trouble you could bring to your family's door.

Creeping along the corridor, I listened to her snores. I cracked her bedroom door open and momentarily looked at her great bulk bundled up on the side of the double bed in which she always slept, as if there was some ghost partner sleeping next to her. If I hadn't been so focussed on not waking her, as I took the car keys from her bedside table, I'd have felt sorry that all she had was a son like me.

For the rest of the world it was the night before Bank Holiday Monday, and the High Street pubs had just called time. Other than some old boozehound at St George's Cross, who laboured under the belief that the cars needed his help in understanding the traffic lights, most of the punters kept off the road. Having exhausted the role of traffic cop, he removed his shirt and presented it like a matador to the snout of the first car. Horns he wanted and horns he should have got. Eventually he settled for a battle with a night bus filled with light, but despite whipping off his belt and lashing at it with chunky buckle blows, he was defeated and was dragged from the road by two of his friends.

I motored towards The Bends, skidding along the wet tarmac as the road twisted and turned and tried to throw me from its back. From the position the trawler had been in, I figured Johnny would have come ashore somewhere along the stretch of beach between Blyth Lighthouse and the town. The more I thought about it, the more it seemed certain that Johnny hadn't ditched me. I grabbed my mobile and tried his number, but it went straight to answer. He'd need a driver, a car, someone to get him out of here. I just needed to find him first. There were only two places you could park a car and get onto the West Beach: the first, the caravan park, I rejected figuring that Johnny would avoid a place with so many people. The second option was a layby above the Smuggler's Caves. It was obvious that this would be the place. The two of us had once nicked a fiver from my Aunt Mary's purse, blew it all on pick n mix bags and sat in one of those caves, Johnny's lighter illuminating arched walls that were tangled with modern graffiti and Pictish runes. We'd made ourselves sick with coke bottles, flumps, gobstoppers and the knowledge that Aunt Mary would be raging. But while we were in that cave stuffing our mouths, we'd felt safe. I convinced myself that the caves' name and our history of hiding out there would appeal to him.

I arrived in minutes and took a spanner from the boot, realising that if the psychos we were working for had been tipped off, or had seen *The Abiding Star* in the harbour, they'd be doing the same thing. Going down the dunes, I stumbled over wiry grass and stubbed my toe on a submerged fence pole that had been put in place to counter erosion. My hand held the spanner out to one side, ready to swing at anything. On the pebbles by the caves something was moving. I hissed Johnny's name and it stopped. After holding my breath for a minute, I tried again. I was convinced that in the dark mouth of the cave, someone was holding their breath too. "Johnny," I said for a third time, but as far as the ear could hear the only sounds were the soft unfolding of the sea and the wind whispering through the dune grass. I fumbled blindly towards the caves and the awful stench of shite. On wild nights, cattle took shelter in these caves, and I figured it was them moving about, watching me with their thoughtless eyes.

The haar was lifting and, as I scanned the moonlit crust of the coastline and the black tumult of the sea for Johnny's dingy, I realised how futile my search was. With the spanner clenched in my fist, I sprinted back up the dunes and didn't feel safe until I was in the car and it was moving at a speed that no one was going to catch. On the way back to town, I tried Johnny's number again, but it kept going to autoreply.

Back at St George's Cross, I decided to head down to Nicky's. From outside the flat there was no sign of life and despite banging on her door while shouting my name through her letterbox nothing stirred. Next I dropped in on Dawn to see if she kent what was happening.

Although the lights were on, no one answered her buzzer, so I began pressing all the others. Eventually a voice said, "Yeah?"

"Malky."

"Anyone know a Malky? Right. Come on up." I stepped into a dark close, faces covered in footprints peering at me from the pages of free newspapers.

"Alright, squinty baws?"

Gowser, Dawn's flatmate, looked like his eyes were going to pop out.

"How's it going?"

"Well, we're one pill short of a picnic."

"And your eyes?"

"Not worth the paper they're written on....But It's good to see you man." He got on his tiptoes and kissed me wet on the lips, his stubble crawling all over my chin.

The flat was open and I pushed my way into a hall busy with bin bags. Music was coming from Dawn's bedroom, which reeked of poppers and fag ends spawning at the bottom of half empty beer cans. They were obviously still on it from the Gala Day party.

I found a bit of carpet next to Dawn, whose hair had been shaved so short that she looked like one of those French women who were punished after the war for having sex with Nazis. They were playing that Billie Eilish song. A gangly girl swung her bare legs next to the stereo, tunelessly chanting the chorus with a stoner's inability to keep time. Her face was obscured by a pink baseball cap on which was written the word BOSS, but when she waved at me, I realised it was Zoe. Looking at the nick of them, my first instinct was to grab her hand and go. A man in a hideous tie-dyed T-shirt, his face totally drained of colour leant close to her. He raised an eyebrow and I turned to Dawn

"So, what happened?" she asked.

"Electrical failure."

"Good. I dinna ken what possessed yous. Hopefully that's you got the going to sea thing out of your system."

I nodded and she sarcastically clapped her hands. Many of the grimiest moments in my life had happened in this flat, but some kamikaze compulsion kept me coming there.

"So, you've not seen Johnny?" I picked fluff from the carpet sounding disinterested.

"Not since this morning."

By the casual way in which she answered, I could tell she hadn't a clue.

She opened a bag of MDMA crystals. "Want some?"

I shook my head.

"Ketamine?" suggested Gowser, like a kindly GP, but I explained that I had things to do and places to be and that ketamine and cars were rarely a good combination.

Dawn started giving me a head massage and placed the wrap in my hands. There was hardly any left and I flattened out the paper to get at the creases. The wrap was made from a magazine picture of Kate Moss. The mandy was all but finished so I lifted her silent sneering pout to my mouth.

"Never says a thing, that's her secret," said Dawn, looking at the wrap.

"Course she doesn't," snorted Gowser, "She's a picture in a magazine."

"I know."

"Well try telling that moon cat."

He pointed at a lump in the bed and started off on some story about having to boot the toilet door in because Corky had been deep in conversation with a Bella front cover. "Comes out mumbling shite about how Meghan Markle's actually a nice person."

"Corky's here?"

"Taking a disco nap."

I felt a surge of gratitude that he'd made it off the boat coupled with the fear of the trouble he could get us in. "Poor fucker," Gowser said, giving the lump in the bed a thump. "He'll be selling Big Issues in a year."

Zoe started shaking his shoulder. "Corky. What have you got?" Her voice chimed and lulled, as she tugged the covers from him. He curled up like a slug when you run a knife down its belly to see if it really turns inside out. "Corky what is it?"

He shivered and a voice sluicing round clenched teeth said, "A special book."

"Show me."

"No. It's a book with the names and numbers of all the friends Corky hasn't met yet."

The man in the tie-dyed t-shirt strode across the room and wrenched it from him.

"Fucking phonebook, ya tube." He sat back down, balanced the book on his knees and started skinning up.

Tie-dyed flopped back with a joint squeezed between tight white lips. The phonebook fell from his knees scattering creepy crawly tobacco.

Corky rolled out of bed and stared at me. He started rubbing his jaw muscles, opened a Venus flytrap mouth, then slowly, carefully, clamped it shut.

"Harbour was full of feds after you left me. Pig mobiles, an ambulance, plain clothed police. Reckon they ken what we were up to?"

"How'd you get out of there?"

Corky shrugged like an expert weary of explaining their unique talent. "Fog."

"Shite. We should get out of here."

"What do you think I've been trying to do?" He drawled, his eyes rolling back into his head.

"Dawn. A word. Somewhere private."

She uncrumpled herself, wrapped a rug round her bones and penguin shuffled to the toilet. I followed, pretending not to watch as she threw the rug into the corner, dropped her shorts and sat on the pan. She wrapped sinewy arms round her bruised knees and motorway-blue veined thighs, resting her head on them 'til I thought she was either asleep or crying. The needle marks on her forearm had all but healed but she had always been vain and could easily be shooting into the top of her feet.

"Dawn," I said not sure if I could reach out and touch her.

She looked up and slurred, "Christ, my head is in fucking bits."

"Are you sure you've not heard from Johnny? Could you check your phone?"

She rummaged in the pockets of the shorts around her ankles, pulled out her mobile and shook her head. "What's going on?"

"Nothing."

I focused on the wall above the cistern, on which someone had sellotaped a postcard of the Pope rising like a colossus from behind St Peters. Scrawled below it in red lipstick, the words, 'Every time you masturbate god kills a kitten. Think of the kittens.' Dawn started pishing.

I waited for her to stop before asking, "Could I borrow some money?"

"How much?"

"How much you got?"

"Well, I'm hardly sitting on a pot of gold," she let off a dirty laugh. "Maybe the filth's daughter in there'll lend you a fiver. She's been going on about you all night."

She stood and pulled her shorts up in one movement, a quick swatch of neatly trimmed pubic hair. After picking up the rug, she sat on the rim of the bath next to me and offered me a wing. "Malky, what went wrong? I always thought you were going to be better than this. You were meant to be the bright one. The one that got out." I shook my head. "I could give you a bag of pills on tick, but honey, you were like the Milky Bar kid of dealing last time we tried that."

"It's alright," I said

With that she unwrapped me from the rug's wing and shuffled back to her room. I flushed the toilet for her.

Back in the bedroom Gowser was trying to play a song on an acoustic guitar whilst muttering like a forgetful joke teller; "No that's not it, not it at all." When he saw me, the crusty in the tie-dyed t-shirt passed the joint and soup bowl ashtray to Zoe. She took a long, exaggerated toke, looking at the milky smoke shimmying from the end as if she was raising the dead.

Dawn took the guitar and sat down to tune the strings.

"It's fucking dark in here."

Gowser looked at the bed sheets taped over the window in terror. "Can't open the curtains."

"How?"

"Just dinna. I can't stand the sunlight when I'm feeling like this."

"It's the middle of the night, you rocket."

She lent down next to the bed and put a plug in the wall. A torn section of fishing net, which was strung across the ceiling and woven with multicoloured fairy, lights burst into juicy glow. Zoe stretched out her leg and placed her foot on the table in front of me.

Showing me her ankle she said, "Do you like my tattoo?"

"Is it new?" She nodded like a doll when you shake it.

"It looks sore." I touched the red skin around an intricate Celtic cross. Dawn started fingering a tune and I caught her scowling at me.

Zoe drew her foot slightly back as Dawn sang, a cracked eerie old lady's voice, a couple of octaves higher than she spoke. Zoe swung her bent knee gently in time. She was wearing a pair of pants that she'd nicked off a mannequin advertising closing-down discounts in the shop window of Henderson's. The pants were red with the words SALE written across them in white. I tried to concentrate on Dawn's song but my eyes wandered over Zoe's stoned blank face. Dawn stopped singing, a strange silence as the last notes tossed and turned before settling to sleep.

"That's fucking beautiful, by the way," said tie-dyed t-shirt man, stubbing a new joint in Dawn's direction, his eyes daring any of us to deny that Dawn's singing was, indeed, beautiful.

"Where's Corky?" I asked.

"He wanted some peace and quiet, so he's gone through to Gowser's room," Zoe replied."

"Peace and quiet," chuckled Dawn. "Is that what they call it these days?"

"Right, I need to boost," I said, but for some reason – Zoe's feet resting on my lap, Dawn strumming a new tune, the smell of a freshly rolled joint being lit – I didn't move. That was not until we tuned in to the racket that Gowser was making through the wall. We staggered through to his room to where he and Frenchie were shaking and slapping Corky in an attempt to revive him. His face was the colour of three day old porridge.

Gowser put his cheek right up close to Corky's nose. "He's still breathing," he said with a weary tone of professionalism, "but slapping seems to be having no affect."

"Should someone not take him to hospital?" I suggested.

"Good idea," Frenchie sarcastically said, as if I'd just proposed they man a spaceship to the moon.

"I'll call an ambulance."

"No ambulances," Gowser snarled.

"Malky's got a car," Dawn reminded everyone.

Gowser grabbed Corky by the oxsters and told me to take his legs. Corky's head flopped as we picked him up, a string of saliva or sick trickling out of his mouth. I had a gut-wrenching flashback to the last time I'd carried a body like this. We lugged him down the stairs and out to the car. As I opened the back door he threw up on my trainers.

"At least he's not dead," Dawn announced, as if that was some form of consolation.

Eventually we slung him onto the back seat, the top half of his body propped up against one of the passenger's doors.

"Are none of yous coming?"

The others backed away, shrugging, desperate to return to the warm oblivion of the flat.

"Let me get my shoes," said Zoe rushing back into the flat.

But I stuck the keys in the ignition. This was a solo mission.

Gowser shouted: "Remember, you found him on the street, you've never been here, you don't mention any names."

As I slung the car down the road, Corky started hiccoughing, his head banging against the window with each convulsion, while his mouth gasped for air like fish when the cod end is first opened.

The hospital was only a 5 minute drive, but I fired the radio on in order to drown out the awful throttled noises from the spasming body in the back. I floored it, a left down a one way road to avoid the lights at the roundabout, down Union Street in case there were any taxis turning on Bridge Street, breaking at the last minute Formula 1 style before turns. Half of me wanted to be the hero that got Corky to hospital - another thing to be known for. The other half just wanted shot of him, so I could get out of here. As I drove, I thought about Nicky. The last few months in which she and Johnny had drifted apart and bad mouthed each other. Had it all been an act? Could she have moved somewhere in preparation for all this?

I parked the car right up by the Hospital's entrance and dragged Corky from the back seat. My plan had been to drop him there, but two paramedics came rushing towards me with a trolley and a barrage of questions.

"What's he taken?" One of them shouted.

"I don't know … heroin I think and probably a whole load of other stuff."

Like VIPs of this twisted scene, we were whisked straight past the check-in desk and the clamour for attention of a busy night in A&E.

As a nurse swabbed Corky's arm, she noticed the tattoo around his bicep.

"Carpe Diem?"

"Seize the day," his colleague smirked.

"More like a seizure a day."

Noticing me gawping at their laughter, the male nurse snapped, "Right this one doesn't need to be here."

And he was right, I didn't. I strode past the receptionist as she shouted at me for details, through the waiting room with the old bruiser picking at the shards of glass in his fist, a girl curled up and sobbing round a sick bucket, a boy with a burst nose, his eyes daring anyone to look. They looked like the dried-out remains of some primordial soup from which the rest of mankind had evolved long, long ago.

My car was where I'd left it, the engine still running. I climbed in and closed the door on all the chaos. It was 2am. With any luck, I'd be half way down the A9 before the shit storm hit town. As I steered around the car park's one way system, a black transit van reversed out of a parking bay blocking my way and a heavy arm wrapped around my throat - the back of my skull whiplashed against the headrest. Souter's cratered face appeared in my rear mirror; the button on the cuff of his jacket pressing against my neck as he crushed my wind-pipe.

"Feet off the pedals," he hissed, spittle and hot breath in my ear, the prickle of his stubble on my cheek.

Grinning at my reflection in the rear view mirror, he eased the pressure, slipping his arm around so that the metallic edge of a Stanley knife scrapped against my skin.

"You're going to follow that van."

CHAPTER EIGHTEEN

First on the scene, they parked behind the fish market as Stark had instructed. Gourlay was out the car like a shot. They'd lost radio contact with the Detective, and PC Carmichael peered apprehensively through the windscreen.

"Should we not wait for back up?"

"If the Campbells' trawler's in. Stark'll have eyes on it."

Amorphous buildings loomed large, as spectral veils of fog drifted over. The damp gossamer touch chilled Gourlay to the bone.

"Help. Somebody help."

They peered round the edge of an old stone warehouse to see a prone body, a big man waving his torch wildly.

"It's Stark."

They raced over to where the Detective lay amidst smashed glass and beer suds.

"He's out cold," said the man, identified by his Harbour Master jacket.

As Gourlay manoeuvred Stark into the recovery position, he murmured something.

"It's me Sir, you're going to be alright."

Stark muttered again and Gourlay with her ear against his mouth made out the words, "Trawler."

"Which one is it?"

Through the haar, Rafferty's torch indicated the vague outline of the boat.

More footsteps and PC Carmichael shouted, "Over here, man down."

"We need to check that boat. How long's it been in?"

"Not much more than five minutes."

"Did the crew get off?"

"Some of them."

Sergeant Grant and PC Mathie emerged from the fog.

"Sir, that's the trawler Stark was monitoring. There might still be crew aboard and smuggled goods."

"Shit," said Grant.

"Serge, we should seal off all roads approaching the Front."

Annoyance at being advised by such a junior officer flickered across the Sergeant's face before he issued the instructions through his radio. Assessing the available officers, he commanded PC Carmichael to call an ambulance and wait with the injured Detective while the others followed him.

Sergeant Grant splashed his torchlight across the trawler's deck, pouring the powerful beam into the wheelhouse.

"Police, come out with your hands where we can see them."

Nothing, but the soft slosh of becalmed water.

"Should we wait on an armed response team," whispered Mathie.

"That could take hours. Let's go in."

Gingerly, they clambered aboard.

"The cabins are down here," Gourlay indicated a door beneath the wheelhouse.

"Mathie, you stay on deck in case one of them makes a run for it."

They systematically moved through the boat, but the crew had gone.

"Sarge," PC Mathie shouted as they emerged from beneath deck. "There's something you should see."

"Now that's weird," Grant observed looking at the smashed up satellite phone. "Bits of it still on the floor too, so it's just been done. What got Stark so excited about this boat?"

"It's the one that pulled in Joe Campbell," PC Mathie said.

"Aye, but that was months ago. What was he doing down here at this time of night?"

Sian thought of the text message. M. The phone company hadn't been able to identify the number, but Stark had clearly figured it belonged to Malcolm Campbell and decided to check on the trawler.

"He was in the station half an hour ago. Said he was going home. Maybe he saw something?"

"Or was keeping information to himself. We've been down that road before with Stark."

Grant's radio crackled into life. "Golf Four Two, Golf Four Two, this is Uniform Bravo, anything to report, over?"

"Uniform Bravo, this is Golf Four Two. Target location has been searched and is empty, over."

"Golf four two, received, thank you, over."

Grant clambered clumsily onto the harbour. "The serious crime boys won't be happy with this. If there actually was something going on here, we've not only missed it but alerted the OCG that we're on to them.

The ambulance bleared along The Front smearing its blue lights through the haar. Gourlay found herself accompanying the semi-conscious Detective, as he daubed his head with a crimson square of gauze.

"Call me the minute he's got something sensible to say for himself," DI Hillman shouted through the ambulance's closing doors.

Although a Sunday, tomorrow was Bank Holiday Monday and, if A&E was anything to go by, the good people of the Port had been taking advantage of the long weekend. Gourlay had to clamber over a girl who was upset about breaking one of her high heels, and maybe her ankle; a beetroot coloured bruiser, who judging by the state of his knuckles had been in a fight with a mirror; and a topless ginger boy, who'd fallen asleep in the afternoon sun and burnt his eyelids.

The same receptionist sat at the hospital desk engrossed with the painting of her nails.

"Nice work," Gourlay said.

175

"Cheers," the receptionist replied. "Got to express yourself someway, don't you. That was Detective Stark, wasn't it? Head injury? Grab a seat and once they've patched him up the Doctor will come through and tell you how he's doing."

Gourlay clambered back over the waiting room walking wounded. Being a doctor looked shite. All that studying and you couldn't even lock up these idiots.

Two hours had passed and she was about to get up and ask what was taking them, when Doctor Houston came out in a flurry of white coats and clipboards. "PC Gourlay, the patient would like to see you." Ushering her to the curtained room, he muttered out of the side of his mouth, "We've got the glass out of the wound and stitched him up, but he's concussed. He's very insistent about speaking to you though, says it's police business. But don't over excite him, and don't let him fall asleep."

Stark was wearing one of those hospital gowns exposing his scrawny neck and collar bones, unsettlingly visible beneath translucent unweathered skin.

"How are you, Sir?"

"Embarrassed."

"Sir, you should have got me to come with you? You knew that message was from Malcolm Campbell, didn't you?"

"Was it?"

Gourlay gave Stark a don't-you-start look. "The phone company couldn't confirm who the number belonged to." Stark issued a grunt of disappointment. "Sir, would you like me to contact your wife, to tell her you're here?"

Stark closed his eyes and groaned like a man waking with the sort of hangover that is going to take 48 hours to shift. For a minute Gourlay thought he'd fallen asleep and was just about to give him a nudge when he opened one eye. "You didn't see anyone on the harbour or notice any vehicles?"

"There was the harbour master, you and lots of fog. The boat was empty when we go there." Stark closed his eye, his features showing the sort of concerted effort of someone trying to remember a forgotten name. "There was one weird thing. Someone had smashed up the satellite phone in the wheelhouse."

Stark opened both his eyes. "Interesting. Did Nicky Skelton get charged?"

"Sergeant Grant let her off with a caution for possession." Stark's eyes dropped shut, but Gourlay could tell his mind was racing. "Sir, what made you so sure the boat was involved in smuggling? Sir?"

"A hunch. You can pass that all on to the serious crime boys."

"Sir, that's not fair." Stark clenched his teeth, his mind still evidently whirling. "DI Stark, you can trust me if there's anything else?"

—

"Well if that's how it is, I'm going to call your wife. She can wait until you're discharged."

Stark's eyes flashed at her. "I don't trust anyone at the station. The person who did this. How did he know I was there? Unmarked car, bunnet on as I went to the control tower - in that fog. How could anyone have seen me?"

"If the trawler actually was bringing drugs into the country, there'd be people waiting at the harbour."

"Did Grant tell you not to use your sirens?"

"What?"

"I expressly told him, no sirens. And how long did it take you? I checked my watch before I was attacked. Ten minutes after the call and not a sign. It's a four or five minute drive at most. What took you?"

Gourlay felt dizzy. The hospital lights, late nights, too much caffeine. "Are you sure about this? Grant told us to use our sirens, and we got there as quick as we could. Honestly, it can't have been five minutes from when we got the call to us arriving at the crime scene."

Stark puffed up his pillow in an attempt to sit upright. "I'm not interested in going after the Jazmynes, or the Nickys or even the Malky Campbells of this world. As far as I'm concerned, they're just vulnerable kids who are easily manipulated. What I want are the ones controlling them. The ones making all the money and taking none of the risks. And we almost had them tonight. I saw Pete Kerr get off that trawler. Before today, I'd bet he's never been to sea in his life. We need to get to them. Malky Campbell especially. He's no criminal, but he's in this deep."

The ringing of Gourlay's phone gave her the excuse to step out of Stark's curtained room and away from his plots and paranoia. It was DI Hillman.

"Stark talking?"

"Just about."

"What's he saying?"

"That he saw Peter Kerr get off the trawler. It was a message on Nicola Skelton's phone that alerted him, but he only figured out its significance on the way home and thought he'd check his theory before calling it in. The trawler belongs to the Campbell family. You know, the ones that pulled in the body."

"I remember. And he thinks this is connected?"

"He's a bit all over the place."

"But there's no actual evidence of smuggling. I've got the transcript of the messages from that girl's phone, and I don't see the link."

"DI Stark is pretty certain, Sir."

"We've got road blocks set up on the routes leading south, but we've not picked up the OCGs vehicles for days."

"What about the harbour master?"

"He's confirmed that the trawler was acting unusually, but he spoke to Malcolm Campbell who mentioned electrical problems and that he was trying things out in the wheelhouse as part of his training. He reckoned it sounded plausible."

"But someone didn't want Stark on that harbour at that time. Have you spoken to any of the crew?"

"Not yet. There's not enough manpower to carry out simultaneous raids. In any case, if there really is something going on, they'll know we're on to them. On that front, Sergeant Grant would like you back at the station. If Stark's getting discharged soon, his wife can drive him home."

"Ok, Sir." Gourlay looked at her watch, thinking that her shift should have ended two hours ago and that she'd have to make it to the station on foot.

She poked her head in to tell Stark the news.

"Take care out there young Gourlay. And see if you can be in on the interview with Malky Campbell. He's the one who'll give the game away."

As she braced herself for the soggy night air, a pair of paramedics raced down the corridor with a comatose man on a stretcher. A blue cable knit jumper. Face drained of life beneath ginger hair the colour of a fox that had lain dead by a motorway for a number of days. Gourlay watched as they disappeared into A&E. She zipped her jacket up to the neck and strode out into the car park.

Driving towards the exit was a black transit van followed closely by a car, which, in the sodium light flicker, she could see was driven by Malky Campbell. A man in the back leant between the front seats headrests as if giving instructions. In the street lights, Gourlay was certain it was the man with the rotten teeth she'd seen Grant speaking to in the park.

CHAPTER NINETEEN

Four miles along The Bends and the black transit van signalled left onto a rubbly track, which led to the old quarry that had once supplied the granite rock from which the town's original fishing houses had been built.

"Kill your lights," Souter hissed and as my eyes adjusted to the darkness, I thought of Danny Kerr and the black transit van spotted around the time of his abduction. "A blubbering wreck," Johnny had described him as, 'cowering and whimpering like one of those rescue dogs.' I'd seen him a few times up at Neverland, but always from a distance. A face partially obscured by a curtain, keeping watch on the passing traffic. As I drove, Souter gripped my shoulders with his chunky fingers, while the other hand occasionally scrapped the sharp edge of the knife across the stubble.

"There are some people you just don't cross Malky." He caught my eye in the rear view mirror and looked genuinely disappointed with me. "But if you hadna worked that out before, you're going to find it out now."

I parked the car before a huge unit of a man wrenched the door open, pulled me to my feet and in one sharp motion kneed me in the balls. Through teary eyes I made out The Viking, head bouncer at Enigma, who with his long hair, beard and bandana looked like a celebrity wrestler. For the past two years I'd attempted to get into that club. Sometimes he'd throw the doors open, his thick Scandinavian voice saying, "This way ladies," even though you were a group of boys and he knew you were all underage, while at other times he'd seem genuinely puzzled and ask, "Do you really like listening to this shite?" He looked down at me the way he'd stare at you while saying "no trainers" even though the previous weekend he hadn't let you in for wearing poncy shoes

"On your knees," The Viking barked - unnecessarily seen as there was no chance my jellified legs could lift me up. That wee rat Brian Souter, the man with the crab tattoo and Elham, circled me.

The headlights of a car that had already been parked there were turned on illuminating the whole scene. The neanderthal in a suit from that night at Blythe Lighthouse got out.

"Elham, show him what we've got in the van."

Elham, the pitbull with the crab tattoo crawling up his neck, grabbed my hair, yanking my head back and pressed the cold edge of a blade against the taunt, thin skin on my neck. The casual way the boss had used his name terrified me: men like these didn't give away information like that unless they knew you couldn't pass it on. The Viking and Souter opened the side door of the transit van and lifted out a body. The ankles, wrists and face had been bound in masking tape and the body squirmed hopelessly as they carried it to a car that some of the others must have arrived in. The guy in the suit walked over to the car. He had a smooth ease to his movements like a champion golfer taking the accolades on his approach to the final hole. He opened the boot and the other two slung the body in the back. As Elham marched me over, I became conscious of the warm dampness around my groin, a trickle of piss that cooled as it snaked down my inner thigh. I expected to see Johnny, but the strands of greasy hair smeared over the balding top of his head like a barcode told me it was a hatless Pete. His mouth had been taped firmly shut and a snottery blood bubble formed as he attempted to breathe through his badly burst nose.

"Bang him," the suited man ordered, his accent that odd Cockney-European mix.

I stood over Pete. One of his eyes was already half closed, the eyelashes matted with blood, but the other one pleaded with me as he shook his head and made pathetic gurgling noises. Punching a Kerr. Every instinct said no. I pulled my elbow back and hit him on his masking taped mouth. I'd brought my fist down fast, but at the last had pulled the punch.

"Malky."

I turned and Elham cracked me with a blow that knocked me so cleanly off my feet that the back of my head hit the ground. A molar that had received root canal work shattered and I gagged on bits of tooth, the metallic gritty taste of filling and blood filling my mouth.

"That's how you fucking do it," he brayed one fist held aloft. He balled the front of my t-shirt in his paw and lifted me onto my feet. "Want me to slap you again?"

I shook my head – partly to try and clear the kaleidoscope of stars, partly to persuade him not to hit me.

I looked around the quarried amphitheatre of rock. Behind me a sheer drop, in front a lake and on either side vertical slabs. Crater-faced Souter was laughing and goading Elham to hit me again and I remembered being here as a wee boy and scrambling up a crack in the cliffs with Rosco. It had been a summer's evening and we'd climbed up there because Rosco had heard that the lads who raced cars along The Front brought girls here.

Eventually a red souped up GTI had rolled in and we'd peered from our hiding place above the quarried cliffs on a couple in the backseat grabbing and thrusting at each other. A boy sat in the passenger seat nonchalantly smoking out the window. "They're shagging", Rosco had whispered triumphantly, "They're actually doing it." The whole car had started bouncing, it seemed, to the beat of the music. Eventually the lad in the passenger seat flicked his fag out of the window and it hit a rock with a burst of sparks. The car stopped bouncing and a boy clambered out of the backseat tugging on his white tracky bottoms. The girl in the back swung her bare legs out the door and adjusted her skirt, while the boy in the passenger seat got out and high fived his pal. As they swapped positions, Rosco had said, "Is that not Nicola Skelton?"

The boy who got into the backseat was Souter, whose face was so puckered with pepperoni coloured eruptions that the thought of him getting close to her had filled me with fury. I'd picked up a rock and lobbed it high in the air. It'd smashed down with an incredible bang on the car's roof. The two lads had jumped out assuming action stances. We had ducked down out of sight as Rosco hissed, "Why'd you do that?"

Eventually we'd heard the car doors shut. I couldn't stomach the idea of Souter on that back seat with her and picked up stone after stone hurling them high in the air, hoping that they'd crash down on them. Quickly enough the car engine growled into gear and with a spin of tyres they were gone. I'd felt elated and sick. I'd never thought of Nicky, my cousin's pal, ruffled and tousled and unbuttoned before.

As I got up from the quarry's gravelly ground, I wanted to swing at Souter and run for that scrambly route up between the cliffs, where I could rain rocks on them. But there was no chance I'd make it in the dark, through the brambles, with these sea legs. Instead I walked over to the car and set about Pete, channelling all of my terror, closing my eyes with every punch. His hands were taped behind his back and he attempted to protect his face by bringing his knees up, rolling into the foetal position. I should have said he had nothing to do with their money – that is was Johnny who had stolen it. But there was a roaring in my ears – the noise of a crowd at school goading you to fight - and I kept punching him again and again until there was no knowing whether my knuckles were sticky with his blood or mine.

When I'd done enough damage, I staggered back, half sick with horror, half sick with a hunger for more violence. Souter grinned, baring his rotten teeth. He'd filmed the whole thing on his phone.

The man in the suit jacket nodded to Elham who released the car's handbrake.

"Close the boot," the man said. "We're going to see how strong you are."

"What?"

"You're going to push the car into the lake. Manage it and El won't take that cute wee face off you."

The lake was a huge quarried hole that over the decades had filled with stagnant rain water, dumped electrical goods and stolen cars. On sunny days you could make out the ancient registration plates of the cars that had got stuck on ledges a few metres under the water. We used to come up here and fill poly bags with rocks before dropping them from the cliffs, watching them sink until they disappeared into the water's depths.

Stupidly, I looked at Pete's battered face as he wriggled and groaned. He'd half managed to sit up as I brought the back door slamming down on his head.

"Lock it," El ordered chucking me the keys.

"Lights, cameras, action," said Souter, again pointing his mobile phone at me.

I crouched down and put my shoulder to the back of the Astra. My mouth still tasted of broken fillings, blood, adrenaline, fear. As I pushed the whole of my weight against the car, my trainers scuffled across the broken ground and the car rolled a couple of inches. With a roar I ground my shoulder, arm, head into the metal door. Pete sounded like he was having a fit on the other side of the back door, but the car was moving down the slope, picking up speed. Just before the drop, my feet gave way and I was on my knees when it splashed into the water.

"Fuck," I said, watching the car float out into the middle of the lake.

"We are sailing, we are sailing," El sang in a rubbish Rod Stewart accent, before hauling me to my feet and wrapping his heavy leather-clad arm around my shoulders as if we were best pals. "Mate. Three minutes – that's how long it'll take. The manufacturers make them that way so you'd be able to get out the windows if there's an accident. Not much help when you're tied up in the boot."

He took out two cigarettes and lit both before putting one to my lips. My mashed up hand quivered as I held the tab to my mouth. I took a long, hard draw and started to cowk. As we smoked the fags, Pete beat his feet against the locked

185

hatchback's door. At the last, he must have ripped through the tape on his face, but by that point, even if there had been anyone who cared about his cries for help, there was nothing they could do. For a minute after the car sank, huge belching bubbles disturbed the water's surface. Then it was still.

"You are claimed," Souter goadingly waved his phone in my face. "Captured on camera. One of the Kerrs. You are so totally claimed."

Now seemed like a good time to take a swing at him and make a break for the path up the crack on the quarried cliffs.

As if reading my mind, the suited neanderthal said, "There is no point in running. From this moment on, running is not an option. You understand this?"

He took out a slim mobile about half the size of mine, then a fat leather wallet about double the width of mine. After checking the phone, he slipped it into his jacket pocket and extracted a business card from the wallet. The card was thicker than that used by the Kerrs, the writing embossed, bold, gold. I glanced at the name and looked again at the shiny suit, claw of black hair and swarthy face.

"Call me, Antonio," He grabbed my limp hand, skin much harder, grip much firmer than mine. "The Kerrs are finished," he nodded at the lake, "That dozey cunt and his stupid hats. Jackie Kerr will be an old man before he's out of prison and the only one of his boys who wasn't a total waster is banged up with him. That leaves Mags, some daft kids and anyone stupid enough to stay loyal to them. They lack muscle and, more importantly, after tonight, they've got no money and no gear. The question is, are you with us? Because if you're not, you're with Peter Kerr."

It didn't really seem like a question.

"Now you owe us. After the fuck up on the trawler, you owe us big time. Phone."

For a moment I thought about pretending I didn't have it on us but that kind of fuckery would go down like a sucker-punched loon amongst these lot. I handed it over and he scrolled through the call history.

"Aw, he really didn't know that his cousin was going to do the dirty on them." He pocketed the mobile and handed me one of those indestructible Nokias. "Keep it on you at all times and answer when you're called. Don't give the number out."

I swallowed hard and in a voice that didn't sound brave asked: "Where's Johnny?"

"Johnny? I'd say that boy'll be keeping his head down. Keeping his head down for some time."

"He's dead?"

"See me, I'm a magician. I make people disappear. Pete Kerr, Danny Kerr, Johnny Campbell. But I can make them reappear as well. Sometimes."

"So he's alive?"

"Listen. Enough of the questions. Remember we've just filmed you beating that boy and pushing the car into the water. That footage can be on the internet any minute of any day. Remember that if you run, we can put the police onto you. Remember that there's a Kerr in every prison in the country. But most importantly, remember that we make people vanish, just like that. Your mum, aunt, that girl you go with. I'm not picky."

He came right up close to me, so that even in the moonlight I could see the crudely cudgelled clay-work of his face contrasted with the white regularity of his false teeth. Hairy caterpillar eyebrows lowered as he stared into me.

"A police detective was on the harbour tonight. We took care of him, but I want to know what he was doing there." I must have looked suitably shocked cause after a pause that could have been seconds or minutes, he continued. "That Goth fag-hag you hang about with got lifted dealing in the park today. What could she have told them?"

"Nothing."

"She knows about the smuggling plan," Souter piped up. "She was the one who put us in touch with this lot."

"But times, dates. How'd she know these?"

"She doesn't."

The suited caveman glowered at me. "Could have fucked up everything. Still, it's all worked out in the end. You'll be getting a visit from the filth tomorrow I wouldn't doubt."

"Tomorrow?" I uttered, stumbling towards an understanding that I was going to see such a day.

"They'll want to know why you were at sea for less than a day and what you did when you got back to shore."

"Well, what are you going to tell them?"

"Same as I said to Rafferty, the harbour master. We had electrical problems."

"Good, and when they ask about what you got up to tonight, probably best to leave out the murdering Pete Kerr bit. Stick to the part about going to a party, taking a pal to A&E. Claim you didn't stick about cause you were worried about getting in trouble. They're not the actions of someone who's just smuggled drugs into the country and is worried about getting caught."

"No."

"Are you expected in the park tomorrow?"

"Day after."

"Right. Make sure you show. It'll throw the police. Maddie Kerr will be after you. Tell her that you came back with the drugs and the last you saw of Pete was him running away from the boat carrying them. You got that? You tell the filth, your family, anyone that asks that you all came back together and that Pete left on his own."

I nodded.

"Then we'll see what we do with you."

I was marched back to my car between Souter and the Viking's enormous bulk.

"You're a killer Malky. A double killer," Souter said in mock admiration.

"What?"

"Johnny told us about Joe. The Boss wasn't sure about you. But Johnny convinced him. First Joe Campbell and now Pete Kerr. Fucking psycho. That's what you are, son."

"Bad to the bone," The Viking dryly agreed.

I turned the ignition, the familiar purr of the engine, the unfamiliar buzz of panic in my stomach. The fingertips of my left hand dabbed at the knuckles of the right, sticky with the blood of a man I'd just killed.

CHAPTER TWENTY

PC Gourlay expected the station to be abuzz with arrests, lawyers, interviews, but Michael Carmichael barely raised his eyes from the sports pages as she passed through the secured doors in reception. She almost wanted to shout, Am I a ghost? as her arrival in the Response Room barely registered a response.

The squeaky creak of too tight motorbike trousers announced Sergeant Grant.

"Office," Grant said.

Behind the soundproof glass, Gourlay waited to be invited to sit.

"Last night," Grant said, hefting his bulky backside onto the corner of his desk. "Don't know what Stark was thinking, but the NCA boys are not impressed. Not impressed at all. The Chief Sup is visiting him today. He'll be given sick leave of course. Concussion. Standard procedure. But it's one thing on top of another with him."

"Did the OCG's transit van get picked up, Sir?"

"Without their reg there's no evidence that the van you saw had anything to do with them."

"And the boys on the trawler?"

"Hillman reckons we haven't got enough on them for it to be worth our while. If there was a smuggling operation last night — and it's a bloody big if — the gear will be well away by now."

The Sergeant attempted a consoling tone, which ended up sounding condescending.

"It happens to the best of them. They get sick of picking up the same petty criminals for the same petty crimes. And detectives are the worst. Thinking they can get to the bottom of things, catch the big men. But the likes of us – small town police – we don't get to lay a glove on those people. Stark's always been a fantasist, dreaming of the big case that'll get him a transfer to a Major Investigation Team, while neglecting to do the day to day detective work, the picking up the pieces." Gourlay had never heard the Sergeant say so much. Embarrassed for his efforts, she stared at a drooping money plant over his shoulder. "The vehicles that you saw leaving the hospital, you're certain you couldn't ID anyone other than Malcolm Campbell?"

"As I said Sarge, the black van was too far away to see the driver and any passengers. There was a man in the back of Malcolm Campbell's car, but he didn't match any of the known members of the OCG."

Technically, Gourlay told herself, this wasn't a lie. Grant, in any case, didn't doubt her.

"Very good Sian, very good."

"Sarge. Sorry for speaking out of turn, but shouldn't we put a patrol car in front of the Starks? It's too much of a coincidence them turning up at the hospital. Perhaps they thought he'd seen something."

Grant laughed. "You've been spending too much time with Jim. Malcolm Campbell brought a friend who'd suffered an OD into A&E. Hardly the actions of someone who's just been involved in a major smuggling op. There are plenty of black transit vans on the roads. You were right to call it in, but it was just a coincidence. As for Stark being attacked, he's got enough enemies in this town. My theory is someone coming home from the pub saw him skulking about the harbour and with it being a foggy night thought they'd take a pop at him. Happens to most of us at one time or other."

"You're probably right, Sarge," Gourlay heard her voice saying, and was surprised at how convincing she sounded.

"Course, I'm right," Grant shuffled off the desk and typed a password into his PC. "Once you've done the paperwork on last night's fiasco, you and Carmichael are to take a car to the usual speed trap on Southgate Road. The school year starts tomorrow, and there are a lot of inconsiderate drivers out there."

Later, sitting in a layby that Carmichael told her the police had used to catch speeding drivers for decades, and which consequently amounted to a sort of tax on tourists seen as none of the locals would ever get caught, Gourlay started to feel uneasy. She didn't understand why she'd withheld information from the team, didn't understand why she'd taken those drugs from Nicola Skelton. This wasn't her. But in both cases, she'd got away with it. Getting caught wasn't the issue. The problem was knowing who to trust. Stark was right: they had stumbled upon a major smuggling operation, which probably did have connections to Joe Campbell's death. But what had being right done for Stark?

"That's another one," Carmichael announced looking at the speed gun that he held out of the window. "Thirty-two in a thirty zone. We'd have made a fortune if we'd gone after all of them." Gourlay had already had this discussion. Carmichael ripped open another cereal bar from the supplies he'd insisted they buy from the petrol station. "Schools are back in tomorrow as well. That's when speeders become a real menace. That'll be why Grant's got us out here."

Gourlay didn't think so. "Michael, could I ask a question?" She'd noticed that her colleague, previously the least experienced officer in the station, loved being asked for advice.

"Anything," he replied, wiping cereal bar crumbs from his lips.

Carmichael was no genius, but Stark had pointed out that he was the most useful person at the station in one regard. He was local, with a mum and sister that ran a hairdressers on The Front. As a result, he had a knowledge of names, intel, background histories more detailed than any criminal database.

"During the Gala the Sergeant was talking to a man in the park. I'd seen him before but can't remember if he was undercover or some local grass."

"Go on."

"Well, he was smaller than Grant, 5'9 or 10. Thinning blonde hair that he'd gelled. Craggy face like he'd had really bad acne. He was wearing a Rangers top but a really old one from like ten years ago." Carmichael closed his eyes and hummed as if he was a machine processing information. "His teeth," Gourlay continued as if just remembering. "Really rotten teeth. He didn't look, you know, like one of us."

Carmichael's concentrated concern that he was being asked to ID someone he didn't recognise, broke into a look of relief once the teeth were mentioned.

"Got it," he said. "That's Colin Souter. You've got a really good memory for details Sian Gourlay. You should think about becoming a police officer."

"Who is he? Where do I recognise him from?"

"Well, you were right. He's definitely not one of us: local, did time for a serious assault involving a knife. It was before I'd joined up, but there was some sort of altercation in the chip shop down The Front. The Kerrs were involved. Mikey Osborne, who's married to Tamara Kerr, got cut up. Nothing life threatening, but the police were called, and it was all on the chippie's CCTV. Colin Souter's bad enough, so probably already had a record. Sentenced for two years if I remember rightly. He's been out for a while now, but the word was he'd moved down south."

Gourlay reached for one of the cereal bars and read the ingredients. "Guess someone must have pointed him out when we were on patrol."

"Good chance. It's that type of local knowledge you have to accumulate."

Jim Stark awoke with a headache so blindingly intense that he was momentarily unable to remember its origins. They'd kept him in hospital overnight for observations, but his wife had collected him in the morning. He didn't expect much in the way of sympathy, but once they were ensconced in the car she'd looked at him with a mixture of pity and contempt before saying, "You daft old bugger, when will you learn?" Rubbing the sleep from his eyes, he was aware of a ringing sensation which he eventually realised was in fact the front door bell.

The hushed voice of his wife was followed by the professionally concerned tones of Chief Superintendent Jackson as she ushered him into the sitting room. Stark had anticipated this moment. Before Linda could knock on the door, he'd thrown on some clothes, splashed his face in the en suite bathroom and swilled some mouthwash.

"Jim, it's Chief Superintendent Jackson," she whispered, as if his presence or rank was some sort of secret.

The Chief couldn't have looked more at home. Instead of sitting on the settee or an arm chair, he'd taken one of the chairs from the dinner table. He stood as Stark entered the room, brushing scone crumbs from his perfected pressed trousers.

"Jim," he said, "How are you?"

He indicated that he had permission to sit on his own settee and for a moment, Stark thought he was going to ask if it wasn't too warm in here, before opening a window, or some other wanky power move learned in a management manual. Even sitting upright on the soft cushions of his sofa, Stark was at a distinct height disadvantage.

"I didn't want to inconvenience you, Jim, not after what you've been through. But I thought it right to pay a visit."

"Thank you, Sir."

Having been through training at the same time, Stark still found calling Jackson, 'Sir' to be a challenge. Not that Thompson ever let formalities slip.

"Always an occupational hazard in this line of work, but that shouldn't normalise this. Your colleagues will no doubt be keen to apprehend the perpetrator."

Stark made a marginal adjustment of his head, which just about suggested his agreement with this questionable sentiment.

"There's undoubtedly been a lot going on in this area. And we're overstretched, that's no secret. I can see it's all got a bit much."

"I wouldn't say — "

Thompson held his palms up as if placating an untrained dog.

He continued, "We've had the NCA monitoring things for a couple of months now. What we really need are a couple of detectives from the Organised Crime Unit, especially as you'll have to be signed off sick for at least a week. We need to show this OCG that we're not a soft touch."

"Definitely, Sir and that's why ..."

"But the lead you were following," Jackson dismissed it with a disdainful wincing of the nostrils. "Your colleagues at the station and DI Hillman feel that you'd got ahead of yourself. The NCA have spent months tracking this group. Non-procedural actions like yours risk jeopardising their whole investigation. There's a London based OCG running county lines in this region. We know that. There's no intel suggesting they're smuggling drugs into the country from here. Our job, your job as a DI, is to assist the NCA in disrupting their operations on the ground."

"Sir."

"We need to clear this up and shut down any stories about smuggling. I had that runt Rory Tan phoning my office asking about the police activity around the harbour last night." Jackson suddenly looked exhausted. "He's not the only one. If you knew the pressure I'm under. Council leader, local MP, MSPs, all on at me. If Sunnyside Homes pull out of the development of The Burnside Estate, there'll be hell to pay. 250 new properties. Both affordable and luxury homes along with a new leisure centre on the site of the old primary school." The barrage of property development speak made Jackson sound like he'd lost the plot. "Local jobs, new families attracted to the area – professional people and holiday goers. That estate's got the lot: salubrious location, sea view, easy access to the marina, five minutes' walk to the Links. It might be a total sink just now, but if this development goes through, the whole town changes. Port Cawdor has got potential. Everyone says it. Miles of unspoilt beaches. The most hours of sunshine in the country. Quaint old fishing cottages. But that's not what people think when they hear its name. They think drugs problem, crime, a fishing industry on its knees."

The Chief Superintendent paused to sip at his cup of tea. Stark momentarily felt annoyed that he hadn't been supplied with a similar prop.

"Jim, I know you want transferred from this area. You've applied before and your wife mentioned it earlier. I can process this. But let's keep a lid on things. The Joseph Campbell case. The pathologist's report was inconclusive and there's no evidence that foul play was involved, yet people at the station are telling me you're trying to connect it to this smuggling conspiracy you've cooked up. I've had complaints from the family about police harassment. It's madness."

Stark felt stung by the word and for a moment considered laying out the case as he saw it. But he knew he didn't have enough.

"Sir, I went down to the harbour as something occurred to me at the end of a long shift. A couple of bits of evidence made me think I was on to something and I called it in, but I can see now that I got it wrong."

Jackson nodded. "Remember the four Ds!"

He looked at Stark expectantly until the Detective realised he was expected to repeat them. "Disrupt, Deter, Detect and . . ."

"Divert, Jim, divert. Let's have them bothering some other regional commander down the road." He drained the last of the tea and exhaled in satisfaction. "An excellent brew. Just the way I like it."

Gourlay's shift had taken a dramatic twist when they'd been called to a suspected fatality. Despite Carmichael sticking to the speed limits down the twisting road that led out of Port Cawdor, they'd been first on the scene. Even now, out of uniform and ten minutes out of the station, Gourlay couldn't shake it from her head. Her second body. A middle-aged couple, who'd been walking their dog, had waited for them by a car, parked where a track leading to a farm house crossed the old railway line. Their alsatian was still going berserk in the boot.

The man, a well chewed dog lead wrapped around his fist, wanted to explain things.

"It was Rannoch what found him. He was off the lead and over sniffing the poor lad. I shouted on him to heel, and he just kept on pawing him, which isna like Rannoch at all. I went over to apologise, and when I saw Rannoch sniffing and licking the laddie's head and him still not moving, I kent something was far wrong."

"He's over there," the women pointed at a path leading down from where the farm track bridged the old railway line.

The body lay on its front, face turned to the side, for all the world like someone who'd gone to sleep in the overgrown summer verge. But no one would choose to lie among the nettles and thistles.

"There's no car," Gourlay observed.

Carmichael was already reaching for his radio. "Don't touch anything," he ordered.

Gourlay semicircled the body. The navy blue jumper was still rolled up around the right arm, where a shoelace that had been used as a tourniquet remained tied to the man's elbow.

"Looks like a drugs overdose," she said.

"Is he definitely dead?"

She moved close enough to check the breathing and in doing so recognised the face, the ginger hair and blue cable knit jumper from the body who'd been rushed in to A&E the previous night.

"Christ, it's Josh McCormack."

"Was he not on that – "

"Yep."

"Shit."

Gourlay was brought back into the reality of her walk home from work, by an awareness that a car was curb crawling at the edge of her peripheral vision. She didn't change her pace but glimpsed in the reflective glass front of the Co-op to see Inspector Stark leaning over the passenger seat.

"Get in."

She opened the door and ducked into Stark's snack wrapper strewn car.

"Like climbing into a bin."

He accelerated smoothly away checking his rear view mirrors. "I've been put on leave for the next week and pretty much warned off investigating anything to do with the boys on *The Abiding Star*. Tell me honestly, Sian, am I going mad? I was so sure I'd worked things out, that everything was clicking into place."

Gourlay took a deep breath. "You're not going mad. When I was leaving the hospital, a boy was being admitted. He'd OD'd. Malky Campbell must have brought him in. Malky Campbell drove out of the hospital behind a black transit van. In the back seat of his car there was a man I'd seen talking to Grant during Gala Day. They'd looked really pally. When I described him to Carmichael, he said that it must have been Colin Souter."

Stark let the car drift into a parking space before resting his forehead on the steering wheel. He kept it there for so long that Gourlay started worrying he'd had some sort of post-concussion black out.

"Sir, there's more." Stark lifted his head. Gourlay stared straight though the windscreen to give him time to blink away the tears blotting his eyelashes. "At the end of my shift, 90 minutes ago now, Carmichael and I were called to assist with a fatality. Dog walkers had found a body dumped in undergrowth by the old railway line. Obviously, we didn't do any more than secure the crime scene, but the body, it was Josh McCormack. I recognised his jumper from ER. It was him that Malky Campbell must have dropped at the hospital."

"The body. Suspicious?"

"Tourniquet still round his arm. But how had he got there? It's miles from anywhere."

"The boy clearly had a fairly serious habit, but this is too much of a coincidence. He was tight with the younger Campbells. Good chance he was on the trawler last night."

Stark spun the car. "Something went wrong with their smuggling operation and I want to know what. Let's have another word with Malcolm Campbell."

CHAPTER TWENTY-ONE

They were doing a military exercise at the Airforce base and our house shook as tornados circled imaginary enemies. Somewhere, up there, young men ripped through the sky at a thousand miles per hour - the ability to annihilate a town the size of this at a twitch of a thumb. Down here, I curled up in my bed afraid of a power that seemed far greater. My body clenched as if all night I'd been bracing myself for the kicking that was coming. I'd love to say there was a moment of contented ignorance before I awoke, but my puce pulverised fist, the ache in my jaw and the jagged gap in my teeth, was with me from the first.

I pretended to sleep for a few minutes, wondering if my mum had gone to work. The TV wasn't on, which provided pretty solid evidence that she was out, but I couldn't understand why she hadn't popped in to share her relief about our early return to land. I crept to the bedroom door, avoided the creaky board above the stairs and snuck down. The house was empty. After double locking the door, and arming myself with the metal bar from some dumbbells that I suddenly wished I'd used more often, I set myself up beside a crack in the curtains. I kept guard there for the rest of the day: counting cars, holding my breath every time a Jeep that looked like the Kerrs' crawled past. Early-afternoon and a couple of Kappa clad Kerr associates, the Ferguson brothers, appeared on the street. I slipped down onto the carpet beneath the window and pressed my back against the wall. The heavy thump of fists here on heavy business announced either their official arrival or an initial attempt at knocking the door down. I held my breath, heard my heart.

"No cunts in."

There was a silence while they listened for me, expecting me to make a move. But I wasn't that daft.

"Round the back," the same voice hissed and the gravel crunched as they crept around the side.

I was behind the couch, so even if they looked through the back windows there was no danger they would see me, but the backdoor was much easier to put in. Looking at my bare feet, it seemed obvious that if I was going to have to fight for my life, it might have helped to have some shoes on.

"You boys," I heard the rasping voice of Miss Maugham who lived next door. "Get out of that garden."

I could see her looming out of her sitting room window with her Havisham hair and mummified face. Mumm-Ra Maugham the ever living, we'd called her as weans, her door a constant favourite for chap and run. Right now I would have kissed those wrinkly chops. The Ferguson brothers scurried down the road in an unnecessary alarm given that Miss Maugham, who'd been wheelchair-bound for years, was hardly likely to give chase.

As the day seeped away I got a pot from the kitchen and filled it with cold water and ice cubes. I kept my lumpy, swollen right hand in the freezing water until it no longer hurt. It was the rest of me that was the problem.

The landline rang nineteen times: always a withheld number. The Nokia that Antonio had given me remained silent and there was no danger I was getting on Whatsapp or Insta on this relic. By the time my mum got home, I was in bits. As she came through the door, I kicked the metal bar under the couch and got to the kitchen in time to empty the pot.

"Well you could at least have opened the curtains," she shouted through from the sitting room. "Fa happened?"

"What?"

"With the boat."

"Electrical failure." I answered, in a tone that conveyed just the right mix of annoyance and boredom. Still, this was my mum: the ultimate lie detector. Keep it short. Keep it simple.

"So that's it then?" She wrung her hands. "You can put those daft notions about becoming a deckie behind you." She glanced at the mantelpiece, at the photo of my old man, who never got to be an old man. "Duffy was in the chippie for his tea. You never told him you were quitting?"

"No."

"That's what I thought. He said there was every chance they'd put you on the lawnmowers once the schools go back. I put a good word in for you."

She bustled into the kitchen and as she filled the kettle, I noticed that her hands were shaking.

"Maddie Kerr was in the chippie."

"Aye?"

"She was asking about you. Wanted to ken if you were back on shore. I telt her that you were home when I got up – sleeping like a log so you were. That daft laddie your cousins hang about with: the one with the hats. She was looking for him. Telt me tae close up the chippie and take her to see you. I wasna having that. I've kent that woman since we were at school and I've never crossed her. But she's no mixing you up in her family's business. So I telt her, 'People have been backing off you for too long Madeline Kerr. Well here's one that's not backing off.' She just scrunched up her face and says, 'Let's hear you say that when I come back with Charlie and Tamara.' 'Bring your whole clan' I says, "Cause I'm no feart ay them.' I was shaking inside – you ken what Big Maddie is like - but I felt that fierce, that mad at her and her brood, bringing the toun doun. She looked like she was gonna swing for us, but then darted for the door. I thought she was off to get those fat daughters of hers until I saw that Francesco had came out the backroom. 'Right, that's it, I've had it with you and your lot harassing my staff. Scoot. And if I hear of you bothering Beth and her family, they'll be hell to pay.' And she was off oot the door – didnae think he had it in him. Just goes to show that if you let a family like that take liberties they'll tramp all over you, but if you face up to them, they're no as tough as everyone thinks."

She took a long breath, as the kettle started to shriek.

"Too true," I muttered, pretending the story held no interest to me.

"Even so," my mum shouted over the kettle, "Nothing good can come fae hanging around with they Kerrs. They're only interested in pulling people down to their level – just look at your cousin Johnny." She came through with two steaming mugs of tea. "Son. Will you promise me one thing? Now that you're off the boats. Johnny, Peter Kerr, that Nicola Skelton – promise me you'll steer clear ay that crowd."

"Sure." I said, sounding plausibly uncommitted, like there was a chance of me seeing any of those people ever again.

She supped on her tea. "That's a good cup of tea," she said, as if it didn't taste exactly like every other cuppa she'd ever made.

The steam evaporated from my undrunk cup. My mum flicked on the evening news. The mugshots of convicted paedophiles, murderers and terrorists blazed into our sitting room. Some looked confused and frightened, but others stared the camera down, as if they'd always known this was how it was going to end.

"What a world," my mum tutted.

A police car pulled into a parking space down the road. I went into the toilet and in the mirror prepared my game face, attempting to make my eyes as pebble-hard as the type of killers who can stare down a mug-shot photographer.

The smart rap-a-tat-tat of knuckles on official business announced them. I waited until they'd been in the house for a minute and flushed the toilet. I had another quick inspection of my face. *Nothing to see here*, I smirked and then felt sure there was something a little twisted about my mouth, a little sneaky around my eyes.

Zoe's dad and the policewoman that had interviewed me were slumped on our saggy settee and easy chair like old family friends. Mum had improbably already managed to furnish them with cups of tea in the couple of minutes since they'd arrived.

"Sugar?"

"I wouldn't normally Beth, but after the day we've had I wouldn't say no."

She brought a pot of sugar through and I watched as the female officer spooned three heaped spoonfuls into her mug. I'd a weird flashback of Stark sitting on that same seat twelve years ago, telling us they'd called off the search for my father. My mum's stormy face, like she was angry with us all. Auntie Mary taking me up stairs, suddenly interested in the picture of mermaids I'd been drawing and which ended up on our fridge, horrifying me for years.

"Hello son, everything alright?"

Inspector Stark peered at me, as if he gave a flying fuck about my well-being. Dinna call me son you condescending fuck, I wanted to reply.

"We've been seeing quite a bit of you lately. You remember PC Gourlay?"

Don't respond to anything except direct questions. When these come, keep it vague. Only lie when you have to. Be consistent. Never admit you're wrong unless they prove it. I minded Johnny's mantra before my first interview.

Inspector Stark presented me with the same smile he'd given me when I went round to see his daughter under the pretext of borrowing a textbook or copying a homework task. A smile that said *I know what you're up to.*

"You were at sea yesterday. What time did you get in?

I shrugged. "Ten-ish."

"See anyone on the harbour?"

"Yeah. Rafferty came out for a word."

"Then what?"

"Went home."

"Alone?"

"Yeah."

"Who was on the trawler?"

Feeling like I was stepping into a trap, I kept shtum for a couple of seconds.

"Me, Johnny, Corky – Josh McCormack – and Peter Kerr."

PC Gourlay who'd been taking notes looked up at the last name.

They turned their attention to Mum.

"Did you see him when he got home?"

"I had an early night," my mum said. "Right enough, I can just about mind hearing the front door closing."

"Any idea about the time?"

"As I says, I was in bed early. Must have been dozing off, so between ten and eleven sounds about right."

"Why were you at sea for less than a day?" The young female officer took over

"Electrical problems." I lifted my shoulders mock apologetically.

"And did you spend the night in?"

"No. My cousin was having a party so I went over there."

"Right. And did anything interesting happen at the party?"

Remembering what Antonio had said about telling the truth about my movements up until the point where I met them, I said, "I had to take Josh McCormack to A&E. He'd taken something."

Inspector Stark scrutinised me for a moment longer than necessary and it seemed certain he knew everything about the gang jumping me.

Noisily he drained his tea and carefully placed the cup on the coaster.

"How'd you describe your relationship with Nicola Skelton?"

"She's a pal of my cousins."

"That's not what I asked."

"I ken her through them. She's their pal."

"Do you text her?"

"Yeah, from time to time."

"She's Johnny Campbell's girlfriend," my mum blurted out. "And I've been telling this one until I'm blue in the face that she's no good."

Stark picked up the cup, disappointed.

"Ok, son. That'll do for now." He was about to clamber out of the depths of the couch but then stopped. "We've actually got a bit of bad news for you. The laddie McCormack. He was found dead earlier this evening. His body had been dumped by the old railway line. Just left there like a bag of rubbish."

My mum gasped and whispered, "What a world."

Goose bumps bead my arms.

"What happened to your hand?"

I looked at my puffy, scabby, knuckles as if noticing them for the first time.

"Dropped a box on it when loading the boat."

"Box tan your jaw an aw?"

I rubbed my swollen jaw.

"Got a broken tooth that's become infected. Show you if you like."

Inspector Stark put his hands up to suggest that wouldn't be necessary and after thanking my mum for her hospitality made his way to the door. I didn't get up. I couldn't get up.

Before leaving the room, he gave me one of those more disappointed that angry looks that teachers and school counsellors had been trying out on me for years. I stared him out, but he genuinely looked sorry for me.

"Just out of interest. What did you do after leaving Josh McCormack at A&E?"

"I went home."

He nodded as if to say that this was what he expected me to say. Before leaving he pressed a card into my hand and whispered, "It doesn't need to be like this." As my mum guided them to the door, their voices slurred and sloshed like the sound when you sank to the bottom of the swimming baths to look at girls' legs.

Once they were gone my mum stormed into the sitting room.

"Do you think my head buttons up the back? I don't know what you're playing at, but there's something not right here, something not right at all. My God, I remember when your pals were nice loons like Alec Mathie and Ross Millar – laddies that are going to university. Now it's all junkie trash and criminals."

I thought of Corky's dad Cal and the number of times I'd caught him sadly shaking his head on the trawler, a confused and hurt look on his face as he watched the sweaty, shaky, shambles his son had become.

"Corky wasn't junkie trash. He was a boy with a mum that you ken well. He made some bad choices. That's all."

I put my head in my hands blocking out the noises she made as she cleared up the cups and biscuits. I'd heard it once said that 70% of communication is non-verbal. With Corky, seen as he was always so melted on methadone it was more like 90%. But he still came out with moments of gold that reminded you of the sharp, funny boy he'd once been. "We are the unprofitable bycatch of humanity" he'd told me in the park like some prophet foretelling his own death, "They'd like to throw us in the sea." I whispered the words to myself as if they were the only thing that made sense.

Once Mum was occupied in the kitchen I took the cordless phone and rifled through her address book for Dawn's number. I stabbed the digits into the phone but waited until I was safe in my room before calling.

"Malky?" She answered. "Where've you been? I've been calling you all evening."

"Lost my phone."

"You've heard?"

"Aye. The police were round."

"The police?"

"Yeah, they wanted to ken about last night."

"He was round at mine this morning after they let him out the hospital. Came round to apologise. Well, he came round to pick up his jacket, but he really was sorry. Said he was gonnae get his shit together. He'd some plan about leaving town. Said he had to get out of here for a few weeks. Get clean. He was different, emotional like. Then he got a text message from someone. On the way out, the last thing I says to him was 'you promise to stay away fae trouble.' I was joking but you ken, serious too. And he looked me right in the eyes and promised. Do you ken what the last thing he said was — 'I love you.'"

"Fuck."

"Exactly. I just canna believe that he went straight out my door and went and bought smack."

I thought about Corky, dumped by the old railway line, and shuddered at the certainty that the text he'd got was almost definitely from my old phone.

"He was an addict."

"No, I'm not saying that I dinna believe that he went and got gear straight after promising me he wouldn't. I'm saying that I canna believe that he didn't take me with him."

"Yeah," I murmured, "that's a bit much."

"That's karma," she corrected me. "If I'd hae been there, I'd have saved him. Not least because I'd hae made him share whatever he bought."

I maintained a stunned silence while Dawn babbled on about who she reckoned had been with him when he'd OD'd. I hated the brittle hardness in her voice. That wasn't Dawn talking, I told myself, it was a character she'd invented that allowed her to deal with things. "We at least got him to hospital. Bastards didn't even do that. Anyway, I'm getting a few folks together – a sort of celebration, or what's the word, commiseration of Corky's life."

"Commemoration."

"Aye that an aw. You game?

"Got work the morrow."

"You not quit?"

"No."

Putting on those sky-blue work trousers with the creases down the front and the council-issue T shirt with PARKIE written in huge letters on the back, I thought that even criminals from days gone by got to wear their own clothes on the way to the scaffold. The only thing I was thankful for were the steelies. Those and the knife I'd slipped from the kitchen drawer were the only things protecting me. I left for work an hour early, took a different route, freezing every time a car passed, my fist tightening around the handle of the blade in my pocket. It was a drizzly morning, but for me everything felt turned up to eleven: the inanity of good morning TV blasting through kitchen windows, the smell of fry ups and damp lawns, the moan of commuting cars. As I walked to work, I thought of all the news stories you read about gangland killings – the victim knowing full well that they were marked men, but were shot or stabbed sitting on the same pub stool that they sat on every night. Idiots, you'd think without realising that the particular pub stool that they sat on was the only place in the world that they were permitted to be at that exact time.

There was no sign of the lawn mower men in the howff. I figured with it being such a dreich morning, they couldn't be cutting grass and that Gav would have them out weeding around the town hall – sooking up to the councillors. I looked over at the corner where Johnny had hidden behind the unusable paddle boats. What I wouldn't give to see that sullen face now. After double bolting the backdoor, I sat down on one of the knackered old chairs that the Lawnmower men had salvaged from houses of evicted tenants. With so much expensive machinery, gardening tools, canisters of petrol and two stroke oil stored overnight, the shed was an absolute fortress. Even if the Kerrs knew I was here, they couldn't get in. I sat next to a salvaged fridge that actually worked. At some early point in his 'career', Duffy had managed to write his name on its side in huge letters by stubbing out countless cigarettes. It was the work of years, the work of infinite patience and non-existent imagination.

I couldn't sit behind locked doors all day. If I didn't show face, they'd think I was hiding from them – that I had something to hide. Cautiously, I inched up the chain that opened the metal shutter at the entrance to the boat shed. From here I could see anyone coming and could release the chain and drop the shutters in seconds. I placed the kitchen knife within easy reach and leant a paddle against my chair. Over amongst the climbing frame of the kids play area I saw a puff of smoke and figured that Leanne Kerr would be texting Big Maddie.

Parked up behind the wall at the back of the war memorial was a people carrier. In the low light it was hard to say if it had the tell-tale blacked out windows. Antonio had said the Kerrs lacked muscle, but he wasn't the one stuck in a deserted park, waiting for a swarm of those nutters to turn up. I minded Old Man Kerr's funeral. Every shop on Bridge Street closed, as the cortege rolled past – shop owners who had paid protection money for decades standing on the edge of curbs heads bowed. The Kerrs had turned out in full force that day. They'd come in limos and handcuffs. The limos were hired for the day. The cuffs would be theirs for longer. But even with their numbers hit by deaths, prison sentences and disappearances they could still terrorise a town the size of this.

I looked left and right. Not a soul. Uncanny. Even in the worst of weather Jimmy could be relied on to be searching through the bins at this time. I looked left and when I looked right a Jeep nudged its way past the broken bollard and drove over the football pitches towards me. My heart battered like a prisoner at a cell door. I put the knife in my back pocket and leant against the boat house entrance, trying to look as if I hadn't a care in the world, while ready to drop the metal shutters the moment things took a turn for the worse. The car skidded in front of us, all four doors flying open before it had even stopped. Maddie, the Ferguson brothers and this big unit who had the misfortune to be huckled to the sumo-sized bulk of Tamara Kerr sprang out. They were coming for us and I was about to release the chain that held up the metal shutter when the people carrier that had been parked behind the War Memorial screeched across the grass. Antonio, Elham and two other out of towners burst out. The Kerr crew sought cover behind car doors, Maddie pulling what looked like a machete from the back seat.

Here we fucking go. This was going to kick off big style - the kind of battle that wasn't going to leave too many of these evil bastards standing.

But Antonio daundered out from his car, empty palms open.

"What's all this?" He asked as if astonished by the Kerrs' reaction. "Take it you're here for a word with this boy." Maddie didn't move from her position. "Because I for one would like an explanation about what the fuck went on the other night." He pointed at me. "Is this one of the little shits that was on the boat?" Maddie nodded. "Any idea where the rest of them are?" She made no motion.

"You," he started towards me.

"One step further and I drop this shutter and call the police." I showed him the chain in my hand.

Antonio paused. "Call the fucking police," he spat like the word disgusted him, but didn't move any closer to me. "Where the fuck is your cousin and that dickhead nephew of hers?"

"I dinna ken what this is about. We came back night before last as planned. Pete wanted off the boat as quick as possible. Last I saw he was running through the harbour on his tod."

"With the gear?"

"With the gear."

"You lying to us?"

"Honestly, I dinna ken what's happening, but I wouldna be here now if I did."

Antonio nodded like he was weighing this up.

"You had a word with the harbour master. Rafferty, or whatever his name is?" Maddie shrugged like she would've liked to deny it, but couldn't. "He knows all these boys. Told me he saw Pete get off the boat. Practically knocked him over he was in such as rush. What he said confirms this one's story. Why didn't he call us? That was the plan. When they were getting close to the harbour, they were to call. Do you know who were told about their arrival? The fucking police. Swarming all over the harbour. Looks pretty fucking shady to me."

"Aye, but …"

"Don't aye but me, you Scottish tramp. Have you seen him?" He snapped at Maddie.

"Naw, I'm down here the same as you."

"Not tying off loose ends."

"Whit."

"The other lad that was on the boat. Died of an overdose last night. Know anything about that? Cos that's suspect. You ripped us off, Maddie? You and that waster with the hats."

For a moment her face collapsed in on itself like my ma's after she takes out her dentures.

"That's not what's happened."

"You thieving tinker bitch."

"I haven't ripped you off."

"Well some cunt has. You better find that nephew of yours. Better find him before we do. Because I will cruci-fucking-fy him. You find him and our gear by tomorrow and there won't be an apocalypse. Repartitions," he barked, "are fucking due. You," he pointed at me, "are coming with us. Drop that shutter and I'll annihilate every fucker you've ever smiled at."

"I want a word with him," Maddie said, "First."

"No you don't. Mind who put up most of the money. Mind whose connection you used. It's your family that messed up here. This was your town, your gig and you fucked it up."

The righteousness of his rage as he prodded his chest with those thick stumpy fingers. He had conned the Kerrs and almost had me, but I kent he was spouting shite. He glowered at her, at the whole lot of them like he'd go to war with them single handed, unarmed and still win.

I shuffled towards their car. One of the out-of-towners grabbed me by the scruff of my t-shirt and practically threw me in the back. They bundled in, wedging me on either side of them. The car stank of fresh leather and stale aftershave. As we wheelspun out of the park, Antonio twisted in his seat and said, "Not bad, son. You could have a career on the stage."

I couldn't understand why they were so pleased. What I could understand was that I'd played my part and was now just as expendable as Pete, Corky and as far as I knew Johnny.

"Dinna look so fucking greetin-faced," Elham cackled. "Here, is it time?" He asked Antonio.

Antonio pulled out his mobile and made a call.

"I've got someone that you might want a word with," he said to whoever had answered. "But mind and stick to what we agreed."

He put the mobile on loud speaker and handed it to me.

"Hello?"

"Malky?"

"Johnny? Fuck, is that you? I thought you were dead."

"Very much not dead. Are you alright?"

"Man, I can't believe it's you. Where are you?"

"I can't say. But I'm alright. You dinna need to worry about me. Listen, we're with Antonio now. You and me. We're playing in the big league. Just make sure you do as he says."

"I will. Jesus, it's good to hear you." I was half laughing as Antonio leant back and grabbed the phone off us.

"I just can't deal with all this emotion." He winked at us. "Johnny, you'll get to see him soon enough," he said down the phone. "The boy's done good ... aye, we're treating him like a fucking king. Yeah, anyway, later."

The car turned onto Bridge Street, the same familiar series of newsagents, hardware shops and pubs repeating themselves through the tinted windows. I was absolutely buzzing. Johnny back from the dead. The Kerrs off my case. Result.

"We run this town now," Antonio said looking out the window. "All these youts with their pay packets from the rigs and the fishing and nothing to spend it on." He gazed fondly at the bored looking shoppers on the High Street, the smokers, lingering at the pubs' doors. "Tomorrow, you call in sick and lie low. I'll put the straighteners on the Kerrs, but there are some head-bangers that won't take a telling. You still got that phone? Hold on to it. You'll get a call."

They steered into the rambling roads of the old town, the fisher-folks squat houses huddled together like sheep before a storm.

"So, you were in on Johnny's plan to go overboard?"

"*Johnny's* plan?" The others chuckled at this. "Do you really think he's got the bottle to come up with something like that?"

"How'd you pick up Pete?"

"Son, you're in the company of pick up artists. You should know that by now. We simply stopped him on The Front. Looked like he was going to brick it to be fair, but we told him there was a tracker packed with the drugs and that we were on our way to catch Johnny. He actually climbed in the car."

When your only experience of big time criminality was the Kerrs putting a dent in someone's head, this was disgustingly brilliant. I almost congratulated him - until I remembered what had happened to Corky.

"That detective turning up could have fucked things up. Still not got to the bottom of which gobby cunt is responsible for that."

Antonio shifted the rear view mirror so he could see my face and for a moment it felt like all the air had been sucked from the car. As we rolled to a stop on my road, his perfectly regular bleached teeth grinned out of his well-worn face and for a moment it felt like I was looking at someone wearing a mask.

In a mock Scottish voice he said, "Look after yourself, wee man."

CHAPTER TWENTY-TWO

"She's alive," Stark remarked as Zoe shuffled into the kitchen, wearing Winnie the Pooh pyjama bottoms and a Pizza Hut t-shirt, which given she'd never worked in Pizza Hut was clearly not hers. "Eighteen hours. That's got to be a record."

Zoe riffled through the biscuit tin, pretending to be annoyed at the lack of choice. Truth was, despite being starving, her stomach was in knots. Keeping her back to her parents, she pulled her denim jacket off a chair and muttered something about going out.

"You are not going anywhere," her dad said, in his best policeman voice.

"Sit down," her mum said, in her best teacher voice.

"I'm going for a walk with Ellie along the West Beach and then …" She stopped, staring at the airtight plastic bag, three pink Mitsubishi pills horribly visible on her parents' kitchen table. She didn't dare look at their faces. "What's this?"

"I rather thought you might be able to tell us that, seeing as they were in your jacket."

Zoe felt a ripple of resentment at the intrusion into her personal property, followed by a surge of annoyance for making such as basic error, both feelings swept away by a tidal wave of panic about what to say next.

"There was a sound system after the Gala. Some of those people from the Lighthouse were there and they were really out of it. The police looked like they were going to move in, and, now I think of it, there was this big sweaty guy bumped into me and sort of grabbed my jacket, I thought to steady himself, but he must have put them in my pocket."Too quick, too breathless, too obviously a story. She risked a glance at her parents who were watching her as if she were an unconvincing theatre piece.

"With your father out there tackling the criminals who sell this stuff. And me, disciplining pupils who get caught with cigarettes never mind drugs. You were head girl for Christ's sake, and you show us up like this?"

"I've never seen them before."

Her mum sighed.

"Go to your room. We'll talk about this when you're prepared to admit some responsibility."

"I'm eighteen next month."

"And while you're living under our roof, you'll abide by our rules. Think I haven't seen kids with eyes like yours when you came in, or heard someone grinding their teeth so hard we could hear you through the walls?"

Zoe stormed off, embarrassed, sorry, resentful.

The Starks sat in silence. The hum of the fridge, the ticking of the clock. Linda Stark loaded the dishwasher.

"I'm meeting a couple of colleagues at the Nineteenth Hole. Make sure she doesn't get out."

"How am I meant to do that?"

Stark took his daughter's purse from the denim jacket and removed her bank card. "We'll speak to her when we've all got clearer heads."

"Jim," Linda said, as he unlocked the door. "Don't be involving yourself with anything stupid. We need out of this town, now more than ever. You're on leave. Remember what Jackson said. Remember your family."

His wife knew him too well. There was no chance Stark was going anywhere near the Nineteenth Hole. He parked round the back of the Co-op, not waiting long before Gourlay climbed into the passenger seat.

"I'm taking a big risk just being here."

"You and me both. What's the news?"

"Two things." Gourlay took a gulp of air. "Josh McCormack's right thumb and forefinger had recently been broken. Cause of death was a massive heroin overdose, but there's also bruising on his forearms consistent with someone being restrained. The serious crime squad are 'keeping an open mind', but with everything else going on it looks suspect."

"So, who'd want him dead?"

"Either it's revenge for something that went wrong during the smuggling operation or someone wants him silenced."

"I keep coming back to the smashed satellite phone, Pete Kerr sprinting away like that. Something's not right there."

Gourlay slipped a sleek looking laptop from her rucksack, and, as the power was coming on, pushed in a USB stick. "It's the CCTV footage from the two cameras that monitor the harbour."

"Look," Gourlay clicked on the first file. "Grant sent round screen shots to see if anyone recognised your assailant. But he's well-disguised. He was cagey about anyone looking at the whole footage though. It's pretty obvious why."

Stark watched himself clamber out of his car and briskly march in the direction of the control tower. Then nothing for three, four, five minutes before a stocky, hoodie wearing figure, bottle already in hand, jogged past the camera's gaze. Two minutes later and he returned, this time walking fast.

"So, he didn't follow me. He knew I was there, because by that time I'd have phoned the station and Grant would have told them."

"There's more. You see our cars arrive on this camera, but no one else either enters or exits the crime scene. The other camera, however." Gourlay clicked the new file. "Here's Pete Kerr, running for his life, by the looks of it." She paused the footage and zoomed in. "There's no way that he's carrying anything like the amount of drugs you'd expect a major op like this to be bringing in to the country."

"No."

She moved the footage forward. "Malky Campbell. He'd be lucky if he could fit a 1 gram bag in the pockets of those skinny jeans." She fast forwarded to Josh McCormack stumbling through the fog like an extra in a zombie apocalypse. "And no one's trusting him to bring their gear ashore."

Gourlay let the footage run. "What about Johnny Campbell?"

"That's the question. What about Johnny Campbell. He's not picked up on either camera."

"Could he have hidden?"

"Not on the trawler. Might have tried some spot on the harbour, but DI Hillman called in the drug squad with their dogs. They'd have found him. Besides, I've watched the whole of this footage. There's an extra three hours on file. Even after we've cleared out, there's no sign of him."

Stark massaged his temples, feeling like he was being asked to complete a crossword for which he had all the wrong clues.

"Theories?"

"Not sure. Looks like neither the drugs nor Johnny Campbell made it ashore. Something obviously happened that someone didn't want communicated when they were at sea. Whatever it was really freaked out Peter Kerr."

"Hold on a minute. Could you scroll back to Pete Kerr?"

"Look. He's running towards Seatown, right? And then, there, show that bit again. Looks like a car's headlights come on and, he stops, looks like he's going to change direction, puts his hands up all defensive like and then walks towards the light and off the camera's range. We've not been able to capture any other footage from the Front?"

"No. Could he not just have heard our sirens?"

"With Grant delaying the call out, you wouldn't have left the station. Clearly someone's waiting for him."

"The OCG."

"And he's frightened of them. Peter Kerr: a psycho. From a long line of psychos. Look at him jigging about like a pavement dancer. Something went wrong on that trawler and it's put the fear into him."

A car reversed into the space beside them and Gourlay let her hair fall over her face.

"So, how do we find out what happened?"

"Think it's time to pay her royal highness a visit." Gourlay looked none the wiser. "We're off to see The Matriarch."

Neverland, as the locals called the Kerrs' mansion due to the rusting fairground rides stored in its garden, was just outside Port Cawdor. Over the years, it had been surrounded by so much razor wire topped fencing and security lighting that the view from the prison cells that family members so frequently occupied must have reminded them of home. Stark drove past the front of the house before parking down a farm track. He knew only too well the location a police surveillance team would use and had seen no evidence of activity.

The entrance gate had three cameras covering the street in addition to one you had to look into when using the intercom.

"It's DI Stark." There was a long pause. "Police," he added unnecessarily. Half a minute elapsed before the gate buzzed open.

Bollards illuminated as they made their way up the gravel pathway. Stark had just about remembered to say, "Watch out for the …", when a no-doubt illegal breed of pitbull bolted from behind a waltzer, a chain whiplashing it back at the last moment, its slavering jaws snapping on thin air.

"That's a warm welcome," Gourlay said.

They were kept waiting at the door until a couple of locks turned and a lump of a man wearing the sort of matching grey tracksuits issued in prison peered out.

"We're here to see Maddie."

The grey track suited giant toddled towards the kitchen. Stark was struck by the silence. Over the years, he'd been inside these walls a dozen times and there were always an indeterminate number of yapping kids and Chihuahuas getting under everyone's feet. The Kerrs were nothing if not clannish. Huge extensions and a whole other annex had been added to the house in order to accommodate the various branches of the family, and those daft wee dogs that all the younger women tottered about town conspicuously carrying in their designer handbags. Where were they now? Their absence made Stark suspect that the family were in defence mode, or preparing for a war.

The Matriarch, as she liked to be known, was sitting at a dining table watching a mounted TV that almost filled the wall, an unfinished plate of spag bol abandoned in front of her. She was wearing a fluorescent pink vest, showing off her huge liver spotted shoulders, which reminded Stark that she was from the class of career criminals who have timeshares in Spain that the family could decamp to in times of trouble.

"What's this all about, then?" she demanded.

"Your nephew Peter was on a trawler we were monitoring two nights ago."

"Strange career move. Can't really see him making it as a trawlerman. It's a hard life, and Pete was always … a bit soft."

"We have reason to believe that he wasn't at sea for the fishing."

"Really. What was he up to, then? A pleasure cruise?"

"You've not seen him since that night."

For an almost imperceptible moment Maddie missed the beat. "How often do you see your nephews or nieces, inspector? For that matter, how often do you see those lovely daughters of yours? Do you even know where your youngest was last night?"

It was Stark's turn to shift tone. "Knowing the whereabouts of your family isn't so hard, I guess, when most of them are behind locked doors." Maddie gripped the leg of the kitchen table with such ferocity that Gourlay thought she was about to flip the thing. "Of course, that's not fair. Must hurt when you really don't know where they are. Seeing that missing poster everywhere. What's it been? Eight months. Tragic. Although I suppose it's the risks you take being born into a family like yours. But then again, young Danny didn't get to choose which family he was born into, did he. Neither did Pete, and I wonder if you'll be seeing him again."

For a moment Gourlay was so certain Maddie was going to upend the table that she stepped back.

"What do you ken?" she growled.

"That's not really what I'm here for."

"I'm no grass."

"No one ever doubted it. But these London criminals are a different breed. They're muscling in. They're unscrupulous. It'd be in both of our interests to seriously disrupt their operations."

Maddie looked hard at PC Gourlay. "Stevie," she yelled, the grey tracksuited unit arriving with surprising speed. "You still watching that reality-TV-shite?"

A shrug like an embarrassed adolescent used to being berated.

"Take this one through with you. It's time for the adults to talk."

Gourlay glared at Stark to see if he was going to let this happen, but he barely registered her leaving the room.

"Youngsters," she heard Maddie contemptuously pronounce. "Obsessed with these reality shows. You'd think they'd get enough reality stepping out their front doors."

Maddie pulled the half-finished plate of bolognaise towards herself slurping the spaghetti into her mouth with what appeared to be a new found hunger.

She chewed before starting. "Peter got put in contact with a group who were attempting to import a significant quantity of goods into the country. They were using lads from round here and wanted to clear it with us. Obviously there were financial incentives, but it was always a high risks high yields type of opportunity." Maddie forked more spaghetti into her mouth. "In order to protect … his investment, Pete was on the boat, but something went wrong: the boys were meant to contact the various … investors, so they could collect the goods. This didnae happen. And now no one has heard from or seen Pete. Josh McCormack is dead and Malky Campbell was seized by Pete's business associates this morning … the weird thing is, he'd gone to work in the park as if there was nothing up. Johnny Campbell's vanished off the face of the earth as well."

"So Pete and or Johnny have stolen the goods. And you'd like to get your hands on them before the gangsters you've been dealing with."

"Kerrs don't steal from their own. It'll be the Campbell laddie. He was always a sly bugger." She mopped up the rest of the bolognaise sauce with a slice of garlic bread. "Now what have you got for me?"

On the way to the car, Gourlay was desperate to find out what she'd missed.

"It's Johnny Campbell we need to find. Malky too. Maddie Kerr just told me the OCG seized him at work this morning. But that doesn't add up. Why'd they need to do that if they were with him at the hospital after the trawler came in? It doesn't make sense. Still, if he's been abducted, I'll get his mum to file a missing persons. His cousin got him into this, and he's in deep. Too deep. We're at the point where he needs us more than we need him. Just hope he's bright enough to realise this."

CHAPTER TWENTY-THREE

Next evening I was summoned to Monty's. I arrived early, scanning the pub for a seat. I'd planned on a corner spot, back to the wall. But it was Tuesday - Death Metal Night. You might think that an outpost this size couldn't sustain a Death Metal Night in the middle of the week, but you've never been to this town. The place was mobbed. Underage kids with statement-making hair, bits of metal in their shocked doughy faces, stood about blinking as if they'd crawled out from under a stone and found, not sunshine, but, a whole host of other people who lived under stones. At the bar, a fat goth, whose entire get up seemed to be a reaction to her parents having named her Daisy, sucked a Bloody Mary through a straw, pouting furiously to avoid ruining her purple lipstick. Once she'd finished drinking she deigned to serve me.

A band started up in the far corner, the drums – machine-gun loud – obliterating any sound from the singer or guitarist. According to a handmade flyer on the bar, they were called Captain Wankhands and his Atomic Accordion Orgasm. Beneath a black and white photocopy of a mushroom cloud they described themselves as sounding like an elephant making love to a poodle, or Joan of Arc's last minutes. I supped my pint trying to decide if either of these comparisons did them justice. Like every band from up here, they wouldn't go anywhere. I minded Johnny once saying: *the question isn't so much does a tree falling in a forest that nobody hears really fall, as does a band playing in a pub in a small town in north east Scotland really make a noise?* The drummer, veins bulging on his shaved head and his black vest clinging to his sweaty torso, pounded the skins with the intensity of someone who knows that the world won't listen.

After twenty minutes The Viking arrived. With his dirty blonde shoulder-length hair, tattoo revealing vests and leather trousers, this was about the only place for miles in which he didn't look out of place. He creaked his neck in a way that indicated I should follow him to a table that had just been vacated. On the beer sodden surface, his huge fingers, decorated with chunky skeleton rings, kept time with the drummer in the band. Suddenly, he stopped and downed the rest of my pint.

"That your first one?" I nodded. He belched. "Antonio has got a job for you. If you do what you're telt it's a piece ay pish. Simple driving job."

"Ok."

"There's a car parked up on Fairacres Road that wants driving – a navy blue Astra, registration SD57 KGN. You're to drive straight to Northampton Service Station."

He held out his hand and I thought he wanted to shake on it till I felt the serrated edge of a car key.

"Northampton in England?"

"That'd be the one."

"Tonight?"

"You're to go straight there. You've still got the mobile we gave you? You'll get a call to tell you the exact location of the drop. If you don't hear from us, sit tight in the service station. Oh and one thing. You don't look in the boot. Don't ever look in the boot. If our associates down south think you've been in there." He made a noise like a neck breaking. "Antonio wanted me to make the point that we own you. If we say go, you go. If we say shite, you shite. Or bad things happen." And then he smiled, rubbing ringed fingers over his stubbly head. In his role of head bouncer at Enigma, I'd never seen him do more than grimace. "But he also said that you're to think of this as an initiation. Manage not to fuck up and you're in. You get me?"

"Do I pick anything up?"

"No, it's a drop off, that's all."

"I'll have to go home first. I've not got my wallet."

"No, you don't. There's petrol money in the car and enough to get you back up the road. If you've got a card on you, don't use it."

"Right."

"Drive within the speed limit, lights on, use your indicators."

"And remember to buckle up!"

"Ha. Dinna fuck up. This isna a joke and these aren't jokers."

The last part rattled in my head as I walked through the gloaming of a late summer's evening to the posh part of town. Down at the marina, bunting bedecked yachts bobbed in that low light, while on the perfectly manicured greens old ladies in white strode softly amongst the kiss of bowling balls and murmur of encouragement. A group of laughing bodies – brainiacs, who had gone to uni the previous year- walked towards me, the girls tossing manes of long hair. I stepped off the pavement for fear they might trample me underfoot. They were all wearing sandals. I was always suspicious of people who wanted to show off their feet; if they were prepared to do that, what else might they reveal.

I took a detour before reaching Fairacres Road in order to see the pebbledash bungalow with the yellow door. Relieved, I noticed the curtainless windows, the overgrown patch of grass around the front. I didn't trust Antonio, El, Souter, any of they cunts, but the moment I was back from this job I was going to demand my money. Hopefully, by then it wouldn't be too late.

On Fairacres a group of wee girls were drawing with chalk sticks on the middle of the road. Inside a dozen bay windows, TVs flickered, classical music wafted and professional people drowned the day in glasses of wine. I pressed the button on the key, and the lights on the blue Mondeo flickered to indicate it would open. I clambered in, the engine starting with a purr. The girls got up and stood at the kerb watching me, as I drove over their huge multicoloured butterfly, its wings spread out like a warning.

It wasn't until I was on the A9 that I stopped expecting to see the strobe of cold blue lights, the wrenching wail of a police car with siren lassoing around itself ready to drag us back. The car smelt of shampoo. Forecourt clean, no CDs or leaking pens. Out of a Road Atlas on the passenger's seat stuck a brown envelope containing £200 in fresh bank notes. More than enough to pay for petrol and get me back up the road. I stuffed the money in my pocket. Placing my hands on the steering wheel felt like signing a contract without getting to read the details: the car was definitely dusted down, no fingerprints but mine.

The noise started once I was out of the 50-mph speed limit. At first I told myself it was my imagination. Then during a road report I heard it again. A fat rat-a-tat-tat. I switched off the radio, heard it again and then after an interval, one more time.

The banging was sporadic, like a person beaten up or tied up or both. I tried to imagine what it would be like being locked in pitch blackness, feeling like you were falling forever, that you'd never hit the bottom. I gave myself a mental slap in the face. Chances were it was a can of de-icer rolling about in the boot. But these people had history. I thought of Pete's panicked, bloodied face as I slammed the door on him, of Johnny's reluctance to tell us where he was and The Viking's insistence that I didn't open the boot. My swollen right hand gripped the steering wheel. *How'd you get here, Malky? Driving a car that isn't yours through the night. Two bodies behind you, a possible third in the boot. Because this really isn't you. This really isn't what you wanted.*

There were no major junctions for the first twenty miles on the A9. You just hammered down as fast as you liked until you hit these identikit Highland tourist towns with their shortbread tin High Streets and wistful nostalgia for a fictitious past. I flicked the road atlas open at the page where the A9 hit the Central Belt and frayed into all the other major roads and motorways connecting millions of people in anonymous cities and towns. I'd never driven this far south, but just one turning and I'd be off the road they'd set me on. I didn't have to make the drop. I could open the boot and see what they had me carrying.

It was getting properly dark as the car drove through the Cairngorms. Lonely houses nestling in hills that melted into the night, winked their windows as blinds were pulled.

There were no services for miles and I was busting for a piss when I pulled off the road near Perth. At the pumps, I pulled the hood of my jacket over my head and stared at the ground as the petrol chugged into the tank. On my way to the cash window I opened the brown envelope, wondered why bank notes smelt dirty even when they were new. As I returned to the car I squatted down to close the petrol cap and chapped on the boot. "Hello."

Nothing. Something rolling about in the back I figured, or a person dead from suffocation, whispered a falling voice.

I wasn't meant to leave the car but went for a slash in the service station. A big trucker wearing a tartan body warmer stood uncomfortably close before letting out a torrent of pish that sounded like a bull urinating. He grinned like one of those contestants on Britain's Got Talent, who the audience has written off for being fat and ugly, but who reveal a previously hidden and extraordinary skill. I focused on shaking the last droplets into the foaming, flowing trough.

It was approaching midnight – closing time. Only a canteen with chairs on most of the tables remained open. Dehydrated Pasties and Pies sat sweating out the last of their grease in hot glass containers. I went for a couple of sandwiches. An old woman came out looking at me as if I was some sort of degenerate for wanting food at this time.

"You get a free cup of coffee with every sandwich. D'ya want three cups of coffee?" I didn't want any but the woman was already at the machine.

"Na, just the one."

I paid and found myself a seat in sight of the car. The place was deserted apart from a girl curled up in a booth, her head resting on a backpack that she was using as a pillow. A torn piece of cardboard on which she'd written LONDON, in what she would later tell me was the last of her eye-liner, was propped up beside her head.

The old woman who had served me, walked over to the girl and gently shook her awake. "We're not a hotel love … closing in 5."

The girl flicked her hair out of her eyes and turned to me.

"Malky?"

"Zoe?"

I walked over and picked up her cardboard sign.

"Hitchhiking? Are you not taking this Eighties revival thing too far?"

She shrugged. "Did you finally get my messages then?"

"What messages?"

"On your phone."

"I've lost it."

"So, what are you doing here?"

"Driving a car down south for one of my uncle's pals," I quickly improvised.

"Are you aye," Zoe grinned, not buying it for a second. "So, you'll give us a hurl then?"

"No, I canna. Really, I'm on a business trip."

"A business trip," she scoffed as if I was on the wind up. "So, you'd leave me here?" She pursed her lips. I followed her gaze towards the fat trucker, wearing the tartan body-warmer with nothing underneath but a thick rug of chest and back hair. He leered at the both of us.

"If you don't take me, he will."

With those eyes, with that mouth – it was hard to tell if she was joking.

"Fuck it. Come on then."

With a whoop, she slung the backpack over her shoulders and we walked to the car. I opened the backdoor, watched as she bent down to put the rucksack in, her jumper riding up, exposing low-slung jeans and the top of black lace knickers with pink ribbons tied round the thin band. For the first time in months I considered the possibility that there was someone bearded and benevolent up there looking out for me.

"This isn't your mum's car. You've not gone and nicked a car just to drive me London?" she asked as I accelerated down the slip road.

"Brilliant," she laughed. "You are properly mental."

"What about you?"

"My parents found pills from the Gala day in my pocket and grounded me. I'm almost eighteen! I mean, I get that they were mad with me, but I had an excuse."

"So you're running away?"

"Sort of. My sister's house sitting for a rich pal of hers from uni while she's doing an internship at a publishers. The girl's away to some Greek island with her family and they needed someone to look after their cats. So she's got this mansion in some posh part of London called Highgate with views over the city and half a dozen bedrooms. Said I should visit."

"Sweet."

"Anyway. I needed to get out of that shithole. Small town, small minds. Everyone knowing everyone's business." She rubbed the valeted interior of the car. "So, tell the truth. Did you nick this and come after me?"

"Well I think it's romantic. Probably the most romantic thing anyone's ever done for me." She pulled out her phone. "Mind if I put some music on?"

"What you got?"

"Ugh, anything. Everything." She hummed a tuneless accompaniment to Lil Peep's *Awful Things*, drumming along on her thighs.

After a bit, she pulled out some skins, rolling tobacco and a Clingfilm wrapped lump of hash. Using her lighter to soften the resin, she picked off bits of it with her long lacquered fingernails.

"Do you mind?"

"What? Am I supposed to ask permission?"

"You could at least open the window."

"At this speed?" She lit the joint and exhaled a great billow of smoke with huge satisfaction, really working the good girl gone bad look. "Apparently this stuff is laced with opium." She took another toke. "Probably bollocks. Still," she mused, "sometimes I think that getting fucked up was the one thing I was put on this planet to do." She dragged theatrically to make the point, the loosely packed joint crackling like old vinyl. "Want some?"

I was sorely tempted, but managed to paw away her offerings.

"You know, I wasn't joking back there. You really saved me. Guy I'd hitched with from outside the Port was a total creep. Had to hide in that service station's toilets." The side of my face tingled as she leant over and pecked me on the cheek. She was wearing lip-gloss, lots of it. It felt like someone touching your skin with the end of a lollipop they've been sucking for a long time. "Ha, you're a nice boy," she laughed, part sarcastic, part scolding.

She fiddled with her phone and as some other non-descript mumble rap came on, went into production mode, her face twisting in concentration like a virtuoso practising a difficult riff on a guitar.

"Making preparations for the long road ahead," she mumbled to herself.

"If you smoke all of that I'll need to put my fog lights on," I complained, but I wasn't really bothered now that we were on the M74 and heading through deepest darkest Lanarkshire.

After rolling half a dozen joints and storing them in the glove compartment, Zoe bunched her puffer coat into a pillow and rested her head against the window. She started snoozing, waking only to tell me that she couldn't sleep without the music. A couple of times, I caught her watching me through half-shuttered mascara gunged eye-lashes, but eventually she fell asleep.

Her phone, propped up in a drinks holder, buzzed again, another missed call from home.

A faint pitter-patter of rain blossomed on my windscreen and I resisted using the wiper to clear it off until I could barely see. This woke her and she muttered in a snug voice: "Raindrops at night. Aren't we lucky to be inside?" She uncurled and stretched her neck.

"Have we crossed the border?"

"Not sure."

She peered out at the darkness.

"I thought I'd remember it from all the Christmas and summer holiday trips to see my aunt and other relatives. Strangers who hugged my mum and were in a continual state of shock at how big me and my sister had grown. Boring holidays with no friends, kids that took the piss out of our Scottish accents and got us to say words like "jobbie" as if we were performing monkeys. We cheered when we crossed back into Scotland. My parents had this tape of old Scottish songs – *The Bonnie Banks of Loch Lomond, The Skye Boat Song, Wild Mountain Thyme* – that type of sentimental pish. They'd get Sophie and me to sing along as we motored back to Port Cawdor and their hated jobs."

Her phone buzzed again. "If you speak to your parents, don't mention us. No one's to know I've got this car."

By way of an answer, she sparked a joint and this time when she offered me a drag I took it.

"Do you not love those signs?" she pointed at a junction overhead saying 'THE SOUTH.' "Makes it sound like some epic voyage."

We hurtled down the M6, by-passing Preston, Manchester, Stoke on Trent, occasionally cracking open the window to let out the eye-stinging smoke, to help me see the road.

"Where are we?"

"Just north of Birmingham."

"Mm" she purred, as if I'd just told her we were just north of Bermuda. "Is there anywhere we can stop with a toilet?"

"Just passed a service station a few miles back but we'll see."

After ten minutes she squawked in a little girl's voice, "Daddy, I really need a wee wee." I pulled into a lay-by. "Got any tissues?" I made a desultory attempt to look through the empty car pockets. "Right then, I'll just drip dry." She got out and scrambled up a dark tree lined bank. I stood by the side of the car, shaking life back into my legs. Under the branches there was a rolled up carpet slumped against a tree. It was the sort of place people dumped bodies, I thought, shuddering at the image of Corky, discarded Zoe's dad had said, like a piece of rubbish. Lorries rumbled by, shaking the car and I got the fear that she could be on the phone to her parents, telling them who she was with. I went back to the motor and turned the engine on. Now was the chance. She appeared further down the lay-by looking disorientated and shielding her eyes from the headlights. It was as good a place as any. With those tight jeans and that loose mouth, she'd get a pick-up no problem. A squall of rain hit the windscreen and I looked out at the dark countryside, unmoving cows still as cardboard cut-outs. I put the gear stick back in neutral.

"Jesus. I thought you were going without me."

Rubbing her nose, she opened the glove compartment and took out the two remaining joints. She put one in my shirt pocket and said, "I think you'll need this later." The other she lit up. After a contemplative silence, she asked, "What are you thinking?"

"Nothing."

"It's strange how thoughtful people look when they tell you that. When we get rid of this car, let's hit the city. I can show you the sights."

"What do you mean, get rid of this car?" I asked, trying to look at her face while overtaking a couple of trucks.

"Well, you're not driving a stolen car into the centre of London, are you?"

"Who knows what I'm planning."

"Fine then." She French inhaled. I'd practised this trick for years and could never pull it off. "Are you planning on staying down here? I mean, I could ask my sister. She said there's loads of room."

And for a moment, I imagined it. The City vs Malky Campbell and the £100 in his pocket. It had been done before and had done in people before. I thought of Nicky and the bungalow that I still hadn't put a deposit on. Maybe — once I'd got paid for this job and set her up. With a bit more money I could sort things up north and come down here or Edinburgh once Zoe had started uni. I'd back myself to make a go of it.

"Sounds sweet."

She reached out and grabbed my hand off the gear stick. "When you didn't answer my calls and I was thumbing a lift, I thought you were just like all the other bastards. All those lovely things you'd said over the summer. All the plans we'd made – I thought for the first time, here's someone just like me. Someone who's not going to accept doing what everyone expects them to do. And when you never got back to me, well I just thought they were only words. That's all they were: words."

I tried to remember what I'd been saying, but most of the time I'd spent with her, I'd been spangled on pills. I smiled and gave her hand a squeeze. Zoe Stark didn't need anyone making plans for her. She'd her whole life mapped out. A few years from now she'd look back on this as her rebellious summer, a brief interlude that provided her with a couple of outrageous stories to shock her fellow medicine students.

As we rolled down the M1 she curled up again, her stoned-blank face dipping in and out of sleep. I drove into the car park at Northampton service station not long after five. After checking to make sure my phone was on, I let my seat go back and tried to get some sleep, but even keeping my eyes shut proved difficult. Instead, I watched Zoe. She was even prettier asleep, her nostrils flaring slightly as she took long deep breaths. At 5:30 my phone shook me awake and a man with an accent I couldn't quite place spoke.

"Malky."

"Yeah."

"You at Northampton?"

"Yep."

"Nice one. Drop off is in Stanmore at 7. We'll give you more details in an hour."

"Stanmore," I muttered straightening my seat and looking at the road atlas. As we drove out of the service station, a faint morning light caught the tinder of a distant horizon. More cars appeared on the road the closer we got to London. I'd never driven on a motorway with so many lanes and felt a growing panic at the country waking up, everyone rolling towards the city, that I was part of them, like water down a plug hole.

Looking at the sunrise, Zoe said, "School starts today."

"Not for us it doesn't."

"I couldn't take another year of it. It'd be like Groundhog day – going into Mr Fitzwilliam's English class for the fifth year in a row. Being asked to write a short essay on what you did with your summer."

"Christ. That'd make grim reading."

"Yeah, if you wrote the half of it."

As we approached Stanmore, Zoe turned on the radio, tuning in to the city's pirate radio stations, the DJs giving shout outs in a language we could barely understand.

"London," I said, guessing at what we had in our boot. "We are going to fuck you up."

At 6:30 my mobile rang and I pulled onto the hard shoulder.

"You near Stanmore?"

"Just outside."

"Be at the train station car park in thirty minutes. Park at the far end away from the cameras. Take your stuff out the car. Leave the keys in the ignition. You can get the first train into town."

I put the phone into the glove compartment, my hands shaky.

"Who was that?"

"Just a friend." I concentrated on the road.

"The conversation didn't sound very *friendly*."

"Listen, when we get into this town, I'll have to drop you off. Can't risk being seen."

"Whose phone is that?" she asked rubbing sleep out of her eye. "Are you in trouble? You sound scared."

At traffic lights on the turn-off she rested her cold little hand on top of mine as I shoogled the gear stick. I looked at her hand with rings on every finger, like a little girl trying to show off all her jewellery at once.

"Are you still on for hanging out in London? See, I don't really know anyone other than my sister and I thought, you know, it'd be fun." I concentrated on the traffic, ducked in to a parking space on the High Street.

"Sure. Meet you at ... Nelson's Column at 12?"

"You better be there."

"Just you try and stop me."

She nodded as if trying to convince herself. "You couldn't shout me a tenner? My control-freak of a dad hid my bank card when he grounded me."

I pulled a twenty from the wad and she ruffled the hair on the back of my head. "You'll do." She got her bag out the car and daundered down the High Street, no idea where she was, or where she was going. A bin lorry tooted as it went past and she gave them the finger.

I arrived at the station ten minutes early. The car park was massive. Rush hour cars already filled the parking bays nearest the platforms. I drove past them, past the mounted CCTV cameras and onto the dusty waste ground at the far end.

I tapped a tattoo on the steering wheel, adrenaline fizzing through me. I remembered that awful crack The Viking had made with his neck after warning me about their *associates* down south. Associates! A couple of months ago, I'd have taken the piss out of this cardboard gangster talk. But I'd seen enough to know that these people didn't fuck about. When you were that slick, you could call each other what you liked. After ten minutes, a car parked a few slots away from mine. The passenger's window cracked open a few inches and a man who looked like Antonio's double nodded at me. The door opened and a big bruiser in his thirties wearing a bomber jacket and hoodie got out. I unbuckled and stood on jittery, skittery legs, watching his hands not his eyes.

The driver joined us. They could be related, the way they looked, the way they dressed. "Well?" said the other man, "Any problems?"

"No, none." He peered at me like he couldn't understand my accent. "Absolutely, no problems at all."

"You've not looked in the boot?" I shook my head. "No, I can see you've not looked in the boot. Good. Do you not have a train to catch?"

"Yeah, of course." I turned, checked that they really meant me to go, that I was simply going to be allowed to walk away from this.

"Well, fuck off then."

I hooked my thumbs in my pockets, attempted to swagger as if sauntering away from a pair of heavies was something I did every day. A bang cracked the morning air and I almost shat myself. Twisting round I saw they'd just slammed the boot and were standing laughing at me. Fuckers, I thought, crossing the gravel my whole body shaking.

I walked the path to the platform, no different to anyone else. It was obviously going to be a scorcher: the air warm and heavy in a way it never was so early in the morning in Scotland. The walkway was surrounded by overgrown bushes with their foliage of crisp packets and coke cans and these exotic flowers splayed pink and white, bursting ripe with life, their last days of summer breath sweet as a drunk girl's mouth. Honeysuckle. I breathed it in and there, amongst that foreign smell, caught up by an ankle high breeze brought about as a train wheezed into the station, a faint hint of cat's piss. A commuter jogged past and I stood there taking deep heady breaths, watching the carousel of sweet wrappers spin in the wind. Honeysuckle and cat's piss, I thought. This is what it means to be alive.

On the platform city workers stood staring straight ahead. And I was alive! They were still alive too, but barely knew it. Once I was back in Scotland, Souter or the Viking would sort me out for this. I'd get Nicky that flat, make things right there. She'd stop looking at me like I was the kid cousin then. A station attendant slalomed around legs, chasing the occasional piece of litter, never once looking above waist height. And then there was Zoe, waiting for me in London. I was a man with choices. With my finger, I traced my route to Charing Cross, following the bright lines and famous names on the Underground map. There was a sign saying TFL – EVERY JOURNEY MATTERS. Not mine I thought. My plan was to fanny about on the trains, jumping off at any station whose name appeared in a song, until it was time to meet Zoe. Antonio, the Kerrs, all those wankers who thought they owned me were at the other end of the country. My phone buzzed in my pocket.

GLASGOW – BUCHANAN STREET BUS STATION. STANCE 22. 6PM TONIGHT. TAKE THE TRAIN FROM EUSTON. DON'T TAKE CHANCES.

For a moment, quick as a muscle twitch, I thought about chucking it. 6pm. There was no chance I could meet Zoe at Nelson's Column for 12 and still make it up to Glasgow for six. There was no chance I was going to see any of London. I wondered how long she'd wait and what she would make of my no-show.

A train terminated unloading a few night workers from the city. The suits filed on and found their place. We sat on seats that were patterned like an enormous game of Tetris. And suddenly I was one of them: controlled, moved to where I was needed, where I could fill a gap. The only difference was that if I didn't meet my deadlines, I was actually dead.

The suits stared at the floor or their mobiles. I'd read about this – the lack of eye-contact on the commute, the angry rustle of territorial newspapers. And of course, I was happy to keep my head down, but I couldn't stop myself from watching their ghost reflections while pretending to read adverts. With their expensive suits, slicked back hair and eyes screwed tight, they looked like a race of people who were flying into the future at enormous speeds, which was ironic given that the train was delayed for thirty minutes outside Wembley. A suicide on the line someone speculated. Bloody inconsiderate during the rush hour another said. Everyone sat holding their briefcases on their laps and looking important. At Kilburn, I gave my seat up to an old lady who thanked me in far too loud a voice. But nobody looked up. At the end of the journey, I could safely say that not one of the passengers who'd sat opposite me for the last hour would have been able to pick me out from an identity parade. London, I thought, must be a great city for a criminal.

I exited at Baker Street, the statue of Sherlock Holmes studying the commuters with his bronze blank eyes. On a back street near Euston a van was unloading boxes of frozen fish. A man carried a box of cod into a fancy restaurant, owned no doubt by some bugger who'd make far more money from the fish than the men who'd risked their lives catching them. I elbowed my way against the tide of commuters flowing from Euston station. Feeling out of place in this congested and contested space, I stood looking at a list of cities I'd never visited: Manchester, Liverpool, Birmingham. All the places I could go where no one would know my name. The queue edged me to the ticket machine and I dumbly fed notes into its mouth. My fingers found Glasgow, confirmed the choice. The machine spat out my ticket. I walked towards the trains, looking at the enormous departures board, waiting to be told where to go.

CHAPTER TWENTY-FOUR

At Buchanan Bus Station, the malfunctioning automatic doors snapped shut on tired mums with buggies, pensioners laden with shopping, and a man begging enough change for a single to Elderslie with such intensity you'd have thought it was El Dorado.

I was sitting next to a bronze life size statue of a couple kissing, the man holding a bunch of flowers as if he knew what to do with them, the girl her left foot raised behind her as she leant into him. It made me wonder how long Zoe had waited and, for the hundredth time, I cursed myself for not having taken her number. Real life people started spilling out of the London Mega Bus. I sifted through the passengers as they drifted by with barely a glance.

There weren't many people waiting. A couple hugged awkwardly and spoke in hushed tones as if they thought the world was listening. Bags bustled out into the city, suitcases rolled off with the night. From this angle I could see the tangle of footprints they'd left on the recently mopped floor. I tried to catch the cleaning woman's eye but she was standing sentry-still, chin propped up on the handle of her mop. A shabby pigeon hobbled across her newly cleaned floor, drawing a wing over its face, like a person going to court trying to hide behind a blanket.

A pair of policemen walked by, tailing a squad of boys who were loudly stubbing out words on the night. As my eyes followed them out of the station, I noticed a mop of black hair, sunken eyes peering through his fringe. He was pretending to read a timetable, but in reality was checking me out

Johnny walked towards me, eyes as friendly as ball-bearings. It was only three days since I'd seen him, but I still wanted to jump up and hug the mad bastard.

"Sit still," he hissed, sitting next to me. "We're being watched."

"How? Where?"

"Dinna ken, but I can feel it. Don't look around."

"I'm not," I complained. "I thought you were dead."

"Aye, sorry about that." He scratched his stubbly chin. "It was necessary."

I felt myself seethe.

"Necessary?"

He nervously tapped his smart pointy shoes and out of the corner of my eye I took in the new jeans and trench coat. "Necessary for who?"

"Shh now. We're being watched. It needs to look like we've never met."

For a second I was speechless.

"Shh now? They killed Peter Kerr."

"Collateral damage," he shrugged.

"They put him in the boot of a car and made me push it into the lake at Ardleigh quarry."

"Pete was a bad bastard. Think he wouldn't have done the same to you? Mind on the cinder pitches when we were weans and he poured lighter fluid over that hedgehog we were going to take home? If you're feeling sorry for him, think of him booting that burning hedgehog about singing Great Balls of Fire."

I'd more or less managed to forget that particular heart-warming memory: the smell of singed pines, the noise the hedgehog made, like the whine of damp driftwood on a bonfire.

"It's not him I'm feeling sorry for; they filmed me doing it. I make one wrong move, and they send that video to the Matriarch."

"Well don't make any wrong moves."

"Corky. Did you hear what happened to Corky? There's no way that's a coincidence."

Johnny clenched his jaws so tight that the muscles looked like they might burst through his face. "I'd heard he was dead."

"He was found dumped by the old railway line. A needle hanging out of his arm. They'd taken my mobile, so could easily have set him up."

For a moment his face struggled to control itself. "They promised me that you and Corky wouldn't be touched. I made them promise. And I didnae ken they'd get you to do Pete. But Corky ... there'll be a reckoning for that. We'll make them pay."

"A reckoning? Have you seen the people we're dealing with? We're Campbells, not Corleones."

My hands gripped the metal bench in anger. Johnny slid his fingers between the knuckles of my hand and as he squeezed, my heart tolled in my throat. I didn't breathe for what seemed like minutes, but I didn't need to breathe.

"I didn't know if you'd forgive me for leaving you like that."

"You did what you had to."

He sat rocking himself like a wild animal in a zoo.

"The rucksack," he said, snapping out of it. He swung the bag from his shoulder and placed it on the ground between us. "You're to take it up the road. Don't open it, don't let it out of your sight."

I unclenched my hand, straightening out my cramped fingers the way you do after an exam. "You're not coming?"

"I'm to stay here. Those are the orders. And for now we follow their orders, act like everything's ok. But when we hit them, they'll fucking know about it. Listen, we've been here too long. You have to take the train. Don't know why it has to be the train, but Antonio insisted. Give me a couple of minutes before you move."

"I've not got enough money for the fare."

He pulled out a wallet, which held a pretty healthy wad and slipped a couple of twenties into the rucksack's pocket.

"More."

"More?"

"I've got fuck all out of this so far." He stuffed a few more notes into the bag. "Is that it?"

"Souter will sort you out when the time's right. Antonio wants you on the ground, going about life like normal, grafting away. He's paranoid you'll start flashing the cash about. The moment you do that it becomes obvious to the Kerrs that you were in on it."

"Why can't I get out of Port Cawdor?"

"He wants you there," Johnny said. "They need bodies they can trust on the streets. The last couple of kids they've sent up haven't lasted … you can't exactly send black kids talking like they're Stormzy up to the middle of nowhere and expect them not to get nicked. Besides. Once everything's settled, we'll become useful. We've proven our trawler provides a smuggling route into the country."

"The only way that works is if it's in regular use." Johnny shrugged as if to say that this wasn't up for debate. "So you're coming back, I mean eventually, to run the boat and that?"

He shrugged again, only this time in a way that said he didn't know. But I kent him better than that.

"So, I'm going to end up at sea for weeks on end while you rake it in down here?"

"I had to get out. My face doesn't fit up there. Besides, I've been working on that trawler for four years. It's your turn."

"How much did you get?"

"Two grand."

"Two grand? That's a joke." I thought of Corky. "Was it worth it?"

He frowned, putting a great deal of effort into showing that he couldn't give a solitary fuck for my opinion. "There'll be more where that came from."

"I need it now."

"Why?"

"For Nicky. She's about to pop. We need to get her out of that squat."

Johnny laughed. "Christ, she's really done a job on you. Kent you were intae her but this is ridiculous."

"She's pregnant. You used to be with her. There are … responsibilities."

"Responsibilities," he looked at me like I was on the wind-up. "That's a fucking laugh. I can guarantee you one thing - that baby has fuck all to do with me." As I protested, he looked at me as if I was a fucking joke. "Did you never get it? Me and Nicky - we were never like that. I thought you of all people understood that."

He stood up, turned on the heel of his leather soled shoes and strutted out of the station. I didn't know if I believed him. Couldn't believe I'd been so blind. The make-up, the androgyny, the camping about, I'd always thought it was a Birthday Party thing, a David Bowie thing. It had always seemed like such a perfect provocation to Joe and all the macho trawlermen, whose greatest displays of public emotion were reserved for discussing offside decisions in football matches that happened hundreds of miles from Port Cawdor. I thought about chasing after him, tried to detect whether anyone had really been watching us, but amidst the bustle of the bus station his movements were lost and I was left with another bag. I didn't touch it. Instead, I punched a made up number into the burner phone, paced angrily as it bleeped, keeping my eyes on the rucksack. Half-confident that no one was about to pounce I slung the bag over my shoulder and made my move. The night's air frisked me as I walked out. I felt my shoulders hunch up, as my body made itself as small a target as possible. I passed a sculpture of a clock held up by two metal legs. Long, frozen, still, steel. It looked as if it was running. I quickened my stride and side-stepped groups and couples coming out of the multiplex. Lines of civilians descended on escalators behind glass windows, their heads full of colour and excitement; they looked like things being processed in a factory.

I cut down Sauchiehall Street, walked round a pavement artist whose huge chalk drawn mural of Celtic players floating in space and playing football with the planets was being smudged by the rain; dodged a couple of girls handing out fliers; ignored the Chinese couple trying to sell flashing jewellery. At the top of Buchanan Street, the statue of Donald Dewar looked down on us all, his broken glasses hanging from his face like those of a bullied child.

I was in luck: the platform number for the Inverness train was already flashing. Just before we started moving, an old drunk stumbled into my carriage. He walked as though stepping over unseen hurdles, holding onto headrests as if the floor might suddenly jump up and greet him. Despite the carriage being deserted he sat opposite me, his mouth opening and closing like a man ducking for apples.

I fished out *Great Expectations* from the pocket of my army surplus jacket. The old fella was aware of me but didn't dare look. He started placing all his possessions on the table: wallet, keys, packet of polos. He touched each object then checked it was still there with an alcoholic's mistrust of the inanimate.

The train rolled past the dark shapes of abandoned railway buildings, lines that were used for sleeping trains, the crazy places that graffiti artists had gone to get their words seen. I put my ticket back in my pocket and felt the labeless bottle of pills Johnny had given me on the boat. Nicky and Johnny. Johnny and Nicky. For years I'd thought of them as a proper couple, but it was all a smokescreen. I shivered, feeling totally enervated as the last of the adrenaline I'd been living off ebbed from my muscles. But I was still way too wired to sleep, so I unscrewed the bottle and popped a couple of pills. The old fella looked at me and I turned a page of my book, pretending to be lost in it.

"What you reading?" I held the book up but he didn't even look at the cover. "What you reading?"

"*Great Expectations*," I replied, hoping that would shut the illiterate drunk the fuck up.

The old man beamed his carefree smile and said, "That's a fucking laugh."

He chuckled to himself and pulled out a book with a blank cover. He seemed to shape his lips round words, chewed and rolled them about his mouth. I leant over to get a glimpse of the text but instead was faced with a page covered in Braille.

I wanted to lean across and close his eyelids, like a priest with a dead man. I wanted to know what shape my face was in his head. But the pills had done something to my head which felt like a balloon lost at a fairground and it was my own eyes that were shutting, as my body pressed against the seat like it was on the sticky wall at the shows: that ride where you spin round and round and gravity presses you against the sides. Before slipping into the treacle of sleep, I undid my belt, put the strap of the rucksack through it before buckling up again.

During the three hour journey, I woke once out of a dream in which I was in one of the rowing boats from the park, but it wasn't the boating pond. It wasn't a pond at all. Water in all directions and no oars, no tide, no motion. I'd lost something in the water and as I stared into its depths some deep-water beast loomed towards me. As it neared the surface, its hands reached out above its head, fingers stretched out as if it would grab me and drag me back under.

Waking, I wiped at my clammy forehead and stared out of the window, trying to recognise some features in the darkening land. As the train slowed to cross a bridge, I realised we were going over the River Findhorn. In the gloaming, one loan fly fisher cast his line in a graceful, fluid motion. Silhouetted in the sunset, he reminded me of Joe. He'd dragged me along with him a couple of times seen as Johnny had made it abundantly clear that standing up to his thighs in icy water while being devoured by midges wasn't how he'd be spending his evenings. I mind standing in the snow melt water, watching the lights of the train carriages flicker by, wishing I was on them. Fly fishing was not a popular pursuit for trawlermen, but Joe took a bizarre delight in the skill needed to land one fish, when just days earlier he'd brought in hundreds of kilos of them. Salmon fascinated him. Not long before the accident, I remembered him holding up a salmon that'd been part of a haul we'd brought in while in the Norwegian Sea. "This," he'd said, "could have been spawned in a river near home. It's like us. It travels hundreds of miles from where it was born, but it'll make its way back to the same river, the same stretch of water. It'll battle tides and jump waterfalls to get home. Then it'll spawn and die." "But this one won't," I'd reminded him, clumsily gutting it with my knife. "No," he'd said, making an odd face, "it won't." Two days later we threw his body into the sea. But still he found his way back.

I sunk back under for the final miles of the journey. When I woke, the blind man was mapping my face. "You alright son?" I pushed his hands away. "Sorry son, we've terminated."

"I'm ok," I said, staggering off the train like I was climbing stairs in the dark and kept taking that one extra imagined step. The blind man shouted after me but his voice sounded like people talking in a lift you've only just missed.

Outside the station a girl wearing Nicky's fake fur jacket, waited at the traffic lights. I shouted on her and she turned. She had Nicky's face, Nicky's hair but a stranger's eyes. The lights turned green and the girl's boyfriend wrapped a protective arm around her. Nicky. I felt suddenly terrified for her. In that squat, behind those bolted doors. She could have been dead for days.

There hadn't been a train station in Port Cawdor since the Beeching Cuts, which, combined with the advent of cheap foreign holidays had destroyed the town as a tourist destination, thus saving generations of Scots from freezing their nuts off in the North Sea. To get there at this time of night I needed a taxi and the rank was typically deserted. Bored, I found the joint Zoe had rolled and seeing as there was no one about sparked up. Although, it had been too loosely rolled and burnt quickly, it still packed a punch. I wondered what she was doing. Her story about the cannabis being laced with opium possibly had some substance because the smoke or Johnny's pills did something funny to my legs and, as I attempted to explain to the taxi driver where I wanted to be taken, it became evident it'd also done a job on my ability to form consonants. But the driver was used to translating such language and eventually he understood me. We were five miles from town when the mobile buzzed.

GO STRAIGHT TO THE OLD ICE CREAM SHOP. KNOCK FOUR TIMES ON THE SIDE DOOR. MAKE SURE YOU'RE NOT FOLLOWED.

I stared hatefully at the message. The capital letters pissed me off – considering who was sending the messages, they were hardly necessary. I got dropped off on The Front, which, now that summer was over, was dead. I moved a couple of wheelie bins and snuck up the side passage, knocking four times as instructed. Souter cracked the door open an inch, half his cratered face peering out.

"You alone?"

"Aye."

"You werenae followed?"

"No."

He hustled us in to the backroom, locking the door behind me before flopping in an incongruously expensive looking leather swivel chair, which wouldn't have looked out of place in a multinational's boardroom. I handed him the rucksack, and he pulled out a briefcase. Turning his back to me, he fiddled with the dials on a safe box that was screwed into the floor and deposited the briefcase. Spinning round on his chair, he caught me gawping at the filing cabinets and desk.

"Like my new office?" He laughed, showing his shit-eating teeth. "I used to love this ice cream shop. Vanilla and raspberry sauce. Bloody brilliant. Gonna get it opened in a few weeks. Not the best time of year for opening an ice cream shop, but it'll work as a front. Pay you in ice cream."

"Aye, very funny. Can I get my cut?"

He screwed up his nose as if I'd just burped in his face.

"Not until Antonio says."

"But I've done everything you asked."

"Asked? We didnae ask."

He flicked his chunky gold braceletted wrist as if waving off some midges and said: "You'll get your money in good time."

"I'm owed it. I need it."

He gestured for me to pipe down. "Keep your heid, wee man." The warning not solely suggesting that he wanted me to simmer down.

"By the end of the week, or else."

"Or else? Just remember who you're talking to. Away home to your mammie, son. She'll have been driven daft with you disappearing like that. Especially with everything else going on." He gave me a significant look. "And dinna look so greetin faced. You've got a future. There's plenty of jobs that'll be needing doing. We just don't want you flashing the cash around town. Not with the Kerrs and that police detective still sniffing around."

So I staggered into the dark empty-handed, shifting the sentry-like wheelie bins back into their positions at the mouth of the close.

I took the back streets through town – the idea of getting jumped by the Kerrs in this state didn't bare thinking about. I hoped my mum would be in bed, but she was up at the door before I could sneak in.

"And where have you been?" I brushed past her and mounted the stairs, but climbing them felt like running up a sand dune in a pair of boots. "What have you done to yourself? What's wrong with you son? Why are you like this?" I continued climbing the stairs on all fours now and sought refuge in my bedroom but she followed me in. "What have I done to deserve a son like you? Tell me that and I'll leave you in peace." I burrowed into my bed, wrapping a pillow around my head. She was silent for a minute, observing me, no doubt raging. But her voice when she spoke was calmer.

"I ken you've had a hard time this summer with what happened to Joe and then the McCormack laddie, but you can't go off like that. I'm only angry because I love you." I squeezed the pillow tighter until I could hardly hear her. "Duffy called. Today was meant to be your last shift in the park. I told him you were upset about the boy that died."

"Thanks."

"He said it was alright. Duffy understands. A vacancy on one of the lawnmower teams has come up. He says you should take the rest of the week off and start on Monday."

"You're best working. It'll take your mind of things. Save you from moping around here, or hanging around with the wrong crowd.

I must have groaned or grunted or let out some sort of signal.

"Well, I'll let you sleep. You must be tired."

And she was right. I'd never been so beat in my life.

CHAPTER TWENTY-FIVE

The train station toilets were surprisingly clean. Pale patches remained on the wooden door where people had kicked the locks in and the walls were covered in anatomically exaggerated sketches of naked women, sectarian threats, attempts at acquiring the services of underage boys and what Jim Stark hoped were implausible claims about cock sizes.

He sat on the lid of the toilet, imagining this cubicle being sent into space on one of those Beagle probes as a sample of modern day Scottish men's interests. Christ knew what the aliens would make of it.

The Inspector had come straight from a meeting with Chief Superintendent Jackson. His GP had declared him fit to work, and with a major team investigating county line activities, the Joe Campbell case still open and the force keeping 'an open mind' about Josh McCormack's death, Stark was certain he'd be welcomed back with open arms. Under a guise of caring about his well-being, Jackson had suggested that neither of the serious crime teams required his services. Indeed, he'd suggested that an opportunity had become available, working as a Wildlife Crime Liaison Officer. A what? Stark had never heard of such a role. Twenty-five years in the service, fifteen in specialist crime squads in the North East division, and they offered him this. His face must have registered his incomprehension because Jackson, with a barely concealed smirk, started to explain that it would involve investigations into the illegal persecution of badgers, poaching, and animal neglect. It'd mean a move of course, closer to the huge nature reserves in the Grampians, and with it a new start: a home in a community where Zoe and Sophie wouldn't always be identified as the policeman's daughter. But Linda would hate it. Even further from civilization would be the way she'd see it.

Stark adjusted his face and unlocked the door. The Aberdeen train was running twenty minutes late, so he went for a coffee. Behind the counter, the barista watched a TV showing a mute journalist interviewing a mute politician, while his hands continued drying a glass that was probably dry half an hour ago.

"A cappuccino, please."

As the man dragged his attention away from the silent TV interview, Stark looked at a poster of a tropical island bearing the message *Destination is unimportant – it is the journey that counts.* Scrawled on the chalk board by the bar were the more urgent words: *Last chance to buy a carryout before your train.*

Zoe had lasted a week in the capital before Sophie, tired of lending her money, asked if they could send her a train ticket back up the road. They'd spoken on the phone and Zoe had been happy to do just that. She'd had her adventure, made her point. There was a fortnight until freshers week, and she'd need to pack her stuff, say her goodbyes. Stark was under strict instructions not to start any unpleasantness.

The Barista had been joined by a severe looking young woman, the two of them lobbing looks at a dreaming duffle coat bunched up in a booth. Encouraged by his co-worker, the barista puffed up his chest and marched across the café to deal with things.

"Excuse me, but you canna sleep here."

The Barista gave a *Will you look at the state of that* shake of his head and repeated, "Excuse me," like he was carrying a tray of expensive drinks through a crowd. He switched tone and accent. "Hoy pal, get up." A tufty brown head appeared, followed by eyelashes, blinking in the bleary light. He tried to smile but someone had recently burst his lip and it changed into a grimace.

"Be gone in a bit. Just need mair…" He flapped his hand, like some sort of sign language, the last word too painful for him. The hood of the duffle coat was pulled back over his head, as if it was all the protection he needed from the world.

"What planet you on son? Canna sleep here and that's that." The barista anxiously wrapped the tea towel around his hand, boxing glove style. "I'm calling the police," he looked at Stark for approval.

The Detective supped the suds at the bottom of his cup and wearily got up.

Up close the boy stank, like opening a lunchbox forgotten about at the bottom of a bag. He was out cold so Stark shook him the way soldiers do in films when their buddies been hit and they're angry at them for dying. The boy gagged, and while wheezing spat out a tooth. It rattled on the cold tile floor and Stark picked it up and pressed it gently into his hard calloused palm. A working hand. A trawlerman or labourer, reduced to a wreck. Somebody's brother, somebody's son.

"Keep it. A dentist could put it back."

But no one was going to put any of him back together again.

The lad squeezed his tongue through the square bloody gap before throwing the tooth across the bar's tiled floor, where it bounced like a bone dice. The boy burrowed back into his hood, freezing Stark with his frosted eyes, the irises shatter-proof glass through which pupil sized holes has been shot.

"Need to get the number 66," he repeated, like some special needs child rehearsing the one line they'd been given in a school play.

His eyes rolled back into his head, a parody of the fruit machine in the corner. Stark imagined them stopping and there being a lemon and strawberry where his eyes had been.

"Call an ambulance as well. Boy's out his skull."

Stark laid the boy out in the recovery position. He was sick of seeing young bodies sprawled out like they'd been hit by a bus. To hell with counting badgers. There was unfinished business here.

PCs Carmichael and Gourlay arrived with surprising speed.

"All yours."

As Carmichael attempted to communicate with the semi-comatose boy, Stark gestured to Gourlay. "Any developments?"

"No one's seen Johnny Campbell, Peter Kerr or anyone linked to the London OCG. There's a total drugs drought as well."

This would normally be good news, but all it meant to Stark was that the case had gone cold and with it his last chance of avoiding a transfer.

"When'll you be back, Sir?"

Stark winced. "I'll be back tomorrow, but Jackson wants me to become a Wildlife Crime Liaison Officer."

"What's that, like? Counting cows and chasing poachers?"

"Pretty much. I'd be based near the Cairngorms. It'd keep me out of trouble."

Gourlay looked sorry for him, and Stark realised this was how younger officers, doing proper police work, would see him from now on.

"Malky Campbell is still around. He's working on one of the council's lawn mower teams. If anyone's going to give us intel on what's going on around here, it's him."

Stark noticed a flurry of activity in the station. "The Aberdeen train's in. I'm picking up my daughter."

"Sir, maybe it's not my place to say, but you were onto something. Don't give up now."

Gourlay blushed, adjusted the bowler that still sat uncomfortably low on her head. With her baggy black trousers and oversized hi-vis jacket, she looked like a wee girl in borrowed clothes, but the intensity in her stare reminded him of the fanatical drive he'd seen in every decent cop he'd worked with.

"You'll do PC Gourlay. I can see you becoming a detective one of these days."

PC Carmichael lumbered up from the sprawled body on the café floor.

"The wanderer returns," he said looking at the passengers passing through the ticket gates.

Stark could smile now. Six nights ago, sitting up with Linda, trying to explain that the police wouldn't do anything until she'd been gone 24 hours, things had been very different. He'd put a brave face on it: telling his wife she'd be out with friends. But there'd been enough people going missing, and he wasn't sure if the old rules about leaving policemen's families out of it applied.

He forced a *welcome home* smile onto his face as his daughter struggled to shoulder a rucksack and to conceal an expression that said *this is what you get for not giving me the money to go inter-railing.*

On the drive home, she nattered on about the inconsiderate behaviour of other travellers on the train. Stark kept his eyes on the road and made sympathetic sounds when it seemed expedient to do so, but he wasn't thinking about his daughter. His head was buzzing with questions about Malky Campbell — the only person from that ill-fated trip who was still around. If he was working on the lawnmowers then he hadn't made any money. If that was the case he'd be angry. He'd be desperate. It gave Stark one last chance.

Zoe had stopped talking and Stark hadn't heard the last thing she'd said. There was an uneasy silence.

"How'd you get down to London, anyway? Can't have been easy without any cash."

"Well," Zoe said, sounding pleased with herself. "That was a bit of a mission. Promise you won't be angry?"

Stark silently acquiesced.

"Well, I totally fluked it. Thought I was going to have to hitch-hike the whole way down when Malky Campbell showed up like a knight in a shiny shell-suit."

She laughed at her own wit, but Stark didn't. Trying to remain calm, he negotiated a treacherous section of The Bends.

"I didn't know you two were still pals."

"Well we're not really, but I've been seeing a bit of him over the summer."

Which bit Stark stopped himself saying. He fiddled with the radio, tuning into a jingle for Waves FM.

"But you must be pretty close if he drove you all the way to London?"

"Suppose."

The winding road wasn't the only thing Stark needed to be careful with. Too interrogatory and she'd clam up until they got home and she could tell Linda how he'd been grilling her from the moment she got off the train.

"In his mum's car?"

Zoe hesitated before saying, "Yeah, I guess so. I mean he doesn't have his own car, so it must have been."

Stark's heartbeat accelerated as he slowed the car. Ten minutes until they were home. Ten minutes to decide whether he was more interested in being a detective or a dad. Clunking down the gears, his mind sped through feverish equations with too many variables. He weighed up the damage that testifying in court could do to his daughter's prospect against the possibility she might have the information that could save a boy with no future.

"What kind of car was it?"

"What?"

"Colour, make, hatchback or estate?"

"I don't know anything about cars."

"You can recognise colours, though."

"I don't notice things like that."

"Did it have five doors or three?"

"It had four."

"And the boot, presumably. Where'd you put your rucksack?"

"On the backseat."

"So, you opened one of the rear passenger doors and put your rucksack on the seat, right?"

Zoe shrugged, eyes fixed on the back streets of Port Cawdor that didn't lead to their house. Stark parked outside Beth Campbell's place.

"Do you see the car that you spent, what, 8 or 9 hours in?"

"I mean, it couldn't be that silver one, because it only has front doors."

"No.

"Well, that's Beth Campbell's car."

Breathing like a man coming up for air, Stark turned off the engine.

"Is he in trouble?"

"Why'd you ask?"

Zoe knitted her fingers. "He'd a phone that wasn't his. An old fashioned thing. Someone called him on it and suddenly he had to drop me off in Watford. He had to take the car to whoever called. He was scared." She unravelled her fingers. Stared at the nails she'd done on the journey up. "He was meant to meet me in London but didn't show."

"This doesn't leave the car," Stark warned. "Malcolm Campbell is back in Port Cawdor, but he's in deep trouble. He's been used by violent criminals to smuggle drugs into the country. The car you were in was moving those drugs down to London. If I can get to him, I can get him out. But he's not helping himself."

Zoe stared pleating her fingers again.

"I've known him since he was a wee boy growing up without his dad's around. He's still a wee boy as far as I'm concerned. But the law won't see it that way and neither will the people he's involved with. Tell me where he dropped the car and it might give me enough to pressure him into testifying."

"He won't get in trouble?"

"It's for his own good. You've no idea how much it'd be for his own good."

"What about me? I didn't know anything about this. Like, maybe I thought he'd borrowed someone's car to help me out, but I didn't know he was into anything like this."

"I'll try and keep you out of it."

Zoe closed her eyes. "Stanmore train station car park about 7am. It was a navy blue car the same as Mr McWhirter's across the road."

"Well done."

His daughter glared at him with that mixture of resentment and relief he saw on the faces of strangers whose secrets he'd unpicked.

CHAPTER TWENTY-SIX

After my random as fuck approach to working as a parkie, I was surprised the Lands Service and Burial Grounds Department were offering me a job as a seasonal gardener, but free fish suppers are a powerful bargaining tool. Duffy talked to me as a potential protégé, which was a good thing seen as I'd need a reference from him if I was ever going to get that bungalow for Nicky. The team I was put in were the same crowd I'd shared the shed with in the park. Most of them had been doing the same job for years. Twenty two of them, as Gav liked to remind us, and not a single day off sick. This in my opinion was nothing to be proud of. As I once again pulled on the ankle-wrecking steel toe capped boots, I told myself I only needed to stick this for the time it took the Kerrs to believe I had nothing to do with the disappearance of Pete and their drugs. I'd hold out for a few weeks at least. By then Antonio would have paid up and Nicky would be about to pop. Even this late in the day, if I could set her up in that bungalow and help sort her life out, she might get to keep the baby.

At the end of my first week cutting grass, I walked into the town to catch my bus. The perspex covering the timetables had all been melted making them unreadable and because we finished early on a Friday I didna ken how long I'd have to wait. It was at this moment that Nicky appeared, fiddling with cold hands at her little girl's purse.

"It's like seeing a ghost." I said. "Where have you been?"

"At my dad's."

She sniffed, looking like death only slightly warmed up.

Nicky's dad lived in a gamekeeper's lodge way out on the MacDougal estate. Since her mum had left, Nicky had spent most of her teens living at Tam and Aunt Mary's seen as she was always getting kicked out of home or doing a runner. Her dad was a weirdo: a poacher turned gamekeeper, who still did a fair amount of poaching. A nocturnal animal, he loved nothing more than spending a night in a ditch staking out some beast. He'd been in the papers a couple of times for setting illegal leg-hold traps, one of which had badly injured a local man. He was not popular. I'd been to The Lodge once with Nicky and Johnny in an ill-conceived attempt to burglarise the place. As Nicky kent where her dad left a spare key, we'd broken in no problem. The house stank of wet tweed and was filled with taxidermy: pheasants, squirrels and a golden eagle strung up so it hovered massively above the sitting room. As Johnny and Nicky rifled through drawers, I tried to move to a part of the room where it felt like the creatures weren't watching me. I was certain they'd report our movements back to Mr Skelton. I'd made a mental note never again to commit a burglary after spending the day smoking blow. On the mantelpiece were school photos of Nicky up until the age of about fourteen and one unframed and crumpled photo of a woman, who, with her angular good-looks and startled eyes, was obviously Nicky's mum – a woman my mum had described as "restless and let's leave it at that." On their way out, Nicky had snatched the photos of herself from the mantelpiece. "Fucked up auld cunt," she'd muttered stuffing them in her coat. She left the photo of her mum. At the time, I'd thought she was only interested in removing the photos in order to sell on the frames. Looking back I wasn't so sure.

Months later Johnny and Nicky went back and stole one of Mr Skelton's shotguns in order to pay a debt that was owed to Stevie Kerr. As a consequence of this, Skelton had taken out a restraining order, barring his daughter from going within a mile of the place – "like I'd fucking want to" she'd replied, lapping up the attention that came with such a ban.

"Why'd he let you back?"

"He didn't. Fucked up old cunt fell out a tree. Apparently checking on fledglings – at least that was his story. Knowing him, he was probably poisoning them or stealing eggs."

"And you've been there all summer?"

"He got out of hospital two weeks ago. Flung me out. Said he couldn't stand the sight of me – the state I was in."

I wanted to ask about the baby but with the big coat wrapped round her, it was difficult to know if she was still pregnant. "Are you alright? You look terrible."

"Ta," she answered with a droll smile. "I'm just fine and dandy. You won't believe me, but I managed to get clean when I was at The Lodge. Went for big walks by the river. Got back in touch with nature," she snorted as if she couldn't quite believe the words. "I was gonnae go to the GP, get a check-up and that. Things fell apart when I came back here though … I've been trying to call but your phone's always off."

"Well I've been knocking on your door and messaging you all summer. I didn't give up on you."

She sniffled, rubbed the pink rim of her nostrils with the back of her hand. "Chucked my mobile in the sea, didn't I. Thought, if I'm gonnae make a clean break, I'm gonnae have to cut myself off from the lot of them. But I've tried to get hold of you since I've been back. Even hauled myself up to your house – eight months pregnant and wearing a baseball cap and sunglasses like some disgraced celebrity. Your mum took one look and telt me where to go. She said fallen lassies like me used to ken what to do with themselves when they were that far gone." Her lips smirked, but her eyes looked like she was about to cry. "She didn't tell you I'd been round?"

"No. I didn't think she would. Malky there's something you need to know."

She reached out her hand, bony fingers perched lightly on my folded arms. She tried to flash those green eyes that had once been so shockingly bright but were now the colour of a stagnant, algae covered pond. She sniffled and this time wiped her nose on the cuff of her mansized sweatshirt that was already sticky with slug- like trails of snot. She looked like someone with bad hay fever, but I kent that wasn't Nicky's problem. And suddenly I didn't want to hear what she'd done with the baby, didn't want to know I was too late, that I'd failed her. As she started to speak I saw my bus sliding in.

"Listen, Nicky I have to shoot. That's my bus."

She looked down as if I'd punched her in the gut.

"Will you meet me at Rick's, this time tomorrow?" She nodded at the cafe across the road. "I'll be waiting."

"Aye nae bother," I mustered a grin and a wink.

It took me ages to find the correct change and the bus driver was the typical sour faced cunt. Tomorrow was Saturday – not that Nicky'd ken this. There was no reason for me to be anywhere near the town centre or Rick's Café. As we turned onto the roundabout I couldn't help catching a glimpse of her standing on the pavement where I'd left her, lonely as a heron, hunched up by a river, waiting.

On Monday morning, Gav had us started down the Bottom End at twenty to eight. You could tell the wife had been nipping at him, the way he was charging about. Iggy had fiddled with the wires in Gav's strimmer so that he got an electric shock every time he tried to start the machine. The rest of the team stood around, trying not to piss themselves laughing.

After he went mental, we started cutting: bypassing the occasional soggy mattress, piles of Advertisers half burnt by lazy paper boys. I was thinking about Nicky, lugging herself up to my house, when this big caveman threw his window open.

"That fucking machines keeping me awake."

"Aye it's keeping me awake an aw," I snarled back, strolling on.

During lunch, Gav told us he wanted me and Iggy to weed the roundabout outside the Town Hall. As he was the only one with the necessary certificates to do weed controlling, he was going to be doing that all day. Even if the plastic backpack containing the weed-killer and the stupid spray gun made him look like he was auditioning for Ghostbusters, getting to daunder about, without being scrutinised by nosy bastards in the council offices was obviously the better job.

"Cuntyfuckingbaws," Iggy said when I passed on Gav's message. I knew exactly what he meant. Weeding on any roundabout was a total embarrassment: the whole town gawking at you while you worked. All it would take was one rogue element from the Kerrs' crumbling empire to see me and I'd be in for a doing.

Iggy, though, had other ideas. After Gav dropped us off, he headed for the flowers in the centre of the roundabout and lay down in the middle of them. Joining him, I realised that as long as we lay flat on our backs, no one could see us.

"Gav'll be raging when he sees we've done no work."

"Gav'll have other things to be raging about by tomorrow," Iggy confidently predicted.

He lit a fag and after cadging a lighter off him, I did too. Far up above, enormously swollen clouds sagged sedately across the sky, while the noise of unseen cars tucked us in on all sides.

"This is the life," said Iggy.

And I guess, for him, it was. Sometime during my second or third cigarette I decided to avoid the bus stop near Rick's Café. The baby had clearly been taken by social services, or it'd been a still birth, or Nicky had put it up for adoption. Besides, even if by some miracle Nicky still had the bairn, there was nothing I could do to help, not until I got the money. All summer I'd reassured myself that all the nasty shite I was doing was for her, that I was decent and kind, not weak and stupid.

I lay there with the back of my head in the soil, surrounded by flowers, daydreaming about pulling out a huge roll of cash, telling Nicky I'd sorted a place for her to stay, that I had come through with the goods, that everything was going to be alright.

"This must be what it feels like getting buried," Iggy chirped, ripping up some flowers and holding them like a bouquet against his chest.

After work, as I trundled along the back road from the Land Services Depot, a navy blue BMW rolled to a halt next to me. Since working on the lawn mowing team, I'd always carried a sharpened chisel in the inside of my steelies in case one of the Kerrs' came for us. As I pulled this out, Souter shouted, "You've missed a bit," pointing at a scrap of grass that wasn't even on our route. He'd clearly not noticed the tool in my hand and for a second I considered holding the sharpened end of the chisel to his neck and not letting go until he coughed up my money.

With the weird telepathy that psychos seem to be blessed with, he straightened his face. "Only winding you up Malky. M'on over here. Christ, you could trip over that face. I've got something that'll cheer you up." I took a couple of steps towards the car, gripping the chisel, checking the back seat.

"At this point, I should probably be shouting stranger danger."

"Ha," he scoffed. "It never worked for the others. Here."

He passed a bag for carrying football boots out of the window and I had the sort of head rush you get after sniffing poppers. "That's you sorted," he said. "There's something there to cheer up those junkie pals of yours too. Tell them to go easy on it. This stuff is far purer than anything they'll have seen." I took the boot bag from him glancing up and down the street, blinking away the needling of tears. "There's more where that came from. The appetite this town has for the stuff. We're gonnae make a fortune." He half closed the tinted window. "The youngsters sent up fae London dinna understand the lingo, so we need someone to punt the stuff. Get someone else to do it mind. Play your cards right and you could be king of this dump." He laughed at the idea and accelerated smoothly off.

I didn't open the bag until I'd bolted myself behind our bathroom door. First, I counted out the roll of fresh English twenty-pound notes. Next, I pulled out handfuls of one gram baggies of heroin. Having seen the damage this stuff caused, I should have chucked it down the toilet, but there was one part of my brain that was already totalling the money. Word was the town was suffering from a major drought, so shifting the gear through Dawn and her crowd would be easy. Once and once only, I told myself. Get the money, help Nicky, make all this horror mean something.

There was no way the stuck-up cow who owned the bungalow was going to rent it to me without a job and a reference from my employer, so I turned up at work the next day at 7:30 sharp, feeling like one of those lottery winners who smugly keep working after a big win. Wankers, I'd always thought, but now I realised there was a certain satisfaction to coasting through the day, knowing soon you'd be out of there. Besides, there was no job that gave me a greater chance of spotting Nicky, as we tooled about all the council run parts of town.

After we'd loaded the van, Gav always drove us round the work we'd done the previous day, providing a commentary on how neatly a hedge had been trimmed, or how far up a bank we'd managed to get our mowers. Daft fucker thought this motivated us. That morning he was going to see the total lack of weeding we'd done on the roundabout and, if he ventured into the flowerbed, a fairly substantial cemetery of cigarette butts.

Iggy, though, was chill. Gav first wanted to drive along the miles of paths he'd hauled the weed-killer backpack round. Within 12 hours the chemicals started turning the weeds yellow and I could already sense the intense satisfaction he was going to get from seeing the evidence of his work. But as we drove along the first stretch of pavement there was nothing to see.

We curb crawled in a tense silence for the next five minutes. Gav made his feelings known by grinding down the gears as we peered at the green, verdant weeds. Eventually he bellowed out of the window, "I fucking did this part." He stopped the van and ran towards the verge, kicking and chopping at the dandelions with his feet and fists.

"Did you empty his backpack?" Frank asked.

"Aye," Iggy affirmed. "Wanker spent four hours walking round town spraying water on weeds."

"Nice." Said Frank, handing round his packet of fags. "Teach him to bang on about aw the certificates he's got. To kill fucking weeds! Wanker."

As Gav drove back to the base, the flowerbeds on the roundabout were forgotten. We felt pretty justified in just lying back for the rest of the day. Iggy was into wrapping tinfoil around the van's tracker so that we could go and look at girls coming out the High School.

"As any fitba manager will tell you, if they're good enough they're old enough" he cackled.

"Do you mind if we dinna do that and just sit outside Parkside Primary."

"Fuck sake Frank, I knew you were sick but I didnae think you were that sick."

"No it's naw that", said Frank looking strangely embarrassed. "Just the wee wan started school a few weeks back and I've naw seen her in her uniform." We sat outside the school like a squad ay right fucking weirdos. Frank jumped out when he saw his ex. I watched him clumsily running to her. As she waited for him to speak, she made the sort of face people do when opening a dishwasher that has days' worth of plates piled up in it. He picked at an imaginary scab on his elbow as he spoke. Back in the van he watched the kids bundle their way out ay school. "Does she naw look braw in her uniform?" Frank said drumming his fingers on the wheel. "She said she'd get her tae wave." He hit the horn. "Said she'd fucking wave." He sat back and rolled a fag. "That's woman for you all over, they're that bitter and twisted." He pulled heavily on the fag, eyes screwed tight. I noticed for the first time the long dirty nails on his right hand. "Dinna get caught there son," he muttered. "Tear your bloody life apart."

"No Frank", I whispered. "I'll try and not."

Once the day was done, I headed for the bus station. For some daft reason, I had a notion that Nicky would be standing stalk still on the spot where I'd last seen her, but of course she wasn't. I went in to Rick's Café and ordered a fry up and extra-large coffee. Fuck, I could have ordered the whole menu and it wouldn't have made a dent in the wad I was carrying. But I was too nervous to eat the food. I kept an eye on the street, hoping she'd appear. Dawn had been bothering me the past few days with increasingly desperate questions about whether I'd seen anyone selling. Antonio had basically stopped the town's supply of heroin and those after the stuff were out on the streets. Others with the same haggard cheeks the same staggered walk, scuttled around the bus station, arms wrapped around themselves in a futile attempt to find warmth.

I thought of the wraps of heroin under my mattress and for a moment felt dizzyingly powerful. But not so powerful that the girls working in the café were not able to make it clear it was closing time by loudly piling chairs on the other tables and brushing the floor around my shoes with the manic intensity of an Olympic curling team. Reluctantly, I clambered out of the place and headed for Riff Raff Road. I'd no idea if she was still squatting there, but went anyway. Before knocking on her door, I went round the back in the hope of seeing the glint of candlelight on the jagged glass hole in the sitting room window. But the place was in darkness. I climbed the steps. Thumped the door. Pressed my ear against the damp flaking paint and clenched my teeth together to stop their chattering from disturbing the silence.

The next day we were down The Burnside Estate and I felt certain I'd spot Nicky. For some reason, I was carrying the full £1000. I was going to produce it the moment I spoke to her. But mid-morning Gav got a call that halted the van. He turned to the rest of the team and mouthed the word: "Clearance."

Iggy whiplashed his head in frustration.

"What's a clearance?" I asked Gav after he'd ended the call.

"It's cleaning up after mawkit bastards that the council have evicted. This though isn't even an eviction. Squatters by the sounds of it."

He did a three point turn and with panic thickening my throat, I watched through the windscreen as the van turned onto Nicky's estate.

"Riff Raff Road?" Iggy enquired, as Pete steered us onto her street. "The only clearance they should be doing here is dropping a bomb on it."

"Some big wigs at the council still reckon that Armitage Construction Company are going to flatten this place and build luxury homes. Dafties emptied most of the council flats, but they've had reports of squatters in one of them."

Pete parked the car a couple of blocks down from Nicky's and for a moment I thought we were saved, but he squinted through the window and in a hushed voice said, "It's that one. If we park too close, they'll ken we're coming."

Iggy was already pulling on his heavy work gloves. "Lucky we've still got that sledgehammer in the back fae the fencing job."

"That still there?" Gav's face glowed a redder hue. "I've telt you before that tools like that shouldn't be left in the van."

My heart thumped like a bass drum as I said, "Is this not a job for The Housing and Repossession Team?"

"Not feart are you Malky?" Gav twisted round in his seat to eyeball me. "In any case, Duffy has taken charge of The Housing and Repossession Team. They've been amalgamated into The Land Services and Burial Grounds Department."

"Jesus," Iggy said. "That's a bit of a mouthful."

Gav indicated we follow him round the backs of the blocks. He and Iggy crept through the knee high grass and I knew by the way they were carrying their sledgehammer and crowbar that they were having Hollywood inspired visions of themselves patrolling a warzone. As we snuck past the shattered windows and the charred rags of a sofa hanging from rusting springs, it wasn't that hard to imagine.

Gav started muttering, "Some people are nothing but scum. We're cleaning up after fucking vermin." His head, which grew out of his shoulders as if some wean had drawn it on and forgotten the neck, was red raw. On the juicy sides of his lips sizzled bits of spit. He started to swipe away at the overgrown grass with his crowbar.

Creeping into the back garden felt like returning to the scene of a crime: the disembowled binbags, the frying pan that had broken the window, a vomit stained sleeping bag.

I stared at the upstairs' windows, which blankly reflected the sullen sky apart from the jagged blackness behind the broken pane. I had a daft notion that if you could climb up and put your ear to that hole it would be like listening to a sea shell.

"No sign of life," Gav said.

As we climbed the unlit stairs I fought against the seasick feeling in my legs.

"Don't hold on to the bannisters," Gav hissed, "These scumbags tape syringes there to spike intruders."

"Dirty junkie bastards," Iggy muttered.

I stared hatefully at them; in Gav's stupid fat head was the idea that as this place wasn't fit for human habitation then no one with normal human feelings could live there. Gav banged on the door, the two of them standing either side of it, as they'd probably seen police swat teams do on TV. No one answered. Not that they waited. Iggy was already swinging the sledgehammer half a minute after Gav had knocked. For obvious reasons, Nicky had got a pal of hers to install two hefty bolts on the inside of the door. If she was still living here, it'd take a while to break the door down, but with three full-blooded swings Iggy had smashed the mortice lock.

The sweet n sour stench of fresh shite and stale vomit hit us before we went in. Iggy edged into the room, sledgehammer at the ready. I pushed past him, past the binbags filled to bursting, the Sally Army sofa, the blackened spoons, crushed limes, the bottles covered in wax from melted candles. I poked my head into Nicky's room, took in the dried bloodstains on the mattress, the balled-up bloodied towels, the orbiting bluebottles.

"Christ," I heard Gav shout as the sound of his crowbar clattered onto the floor. "It's like Nightmare on Elm Street in here."

In the spare room was a cot or top part of a pram. It had blue corduroy material around the outside and looked bright and clean compared with the rest of the filthy room. On the floor were two packs of newborn nappies, a pile of baby's clothes and a half-finished bottle. Covering the cot was a torn section of a fine mesh fishing net. Inside amongst the frilly lace and stuff was a baby's face. It looked smaller than any baby I'd ever seen and with its waxy, plasticky pallor I had to double take to be sure it was real. There was something ancient and judgemental about its jaundiced face. I untucked the net, realising it had been put there to protect the baby from the rats that clawed at the walls, scampered in and out of the candle light and were the healthiest looking creatures in that place. If she'd been thinking clearly enough to do that, why'd she taken the risk of leaving her baby here? What was she thinking leaving it at all?

"Is it, you know — ?" Iggy faltered.

I crouched down on the ground remembering a time down by the caves being dared to touch a beached jellyfish. I felt it with the outside of my finger. It was cold but incredibly smooth. The baby lay there still, silent, plastic faced. I lifted the blanket so I could see it properly. I never really believed it when folks banged on about babies looking like their parents, but this one had it – the same sullen face, same sunken eyes. A Campbell's face. No point denying it. As I continued rubbing its cheek with the outside of my forefinger, the baby attempted to open its eyes, while its tiny perfect hands reached out to try and grasp something that neither of us could see.

"Get an ambulance." I said, letting the baby's hand weakly hold on to my forefinger, while I begged whoever you beg in these moments that it be allowed to live.

"Do you think we'll get the rest ay the day off pal?" Iggy asked, rolly cupped under hand, eyes creeping up and down my left trouser leg.

"Doubt it."

"Tight cunts", he hissed, "I could go mental in the head fae a shock like that."

An old woman in just about the only occupied house on the street sat gawping at us from her window, her perfectly trimmed privet hedge and pots of flowers a reminder of what this estate had once been. Iggy gave her a wave.

Gav was flapping around the police. "There haven't been tenants here for almost a year. You could try the auld yin over there, but the rest of the flats are vacant. At least they're meant to be. From the nick of the place, I surmise that whoever was squatting there had alcohol and drug problems."

Gav always used words like surmise when talking to suits. I could see PC Carmichael nodding his head, taking note.

"Whoever she was, the poor lassie must have been in some state to do that." He was shaking his head showing his human side. Poor Gav, the head shake said, having to do a shitey job like this with daft loons like us. "Someone'll ken who she was. You canna hae a bairn without anyone noticing." He caught me watching and snapped, "Have neither of youse got ma crowbar out of there?"

Iggy was suddenly busy picking a sticker off the van's dashboard and aware of the old wifey watching us, I went.

I wanted a last moment in that room before the police arrived. Before long Nicky's legendary collection of bottles would be thrown into a skip, the glass smashed, the messages that no one had read lost to the wind. Whoever was clearing the squat would chuck the ghetto blaster that was always giving up the ghost, the blood-stained mattress and the mixtapes of admirers. After picking up Gav's crowbar, I lingered in the room that the baby had been in, leant into its cot and sniffed the milky sickly baby smell on the blanket. Before leaving the flat, I ejected a tape from the soundsystem noticing Johnny's handwriting and the words *Happy Birthday*. I slipped it into my pocket with the useless roll of twenty-pound notes. The floorboards creaked and even before I turned, I knew it'd be Stark in the doorway.

"You again." And the way he looked at me, it was as if he understood everything.

I wasn't sure if he'd seen me take the tape, so held up the crowbar. "Gav sent me here for this."

"You haven't touched anything else? Because this is a crime scene. Potentially a serious crime scene, and we have a duty to preserve crime scenes. The constables should never have let you back in."

I shook my head like his words were irrelevant. "Crime scene?"

"Aye crime scene. Neglect is a crime. What a mess." He was looking around, but it didn't feel like he was talking about the state of the place. "Must hardly feel worth it now."

He examined me like I was some weird specimen dredged up from the deep.

"What?"

"The murder, the smuggling, couriering drugs up and down the country. For what? This? Who did you save, Malky?"

I stared at the empty cot.

"Know who you could save? Yourself. They've used you. The lot of them. And what have you got from it? Nothing. That car you drove down south. It was stopped in Tottenham two days ago. Weapons and a significant quantity of drugs were recovered. Further arrests will be made. The net's been cast, Malky. You either help us haul it in or you'll be caught in it like the rest."

Breathless, I backed towards the fireplace filled with all those bottles, all those stories, waiting to get out. This room had always felt a sanctuary, a safe place, where the normal rules didn't apply. To have it invaded by this much reality made my stomach turn.

Stark looked pleadingly at me. "You can't go on like this. Come in and make a confession or you'll end up dead or in jail. Nothing surer. You don't owe these people anything."

"I'll end up dead or in jail whatever I do."

"It doesn't have to be this way." The sound of other officers echoed up the stairwell. "Come on," he whispered.

"Give me 48 hours and I'll come in. I promise."

"How do I know you won't do a runner?"

"If I could get away from this, would I be here now?"

At piece time the next morning we listened to the local news on the van's radio.

"Police are keen to know the whereabouts of the mother of a baby found by workmen in the Burnside Estate. Reports from hospital describe the baby's condition as poorly but stable. Serious concern for the welfare of the baby's mother have prompted the police to appeal for her to contact them as soon as possible."

"Did ye hear that, fucking mentioned on the radio," Iggy proclaimed

"Naw as if they said your names," said Frank, setting the two of them off.

Gav broke up Iggy and Frank's bickering.

"Right lads. The three ay yous better get started or we're naw gonnae finish the route."

Cutting down the Bottom End was a piece of pish: just under trees, around manhole covers, the bits the John Deere couldn't reach. The machines were motorized so all you had to do was keep them under control. No one could speak to you cause of the noise they made, which suited me fine. I was still going through the motions. From the outside I must have looked like a normal, functional person with a normal, functional future. Now that I knew it was all going to end, I took a weird pleasure in this sort of work.

Once Gav was out of view we sat on the warm engines of our mowers gulping juice. Everyone drank Irn Bru. Each team's howff was full of glass bottles stored till Christmas when they were banked bringing in hundreds of pounds. Frank and Iggy launched into intrigues about who had been thieving fae whose shed and what percentage share each contributor should receive.

Frank enthusiastically started telling me I'd get at least 10% of the team's share if I kept going through ma bottles at this rate. I emptied my juice as if I was going to make it to Christmas. I kept telling myself I was only there on the off chance that some news would come through about the baby, but in truth, I had an idea that every hour of acting like a normal hard-working citizen placed me an hour further away from all the bad I'd done. Eventually, the distance would get so great that no one could blame me, cause the person, who'd done all that stuff wasn't even me. A bit of me thought Duffy might organise us to go to the hospital, or that the local newspaper might want a photo of us with the baby, as if we'd saved it. Even if that didn't happen, I considered trying to persuade the others to pay the place a visit. But they wouldn't be into that and besides, on what grounds did I have any right to that bairn.

"Fucking junkies" sneered Iggy, as a group ay crooked skeletons twitched into view. The lads all hated heroin addicts. Just before I'd started here Iggy had gone over a syringe with his mower and the blades had fired the needle into his leg. He'd waited a week for blood test results.

Nicky was with them: hands stuffed in that oversized fur coat, face too tight as if someone had grabbed the skin on the back of her head and pulled. I'd never have recognised her if I hadn't seen her last week. I thought about the places you'd have to go, things you'd have to see to look that bad. She'd gone from being a girl who you'd know had entered a pub even with your back to the door, to one you wouldn't even glance at in a crowd — except perhaps to wonder how someone could look so rough, so young.

She stalked across the park with this wraith called Deek who used to hang about Pete the Hat's place. I mind thinking that he looked like a picture of this mad wee guy in a painting they had up in the Art Department at school. The Scream or something. Well, gie the boy in that painting a manky white tracksuit and a Burberry baseball cap and that was what was looking at me. I kept my head down. Her baby was in a hospital ward surrounded by sterilised floors, fresh linen, nurses who knew how to look after children and no one who knew his name. Meanwhile she was heading into a block of flats, searching for smack.

That evening, I was heading to the bus stop having decided to do a runner before Stark came after me. I was carrying the money in case of emergencies and had a packed rucksack under my bed. I'd already hinted to Mackinnon that if he could drive me somewhere, I'd be able to pay him in gear. But I still wasn't sure. Once I started, I'd be running forever. A pair of heavy boots clumping along behind me broke into my thoughts.

"Mind if I chum you intae town?"

Reluctantly I fell into step, Iggy babbling on about plans for the night, which I seemed to have become involved in. As we waited at the bus stop I spotted Nicky, staring out of the café window, sipping on a polystyrene cup. Iggy rammed his elbow into me and nodded at this woman from the Day Care Centre pushing a young man with cerebral palsy down the High Street in a multicoloured wheelchair. She was wearing a white nurse's top and leggings of the same colour. Her arse juddered magnificently with each step. Iggy inhaled sharply, "Does that not just make you want to sink your teeth into it?" I murmured an agreement. "And fuck me," he started cackling, "That lassie's arse isn't bad either."

I pretended to laugh before worrying that Nicky would see and think we were laughing at her. Instead, I leant against the shelter tapping my steelies to a tune that wasn't really playing in my head, looking at the chewing gum constellations on the pavement, pretending I hadn't seen her. When I looked up she attempted a smile and gave me a nervous wave.

"Dinna like yours much," Iggy chirped, following my stare.

"What's that" I said pretending not to have been listening.

"Just saying, you dinna ken that lassie do you? She was in the year below me at school. Looks a right state now."

I remembered the Saturday night, the weekend before Christmas, when all of this had started.

During winter the town went into hibernation, but that weekend the School had stopped and the pubs were full of deckies on shore leave, lads back from the rigs and students home from university. I'd bumped into her near the kebab van. "What you up to?" I'd asked. "Trawling for cock," she'd slurred, stumbling into my arms. She was wearing a backless dress and her shoulders were frozen. She'd smelt of singed hair, and only later did I notice she'd managed to burn the end of her long fringe that she was always trying to grow out. Arm in arm we left the Christmas lights of Bridge Street and went back to hers. It was so cold in the squat that condensation had frozen to the inside of her windows, letting even less street light in than usual. We cocooned ourselves with blankets on the couch. The only things we took off were our shoes. After sharing a heavily packed joint, she'd told me to blow out the candles. The permanently dying sound system slowly throttled The Birthday Party's *She's Hit* before the tape clicked to the end of a side leaving us alone with the incessant scurry of rats, searching for food, searching for warmth, where there was none.

"I feel so relaxed with you," she'd kept saying, and in fact she was so relaxed that she could barely keep her mouth closed or her eyes open. "Johnny," she'd said turned round to stare into my eyes, "I love you. Why don't you love me?" And I'd kissed her hoping she would close her eyes, that she wouldn't realise I wasn't my cousin. The last thing she'd said, as she arched her body towards mine was, "keep me warm."

A summer spent knocking on her door, texting her phone, doing whatever I was told by a crowd of mental cases later.

"No, never seen her before." And the bus trundled by and we were gone.

I should have got away that night, but I knew that once I started running I was never going to stop. Besides, MacKinnon had lost his car keys, or his car or something: he was too stocious to explain which. There was still the last bus to Aberdeen, and I had enough cash to go anywhere, but with a fatalistic inertia I'd ended up going out with the lawnmower lads: a last night in Port Cawdor.

First, I met Frank, who was walking along the road like he had a boner.

"What you got there," I said as I walked and he hobbled into the Bottom End. I spied Iggy leaning against a lamp post, hoodie pulled over his head.

"You got it?" he asked. Frank nodded. "I know just the place. Left a few tins there." We daundered down through the estate tasting the night's air: young and free and dangerous. After a bit we nicked into a lay-by near one of the most derelict blocks.

"Nothing but smackheids left in that place," nodded Frank. Iggy crouched behind a grit bin and displayed the beers. I squatted next to him while Frank undid his belt and pulled out an airgun.

Iggy looked along the length of the barrel, fag hanging limply from the side of his mouth, smoke curdling the fresh early autumn air.

"Has there been any news about that bairn?"

"Nothing," I replied.

"It'll be one of they junkies. That's the only type of women who'd do a thing like that. Strange no one's come forward. Must be someone kens the mother."

In the pale orange of the street light his face ruminated on this mystery. I sipped at the cold beer and shivered.

"There's wan ay the bastards now." Iggy hissed.

He had the scummy clothes, the walk that made him look like he was just about to shite himself. I recognised him as one of Corky's old pals, a former deckie, who, before getting totally mangled by smack, had been one of the best footballers in school. Iggy's face tightened as he pulled the trigger.

"Hit." The boy cursed threw a punch at an imagined assailant and scuttled off. "Did you see that?"

"Aye nice one." I snickered to cover the false enthusiasm in my voice. Frank inhaled his rolly appreciatively. We sat back and got stuck into the beers whilst waiting for the next target. Music was coming from one of the further away flats. Silhouetted revellers danced behind windows. It all seemed so far away, like looking at fish underwater.

"Can I have another beer?"

"Dinna need tae ask Malky, just dig in." He flashed me a tobacco stained grin, his face burnt into my memory by an approaching car light.

"Pigs," hissed Frank and we ducked down below the bin.

The lights shone on the tangled brambles and clumps of dusty grass. The engine stopped and I waited for the doors to click open. The amount of actual trouble I was in, I was fucked if I was getting lifted for sitting in a bush with an airgun and these two. I peered over the bin, ready to leg it the moment they moved.

It was a plain car, a man and woman having a blether. I was about to make a cheeky comment about they two shiteing themselves when I saw her pale face, hair as black as a bird caught in an oil slick. The bloke was saying something but she just kept looking out the window as if he didn't exist. I ken that look I thought. He was doing all the talking but she just kept on staring into the darkness. Finally, she turned, looked at him and shrugged. He handed her some money and she unfastened her seat belt. As she leaned towards him I felt a scream crawl down my throat. He made his seat go back and her head dipped down out of sight.

"Is that dirty bitch doing what I think she's doing?" asked Iggy his unshaved cheek brushing close to mine. I had a grand in my pocket and enough gear hidden in my mattress to double that. But even if I had all the money in the world, I couldn't make anything right, not now.

For a moment, I thought about grabbing the gun, smashing the driver's window and shooting the punter in the face, before throwing the money at her. But instead I drank from my can, dank taste of flat beer in my mouth, bile in my throat. I swallowed hard.

"Finished already" said Frank, "must be a real pro." The car's engine started and I felt a purring in ma stomach as it reversed into the night.

"Leaves a bad taste in the mouth, doesn't it," said Iggy wi a twisted smile. I smiled back, stood on legs that felt like they hadn't been used in years.

"Have tae go now," a voice said and I was up and walking not heeding Iggy's protests. Far up above a flight of geese could be heard screeching their way across the night sky as they made their way to warmer lands. I looked but couldn't see them in the moon's pale light. They moved on their chatter growing faint.

I stood outside the end house on a dead end street. A condemned building that no one could be bothered knocking down. In the last 24 hours, metal shutters had been screwed over the windows to stop kids breaking in and worse things breaking out; a jagged memory, cry in the dark, a hurt nobody heard. I moved into the garden, held my breath, trying to catch something amidst the gloaming's lonely noises.

During the daytime, the street had a grand view of the harbour and I watched a lone trawler coming into port. From here you could make out the silhouettes of the old fishing boats, rusting hulks from another age their paint flaking so badly that their names were often indecipherable.

I turned one last time to the tenement. The door at the entry to the close had long since been booted in and the only thing stopping me from entering the building were a couple of strips of police tape. I headed up the dark stair well, crunching over the remains of carry outs and skeletal leaves from last autumn. There was more police tape across the entrance to Nicky's flat, but this now hung in tatters. A sheet of plywood had been nailed to the doorframe in an attempt to prevent entry. Someone had already had a go at it and in the semi-darkness I felt the ravaged wood, the desperate clawing of a creature trying to get back to its cave. I ran my fingers over its surface. A knife or hatchet had been taken to it and there were scars, cuts running here and there. Someone had carved, what felt like letters into the wood. I traced them with the tips of my fingers. They looked newly done, sharp and edgy. "ANIMALS" it read.

I stumbled down the dark stair well as if stung and headed out of town, cutting through the graveyard, ignoring the stones with the same names repeating themselves, generation after generation. Soon, Corky too would have his small plot; a little stone; a piece of scripture; beloved son, brother, friend.

I headed to The Front for one last look, past the sleek yachts with their polished wood and bunting. Down to where the decommissioned boats: *The Silver Harvester*, *Olympia* and Uncle James's old boat, *Coleen*, bobbed about like quines at the edge of a dance floor knowing they're past it, that they're never getting picked. *The Abiding Star* was tethered down there too. Our ticket to proper amounts of money if Johnny, Souter and the London gang had their way.

I watched the boats bobbing until a queasy sea sickness returned to unsettle my stomach. Returned? In truth the feeling had never gone away. Not since my first time as a deckie when we dumped Joe overboard. Nothing had felt solid since then. Even the road on which I stood pitched and plunged as my feet led me to the police station, to the moment where I could put an end to this. Opening the door, I was relieved to see Carmichael on the front desk.

"Is Stark in?"

"DI Stark went home hours ago."

"Can I have paper, pen and an envelope then?"

He looked at me like I was joking. "This isn't a Post Office."

"I've got a message for him. It's important."

PC Gourlay rushed out from their office. "Here," she said, handing me what I'd asked for. "Are you sure, you don't want to talk to anyone?"

"I'd rather write it down."

I sat on a plastic seat next to a plastic plant in their waiting room. The police-wifey hanging over me like some anxious teacher. "It's private. Between me and Stark." I hadn't held a pen since my last school exam four months ago. Four months! A lifetime. No wonder it felt alien in my fingers, but as soon as I started writing the words poured out. I put everything down and as the ink flowed that guilt, which had constricted my throat all summer, released its throttling grip. When it was over, I looked around the room, dizzy with all the oxygen in the world.

I ripped the sheets from the pad and stuffed them in the envelope. Twelve sheets. I thought of the twelve messages in the bottles at Nicky's and felt a weird intuitive twitch that they would contain the same words as those in my confession. The police-woman hadn't stopped watching me, her face smiling like I'd done the right thing. I smiled back. Once the world kent the contents of the envelope, no one was going to smile at me like that again. I closed the envelope and wrote FAO STARK over the seal, while a couple of uniformed cops came in. The one wearing leather biker trousers shot me a look. He leant over the reception desk and growled, "What's he doing here?"

I was up on my feet and out the door before Carmichael could reply. The cop was the fourth man I'd seen on the harbour the morning after the party at Blythe Lighthouse, after Johnny had shown El and Antonio our boat. The fuckers even had the police in their pocket.

The streets of the Port were deserted, as I sprinted towards the West Beach, my confession crumpled in my fist. I squelched over slippery rocks the sulphurous smell of rotting seaweed and the taste of trying not to cry. Beyond the rocks, the soft sand became hard, heavy, and the waves soaked through my trainers. In the failing light, the sea unwrapped itself, the waves hitting the shingle before drawing back, the sound like someone tearing a sheet of paper before crunching it into a ball. I ripped open the envelope and pulled out my confession.

Another trawler made its way through the crimson waters of the sun sunk sea. Gows swarmed in huge numbers as two deckies threw bucket loads of fish that were too small, or that exceeded the boat's quota, or that were simply from unwanted species, back into the sea. Dead, stunned, or alive the fish were a feast for the gows.

"We are the unmarketable by-catch of humanity," Corky had said. "They'd like to throw us in the sea."

Maybe it was the mewing of the gulls or the mournful moans of a seal, but something out there was calling me. Without taking off my trainers I waded further into the water, the waves tugging at my jeans like a child desperate for attention. Without thinking, I pulled the pages from the envelope and threw them into the sea, watched as they floated a while before sinking into its depths. I stumbled forward as the sound of sirens filled my ears. It was a relief to feel the tidal tug, the tremendous strength of heavenly bodies that knew nothing of my past and cared nothing for my future.